'Brilliant and influential science

'Masson is a wonderful storytell

Also by David I. Masson

SF MASTERWORKS

The Caltraps of Time

DAVID I. MASSON

This edition first published in Great Britain in 2012
by Gollancz
An imprint of the Orion Publishing Group
Orion House, 5 Upper St Martin's Lane,
London WC2H 9EA
An Hachette UK Company

1 3 5 7 9 10 8 6 4 2

A CIP catalogue record for this book
is available from the British Library

ISBN 978 0 575 11828 7

Typeset at The Spartan Press Ltd,
Lymington, Hants

Printed and bound in Great Britain by
Clays, Ltd, St Ives plc

The Orion Publishing Group's policy is to use papers that
are natural, renewable and recyclable products and made
from wood grown in sustainable forests. The logging and
manufacturing processes are expected to conform to the
environmental regulations of the country of origin.

www.orionbooks.co.uk

ACKNOWLEDGEMENT

I should like to acknowledge with thanks the encouragement of Michael Moorcock, editor of the magazine *New Worlds SF*, in which most of these stories first appeared.

David I. Masson

CONTENTS

AUTHOR'S FOREWORD

Now, when the frontiers of strict scientific hypothesis read like science fiction, but the conduct of global affairs reads like a set of fifth-rate films dreamt up by moronic scriptwriters, and humanity gets on with the business of running the Sixth Major Extermination of Species, I invite you to relax with the imaginations of a slightly more innocent decade.

The White Queen enjoyed believing in six impossible things before breakfast; here you can believe in a dozen, a few of which may be possible, or at least secrete a truth: the chaos at the heart of language; the fires beneath us; the dimensional complexities of time; parallel universes; the fragility of civilization.

David I. Masson, December 2002

INTRODUCTION

The Caltraps of Time is a collection of short stories, the only book of fiction published by David I. Masson. He never wrote a novel, and every story that he published in his lifetime is in this volume. If for no other reason this is therefore a unique book. However, few writers with only one book to their name have ever come up with such startling and original material.

David Masson's first story, the remarkable 'Traveller's Rest', appeared in the September 1965 edition of *New Worlds*, which at the time was the leading SF magazine in the UK. The story of *New Worlds* and the development of the 'New Wave' has been told many times, but within that context Masson's work was always in a class of its own. Many of the New Wave stories of that period were experiments with form, or with narrative structures, or with subject-matter. Not all these experiments succeeded. Masson was entirely different: he was involved with language itself, in particular with what he called the functions and effects of phonetic sound-patterning. He brought this fascination with language to the science fiction genre, and the results are all here.

In 1965, 'Traveller's Rest' made a profound impact. Its completely original ideas about the mutability of language and meaning had a seminal influence on the small but extremely active group of writers, critics and readers who closely followed *New Worlds*. I was one of them – if I look back and remember my first encounter with this story, I am reminded of the imaginative vistas it opened up for me as a beginning writer: the apocalyptic war being fought across a time-dilated landscape, the feeling that time itself can influence human perception, and that experience of life is, like mass and energy, subject to the distortions of relativity. Nearly half a century later the story still has an extraordinary effect. It feels like a breakthrough, a pioneering work that has influenced many others, but it manages to retain its own lovely mystique.

Within a few months, Masson followed up with a series of similarly original stories, all different in tone and subject matter: some satires, a brilliant pastiche of 17th-century English, other explorations of the human psyche in extreme circumstances. All his stories create a spell: in particular a sense of strangeness, of otherness, in counterpoint to the banality of the ordinary. 'Mouth of Hell' describes the discovery of a huge hole in the world, one which must be explored at any cost. The difficulties are fantastic, and one team of explorers after another comes to grief. But in the end the hole gives up its secrets. What then happens is pure Masson.

Others are superficially less serious: 'Not So Certain' is a conversation piece about the difficulties human beings might have when they try to learn the language of an alien race, and in the midst of the expostulations and gleeful discoveries there are many serious arguments about language and phonetics. And in one or two of the stories ('Doctor Fausta' or 'The Transfinite Choice') the dazzling sequence of puns, allusions and neologisms will make you think you might have somehow backed inadvertently into the world of Masson's contemporary, John Sladek.

The first seven Masson stories were published in 1968, under the present title, in a beautiful and highly collectible hardcover edition by Faber and Faber. A paperback followed a few years later, but both editions have long been out of print.

By the early 1970s, Masson's burst of creativity had come to an end. He published no more stories after 'Doctor Fausta', in 1974.

David Irvine Masson was born in Edinburgh in 1915, to a family of distinguished academics and thinkers. He went to

Merton College, Oxford, between 1934 and 1938, where he read English Language and Literature. After graduation he went to work as an assistant librarian at the University of Leeds. The Second World War interrupted: he served with the Royal Army Medical Corps in the Mediterranean theatre, chiefly North Africa and Italy. After the war he became the curator of special collections at the University of Liverpool, but in 1956 he returned to Leeds to become curator of the Brotherton Collection.

Between 1951 and 1991 he published many articles on phonetic sound-patterning in poetry (especially in the work of Rainer Maria Rilke). His published works include three articles with the Princeton University Press publication *Encyclopedia of Poetry and Poetics* (1965). Also notable is his paper, *Poetic Sound-Patterning Reconsidered* (Leeds Philosophical and Literary Society, May 1976).

In 2002, my colleague David Langford and I decided the time had come for a complete collection of Masson's stories. We knew that he had written three more stories after the Faber book, and these were little known. David Masson was then in his late 80s, and almost ridiculously happy to be remembered (little realizing, perhaps, how *well* he was remembered, and not just by Langford and myself). He enthusiastically collaborated with us on minor revisions and improvements to the Faber stories, and entered into a detailed correspondence with both of us about the less well known extra three. He actively involved himself not just with the quality of the text (which presented amazing demands to anyone who was not David Masson himself, a man proud to proclaim himself obsessed with a level of intricate detail that was above all pedantry) but also with the correct sequence in which the stories should be presented in the book. He wrote a short Foreword for our edition. The new collection was published in the USA as a print-on-demand book, which was unfortunately not widely distributed.

It is therefore not only a great pleasure to bring this book to the Masterworks series, but a genuine privilege to have been able to work with David Masson. He was a good and great man, and his sole book of fiction is a good and great work. More than that: it is memorably different and inspiring.

Christopher Priest

Traveller's Rest

It was an apocalyptic sector. Out of the red–black curtain of the forward sight-barrier, which at this distance from the Frontier shut down a mere twenty metres north, came every sort of meteoric horror: fission and fusion explosions, chemical detonations, a super-hail of projectiles of all sizes and basic velocities, sprays of nerve-paralysants and thalamic dopes. The impact devices burst on the barren rock of the slopes or the concrete of the forward stations, some of which were disintegrated or eviscerated every other minute. The surviving installations kept up an equally intense and nearly vertical fire of rockets and shells. Here and there a protectivized figure could be seen sprinting up, down or along the slopes on its mechanical walker like a frantic ant from an anthill attacked by flamethrowers. Some of the visible oncoming trajectories could be seen snaking overhead into the indigo gloom of the rear sight-curtain, perhaps fifty metres south, which met the steep-falling rock surface forty-odd metres below the observer's eye. The whole scene was as if bathed in a gigantic straight rainbow. East and west, as far as the eye could see, perhaps some forty miles in this clear mountain air despite the debris of explosion (but cut off to west by a spur from the range) the visibility-corridor witnessed a continual onslaught and counteronslaught of devices. The visible pandemonium was shut in by the sight-barriers' titanic canyon walls of black, reaching the slim pale strip of horizon-spanning light at some immense height. The audibility-corridor was vastly wider than that of sight; the many-pitched din, even through left ear in helm, was considerable.

'Computer-sent, must be,' said H's transceiver into his right ear. No sigil preceded this statement, but H knew the tones of B, his next-up, who in any case could be seen a metre away saying it, in the large concrete bubble whence they watched, using a plaspex window and an infrared northviewer with a range of some hundreds of metres forward. His next-up had been in the bunker for three minutes, apparently overchecking, probably for an appreciation to two-up who might be in station VV now.

'Else how can they get minute-ly impacts here, you mean?' said H.

'Well, of course it could be long range low-frequency – we don't really know how Time works over There.'

'But if the conceleration runs asymptotically to the Frontier, as it should if Their Time works in mirror-image, would anything ever have got over?'

'Doesn't have to, far's I can see – maybe it steepens a lot, then just falls back at the same angle the other Side,' said B's voice; 'anyway, I didn't come to talk science: I've news for you, if we hold out the next few seconds here, you're Relieved.'

H felt a black inner sight-barrier beginning to engulf him, and a roaring in his ears swallowed up the noise of the bombardment. He bent double as his knees began to buckle, and regained full consciousness. He could see his replacement now, an uncertain-looking figure in prot-suit (like everybody else up here) at the far side of the bunker.

'XN 3, what orders then?' he said crisply, his pulse accelerating.

'XN 2: pick em-kit now, repeat now, rocket 3333 to VV, present tag' – holding out a luminous orange label printed with a few coarse black characters – 'and proceed as ordered thence.'

H stuck up his right thumb from his fist held sideways at elbow length, in salute. It was no situation for facial gestures or unnecessary speech. 'XN 3, yes, em-kit, 3333 rocket, tag' (he had taken it in his left glove) 'and VV orders; parting!'

He missed B's nod as he skimmed on soles to the exit, grabbed a small bundle hanging (one of fifteen) from the fourth hook along, slid down the greasy slide underground ten metres to a fuel-cell-lit cavern, pressed a luminous button in the wall, watched a lit symbol passing a series of marks, jumped into the low car as it ground round the corner, and curled up foetuswise. His weight having set off the door mechanism, the car shut, slipped down and (its clamps setting on H's body) roared off down the chute.

Twenty-five seconds after his parting word H uncurled at the forward receiver cell of station VV nearly half a mile downslope. He crawled out as the rocket ground off again, walked ten steps onward in this larger version of his northward habitat, saluted thumb-up and presented his tag to two-up (recognized from helm-tint and helm-sign), saying simultaneously, 'XN 3 rep, Relieved.'

'XN 1 to XN 3: take this' (holding out a similar orange tag plucked from his pocket) 'and take mag-lev train down, in – seventy seconds. By the way, ever seen a prehis?'

'No, sir.'

'Spot through here, then; look like pteros but more primitive.'

The infrared telescopic viewer looking north-west passed through the forward sight-barrier which due north was about forty metres away here. Well upslope yet still well clear of the dark infrared-radiation barrier could be seen, soundlessly screaming and yammering, two scaly animals about the size of large dogs, but with two legs and heavy wings, flopping around a hump or boulder on the rock. They might have been hit on their way along, and could hardly have had any business on that barren spot, H thought.

'Thanks; odd,' he said. Eleven seconds of the seventy had gone. He pulled out a squirter-cup from the wall and took a drink from the machine through his helm. Seventeen seconds gone, fifty-three to go.

'XN 1 to XN 3: how are things up there?'

Naturally a report was called for: XN 2 might never return, and communication up-time and down-time was nearly impossible at these latitudes over more than a few metres.

'XN 3. Things have been hotting up all day; I'm afraid a burst through may be attempted in the next hour or so – only my guess, of course. But I've never seen anything like it all this time up here. I suppose you'll have noticed it in VV too?'

'XN 1, thanks for report,' was all the answer he got. But he could hear for himself that the blitz was much more intense than any he had known at this level either.

Only twenty-seven seconds remained. He saluted and strode off across the bunker with his em-kit and the new tag. He showed the tag to the guard, who stamped it and pointed wordlessly down a corridor. H ran down this, arriving many metres down the far end at a little gallery. An underslung rail-guided vehicle with slide-doors opening into cubicles glided quietly alongside. A gallery-guard waved as H and two others waiting opened doors whose indicators were unlit, the doors slid to, and H found himself gently clamped in on a back-tilted seat as the mag-lev train accelerated downhill. After ten seconds it stopped at the next checkhalt; a panel in the cubicle ceiling lit up to state DIVERSION, LEFT, presumably because the direct route had been destroyed. The train now appeared to accelerate but more gently, swung away to left (as H could feel), and stopped at two more checkhalts before swinging back to right and finally decelerating, coming to rest and opening some 480 seconds after its start, by Had's personal chronograph, instead of the 200 he had expected.

At this point daylight could again be seen. From the top bunker where XN 2 had discharged him, Had had now gone some ten miles south and nearly 3000 metres down, not counting detours. The forward sight-barrier here was hidden by a shoulder of mountain covered in giant lichen, but the southern

4

barrier was evident as a violet–black fog-wall a quarter of a mile off. Lichens and some sort of grass-like vegetation covered much of the neighbouring landscape, a series of hollows and ravines. Noise of war was still audible, mingled with that of a storm, but nearby crashes were not frequent and comparatively little damage could be seen. The sky overhead was turbulent. Some very odd-looking animals, perhaps between a lizard and a stoat in general appearance, were swarming up and down a tree-fern near by. Six men in all got out of the mag-lev train, besides Had. Two and three marched off in two groups down a track eastward. One (not one of those who had got in at VV) stayed with Had.

'I'm going down to the Great Valley; haven't seen it for twenty days; everything'll be changed. Are you sent far?' said the other man's voice in Had's right ear through the transceiver.

'I – I – I'm Relieved,' tried Had uncertainly.

'Well I'm . . . disintegrated!' was all the other man could manage. Then, after a minute, 'Where will you go?'

'Set up a business way south, I think. Heat is what suits me, heat and vegetation. I have a few techniques I could put to good use in management of one sort or another. I'm sorry – I never meant to plume it over you with this – but you did ask me.'

'That's all right. You certainly must have Luck, though. I never met a man who was Relieved. Make good use of it, won't you. It helps to make the Game worthwhile up here – I mean, to have met a man who is joining all those others we're supposed to be protecting – it makes them real to us in a way.'

'Very fine of you to take it that way,' said Had.

'No – I mean it. Otherwise we'd wonder if there was any people to hold the Front for.'

'Well, if there weren't, how'd the techniques have developed for holding on up here?' put in Had.

'Some of the Teccols I remember in the Great Valley might have developed enough techniques for that.'

'Yes, but think of all the pure science you need to work up the techniques from; I doubt if that could have been studied inside the Valley Teccols.'

'Possibly not – that's a bit beyond me,' said the other's voice a trifle huffily, and they stood on in silence till the next cable-car came up and round at the foot of the station. Had let the man get in it – he felt he owed him that – and a minute later (five seconds only, up in his first bunker, he suddenly thought ironically and parenthetically) the next car appeared. He swung himself in just as a very queer-looking purple bird with a long bare neck alighted on the stoat-lizards' tree-fern. The cable-car sped down above the ravines and hollows, the violet southern curtain backing still more swiftly away from it. As the time-gradient became less steep his brain began to function better and a sense of well-being and meaningfulness grew in him. The car's speed slackened.

Had was glad he still wore his prot-suit when a couple of chemical explosions burst close to the cable line, presumably by chance, only fifty metres below him. He was even more glad of it when flying material from a third broke the cable itself well downslope and the emergency cable stopped him at the next pylon. He slid down the pylon's lift and spoke with his trans-ceiver close to the telephone at the foot. He was told to make west two miles to the next cable-car line. His interlocutor, he supposed, must be speaking from an exchange more or less on the same latitude as that of his pylon, since communication even here was still almost impossible north–south except at ranges of some metres. Even so, there was a squeaky sound about the other voice and its speech came out clipped and rapid. He supposed his own voice would sound gruff and drawled to the other.

Using his walker, he picked his way across ravines and gullies, steering by compass and watching the sight-barriers and the Doppler tint-equator ahead for yawing. All very well for that man to talk about Teccols, he thought, but he must realize that no civilization could have evolved from anywhere

6

as far north as the Great Valley: it's far too young to have even evolved Men by itself – at least at this end; I'm not sure how far south the eastern end goes.

The journey was not without its hazards: there were several nearby explosions, and what looked like a suspicious artificial miasma, easily overlooked, lay in two hollows which he decided to go round. Moreover, an enraged giant bear-sloth came at him in a mauve shrub-thicket and had to be eliminated with his quickgun. But to one who had just come down from that mountain hell all this seemed like a pleasant stroll.

Finally he came upon the line of pylons and pressed the telephone button at the foot of the nearest, after checking that its latitude-number was nearly right. The same voice, a little less outlandish and rapid, told him a car would arrive in three quarters of a minute and would be arranged to stop at his pylon; if it did not, he was to press the emergency button nearby. Despite his walker, nearly an hour had gone by since he set out by it. Perhaps ninety minutes had passed since he first left the top bunker – well over a minute and a half of their time there.

The car came and stopped, he scrambled up and in, and this time the journey passed without incident, except for occasional sudden squalls, and the passage of flocks of nervous crows, until the car arrived at its terminus, a squat tower on the heathy slopes. The car below was coming up, and a man in it called through his transceiver as they crept past each other, 'First of a bunch!' Sure enough the terminus interior was filled with some twenty men all equipped – almost enough to have warranted sending them up by polyheli, thought Hadol, rather than wait for cars at long intervals. They looked excited and not at all cast down, but Hadol refrained from giving away his future. He passed on to the ratchet-car way and found himself one of a group of men more curious about the landscape than about their fellows. A deep reddish curtain of indeterminate thickness absorbed the shoulders of the heights about a quarter-mile northward, and the bluish fog terminated the view over the valley at nearly half a mile southward, but between the two the latitudinal zone was tolerably clear and devoid of obvious signs of war. Forests of pine and lower down of oak and ash covered the slopes, until finally these disappeared in the steepening edge of the Great Valley, whose meadows could however be glimpsed past the bluff. Swirling cloud-shadows played over the ground, skirts and tassels of rain and hail swept across it, and there was the occasional flash and rumble of a storm. Deer could be seen briefly here and there, and dense clouds of gnats danced above the trees.

A journey of some fifty minutes took them down, past two empty stations, through two looped tunnels and among waterfalls and under cliffs where squirrels leapt across from dangling root to root, through steadily warmer and warmer air to the pastures and cornfields of the Great Valley, where a narrow village of concrete huts and wooden cabins, Emmel, nestled on a knoll above the winding river, and a great road ran straight to the east, parallel to a railway. The river was not large here – a shallow, stony but attractive stream – and the Great Valley (all of whose breadth could now be seen) was at this western point no more than a third of a mile across. The southward slopes terminating the North-Western Plateau, now themselves visible, were rich in shrubland.

The utter contrast with what was going on above and, in top bunker time, perhaps four minutes ago, made Hadolar nearly drunk with enjoyment. However, he presented his luminous tag and had it (and his permanent checktab) checked for radiation, countersigned and stamped by the guard commander at the military terminal. The detachable piece at the end of the tag was given back to him to be slipped into the identity disc, which was, as always, let into a slot in one of his ribs; the other portion was filed away. He got out of his protsuit and walker, gave up his gun, ammunition and em-kit, was given two wallets of one thousand credit tokens each and a temporary civsuit. An orderly achieved the identity-disc operation. The whole ceremony from his arrival took 250 seconds

8

flat – two seconds up in the top bunker. He walked out like an heir to the earth.

The air was full of scents of hay, berries, flowers, manure. He took intoxicated gulps of it. At the freshouse he ordered, paid for, and drank four decis of light ale, then ordered a sandwich and an apple, paid and ate. The next train east, he was told, would be in a quarter of an hour. He had been in the place perhaps half an hour. No time to spend watching the stream, but he walked to the railhead, asked for a ticket to Veruam by the Sea some 400 miles east and, as the detailed station map showed him, about thirty miles south, paid, and selected a compartment when the train arrived from its shed.

A farm girl and a sleepy-looking male civilian, probably an army contractor, got in one after the other close behind Hadolar, and the compartment contained just these three when the train left. He looked at the farm girl with interest – she was blonde and placid – as the first female he had seen for a hundred days. Fashions had not changed radically in thirty-odd years, he saw, at least among Emmel farm girls. After a while he averted his gaze and considered the landscape. The valley was edged by bluffs of yellowish stone now to north and now to south. Even here their difference in hue was perceptible – the valley had broadened slightly; or perhaps he was being fanciful and the difference was due solely to normal light-effects. The river meandered gracefully from side to side and from cliff to cliff, with occasional islands, small and crowned with hazel. Here and there a fisher could be seen by the bank, or wading in the stream. Farmhouses passed at intervals. North above the valley rose the great slopes, apparently devoid of signs of human life except for funicular stations and the occasional heliport, until they vanished into the vast crimson-bronze curtain of nothingness which grew insensibly out of a half cloud-covered green sky near the zenith. Swirls of whirlwind among the clouds told of the effects of the time-gradient on weather, and odd lightning-streaks, unnoticed further north amid the war, appeared to pirouette among them. To the south

9

the plateau was still hidden by the height of the bluffs, but the beginnings of the dark blue haze grew out of the sky above the valley skyline. The train stopped at a station and the girl, Hadolar saw with a pang, got out. Two soldiers got in in light dress and swapped minor reminiscences: they were on short-term leave to the next stop, a small town, Granev, and eyed Hadolar's temporary suit but said nothing.

Granev was mostly built of steel and glass: not an exciting place, a one-block twenty-storey five-mile strip on either side of the road, with overpass-canopy. (How lucky, thought Hadolar, that speech and travel could go so far down this Great Valley without interlatitude problems: virtually the whole 450 miles.) Industry and some of the Teccols now appeared. The valley had broadened until, from the line, its southern cliffs began to drown in the blue haze half a mile off. Soon the northern slopes loomed a smoky ruddy brown before they too were swallowed up. The river, swollen by tributaries, was a few hundred metres across now and deep whenever the line crossed it. So far they had only gone fifty-odd miles. The air was warmer again and the vegetation more lush. Almost all the passengers were civilians now, and some noted Hadolar's temporary suit iron-ically. He would buy himself a wardrobe at Veruam at the first opportunity, he decided. But at the moment he wished to put as many miles as possible between himself and that bunker in the shortest personal time.

Some hours later the train arrived at Veruam by the North-Eastern Sea. Thirty miles long, forty storeys high, and 500 metres broad north–south, it was an imposing city. Nothing but plain was to be seen in the outskirts, for the reddish fog still obliterated everything about four miles to the north, and the bluish one smothered the view southward some seven. A well-fed Hadolaris visited one of the city's Rehabilitation Advisers, for civilian techniques and material resources had advanced enormously since his last acquaintance with them, and idioms and speech-sounds had changed bewilderingly, while the whole code of social behaviour was terrifyingly different. Armed with some manuals, a pocket recorder, and some standard speech-form and folkway tapes, he rapidly purchased thin clothing, stormwear, writing implements, further recording tools, lug-bags and other personal gear. After a night at a good guestery, Hadolaris sought interviews with the employing offices of seven subtropical development agencies, was tested and, armed with seven letters of introduction, boarded the night liner mag-lev train for the south past the shore of the North-Eastern Sea and to Oluluetang some 360 miles south. One of the tailors who had fitted him up had revealed that on quiet nights very low-pitched rumblings were to be heard from, presumably, the mountains northward. Hadolaris wanted to get as far from that north as he conveniently could.

He awoke among palms and savannah-reeds. There was no sign of either sight-barrier down here. The city was dispersed into compact blocks of multi-storey buildings, blocks separated by belts of rich woodland and drive-like roadways and mono-rails. Unlike the towns of the Great Valley, it was not arranged on an east–west strip, though its north–south axis was still relatively short. Hadolarisóndamo found himself a small guest-ery, studied a plan of the city and its factory areas, bought a guide to the district and settled down to several days of exploration and inquiry before visiting the seven agencies themselves. His evenings were spent in adult classes, his nights absorbing the speech-form recordings unconsciously in sleep. In the end after nineteen days (about four hours at Veruam's latitude, four minutes at that of Emmel, less than two seconds at the higher bunker, he reflected) he obtained employment as a minor sales manager of vegetable products in one of the organizations.

Communication north and south, he found, was possible verbally for quite a number of miles, provided one knew the rules. In consequence the zoning here was far from severe and travel and social facilities covered a very wide area. One rarely saw the military here. Hadolarisóndamo bought an automob and, as he rose in the organization's hierarchy, a second one for pleasure. He found himself well liked and soon had a circle of friends and a number of hobbies. After a number of love-affairs he married a girl whose father was higher up in the organization, and, some five years after his arrival in the city, became the father of a boy.

'Arisón!' called his wife from the boat. Their son, aged five, was puttering at the warm surface of the lake with his fists over the gunwale. Hadolarisóndamo was painting on the little island, quick lines and sweeps across the easelled canvas, a pattern of light and shade bursting out of the swamp trees over a little bay. 'Arisón! I can't get this thing to start. Could you swim over and try?'

'Five minutes more, Mihányo. Must get this down.'

Sighing, Karamihanyolàsve continued, but without much hope, to fish from the bows with her horizontal yo-yo gadget. Too quiet round here for a bite. A parakeet flashed in the branches to right. Derestó, the boy, stopped hitting the water, pulled over the tube-window let it into the lake and got Mihányo to slide on its lightswitch. Then he peered this way and that under the surface, giving little exclamations as tiny fish of various shapes and hues shot across. Presently Arisón called over, folded up his easel, pulled off his trousers, propped paints and canvas on top of everything, and swam over. There were no crocs in this lake, hippo were far off, filariasis and bilharzia had been eliminated here. Twenty minutes' rather tense tinker-ing got things going, and the silent fuel-cell driven screw was ready to pilot them over to the painting island and thence across the lake to where a little stream's current pushed out into the expanse. They caught four. Presently back under the west-ering sun to the jetty, tie up and home in the automob.

By the time Derestó was eight and ready to be formally named Lafonderestónami, he had a sister of three and a baby brother of one. He was a keen swimmer and boatman, and was developing into a minor organizer, both at home and in school. Arisón was now third in the firm, but kept his balance. Holidays were spent either in the deep tropics (where one could gain on the time-exchange) or among the promontories on the southern shores of the North-Eastern Sea (where one had to lose), or, increasingly, in the agricultural stream-scored western uplands, where a wide vista of the world could in many areas be seen and the cloudscapes had full play. Even there the sight-barriers were a mere fogginess near the north and south horizons, backed by a darkness in the sky.

Now and then, during a bad night, Arisón thought about the past. He generally concluded that, even if a breakthrough had been imminent in, say, half an hour from his departure, this could hardly affect the lives of himself and his wife, or even of their children, down here in the south, in view of the time-contraction southwards. Also, he reflected, since nothing ever struck further south than a point north of Emmel's latitude, the ballistic attacks must be mounted close to the Frontier; or if they were not, then the Enemy must lack all knowledge of either southern time-gradients or southern geography, so that the launching of missiles from well north of the Frontier to pass well south of it would not be worthwhile. And even the fastest heli which could be piloted against time conceleration would, he supposed, never get through.

Always adaptable, Arisón had never suffered long from the disabilities incident on having returned after a time at the Front. Mag-lev train travel and other communications had tended to unify the speech and the ethos, though naturally the upper reaches of the Great Valley and the military zone in the mountains of the north were linguistically and sociologically somewhat isolated. In the western uplands, too, pockets of older linguistic forms and old-fashioned attitudes still remained, as the family found on its holidays. By and large, however, the whole land spoke the tongue of the 'contemporary' subtropical lowlands, inevitably modified of course by the onomatosyntomy or 'shortmouth' of latitude. A

13

'contemporary' ethical and social code had also spread. The southern present may be said to have colonized the northern past, even geological past, somewhat as the birds and other travelling animals had done, but with the greater resources of human wits, flexibility, traditions and techniques.

Ordinary people bothered little about the war. Time conceleration was on their side. Their spare mental energies were spent in a vast selection of plays and ploys, making, representing, creating, relishing, criticizing, theorizing, discussing, arranging, organizing, co-operating, but not so often out of their own zone. Arisón found himself the member of a dozen interweaving circles, and Mihányo was even more involved. Not that they were never alone: the easy tempo of work and life with double 'weeks' of five days' work, two days free, seven days' work and six days free, the whole staggered across the population and in the organizations, left much leisure time which could be spent on themselves. Arisón took up texture-sculpting, then returned after two years to painting, but with magneto-brush instead of spraypen; purified by his texture-sculpting period, he achieved a powerful area control and won something of a name for himself. Mihányo, on the other hand, became a musician. Derestó, it was evident, was going to be a handler of men and societies, besides having, at thirteen, entered the athletic age. His sister of eight was a great talker and arguer. The boy of six was, they hoped, going to be a writer, at least in his spare time: he had a keen eye for things, and a keen interest in telling about them. Arisón was content to remain, when he had reached it, second in the firm: a chiefship would have told on him too much. He occasionally lent his voice to the administration of local affairs, but took no major part.

Mihányo and Arisón were watching a firework festival on the North-Eastern Sea from their launch off one of the southern promontories. Up here, a fine velvety backdrop for the display was made by the inky black of the northern sight-barrier, which cut off the stars in a gigantic arc. Fortunately the weather was fine. The silhouettes of the firework boats could just be discerned. In a world which knew no moon the pleasures of a 'white night' were often only to be got by such displays. The girl and Derestó were swimming round and round the launch. Even the small boy had been brought out, and was rather blearily staring northward. Eventually the triple green star went up and the exhibition was over; at the firework boats a midnight had been reached. Derestó and Venoyyè were called in, located by a flare, and ultimately prevailed on to climb in, shivering slightly, and dry off in the hot-air blaster, dancing about like two imps. Arisón turned the launch for the shore and Silarrè was found to be asleep. So was Venoyyè when they touched the jetty. Their parents had each to carry one in and up to the beach house.

Next morning they packed and set out in the automob for home. Their twenty days' holiday had cost 160 days of Oluluetang time. Heavy rain was falling when they reached the city. Mihányo, when the children were settled in, had a long talk on the opsiphone with her friend across the breadth of Oluluetang: she (the friend) had been with her husband badger-watching in the western uplands. Finally Arisón chipped in and, after general conversation, exchanged some views with the husband on developments in local politics.

'Pity one grows old so fast down here,' lamented Mihányo that evening; 'if only life could go on for ever!'

'For ever is a big word. Besides, being down here makes no difference to the feeling – you don't feel it any slower up on the Sea, do you now?'

'I suppose not. But if only . . .'

To switch her mood, Arisón began to talk about Derestó and his future. Soon they were planning their children's lives for them in the way parents cannot resist doing. With his salary and investments in the firm they would set up the boy for a great administrator, and still have enough to give the others every opportunity.

15

Next morning it was still in something of a glow that Arisón bade farewell to his wife and went off to take up his work in the offices. He had an extremely busy day and was coming out of the gates in the waning light to his automob in its stall, when he found standing round it three of the military. He looked inquiringly at them as he approached with his personal pulse-key in hand.

'You are VSQ 389 MLD 194 RV 27 XN 3, known as Hadolarisóndamo, resident at' (naming the address) 'and sub-president today in this firm.' The cold tones of the leader were a statement, not a question.

'Yes,' whispered Arisón as soon as he could speak.

'I have a warrant for your immediate re-employment with our Forces in the place at which you first received your order for Release. You must come with us forthwith.' The leader produced a luminous orange tag with black markings.

'But my wife and family!'

'They are being informed. We have no time.'

'My firm?'

'Your chief is being informed. Come now.'

'I – I – I must set my affairs in order.'

'Impossible. No time. Urgent situation. Your family and firm must do all that between them. Our orders override everything.'

'Wh – wh – what is your authority? Can I see it please?'

'This tag should suffice. It corresponds to the tag-end which I hope you still have in your identity disc – we will check all that en route. Come on now.'

'But I must see your authority. How do I know, for instance, that you are not trying to rob me, or something?'

'If you know the code you'll realize that these symbols can only fit one situation. But I'll stretch a point: you may look at this warrant, but don't touch it.'

The other two closed in. Arisón saw that they had their quickguns trained on him. The leader pulled out a broad screed. Arisón, as well as the dancing characters would let

16

him, resolved them in the light of the leader's torch into an order to collect him, Arisón, by today at such and such a time, local Time, if possible immediately on his leaving his place of work (specified); and below, that one man be detailed to call Mihányo by opsiphone simultaneously, and another to call the president of the organization. The Remployee and escort to join the military mag-lev train to Veruam (which was leaving within about fifteen minutes). The Remployee to be taken as expeditiously as possible to the bunker (VV) and thence to the higher bunker (from which he had come some twenty years before, but only about ten minutes in the Time of that bunker, it flashed through Arisón's brain – apart from six or seven minutes corresponding to his journey south).

'How do they know if I'm fit enough for this job after all these years?'

'They've kept checks on you, no doubt.'

Arisón thought of tripping one and slugging two and doing a bolt, but the quickguns of the two were certainly trained upon him. Besides, what would that gain him? A few hours' start, with unnecessary pain, disgrace and ruin on Mihányo, his children and himself, for he was sure to be caught.

'The automob,' he said ridiculously.

'A small matter. Your firm will deal with that.'

'How can I settle my children's future?'

'Come on, no use arguing. You are coming now, alive or dead, fit or unfit.'

Speechless, Arisón let himself be marched off to a light military vehicle.

In five minutes he was in the mag-lev train, an armoured affair with strong windows. In ten more minutes, with the train moving off, he was stripped of his civilian clothes and possessions (to be returned later to his wife, he learnt), had his identity disc extracted and checked and its Relief tag-end removed, and a medical checkup was begun on him. Apparently this was satisfactory to the military authorities. He was given military clothing.

He spent a sleepless night in the train trying to work out what he had done with this, what would be made of that, who Mihányo could call upon in need, who would be likely to help her, how she would manage with the children, what (as nearly as he could work it out) they would get from a pension which he was led to understand would be forthcoming from his firm, how far they could carry on with their expected future.

A grey pre-dawn saw the train's arrival at Veruam. Foodless (he had been unable to eat any of the rations) and without sleep, he gazed vacantly at the marshalling yards. The body of men travelling on the train (apparently only a few were Remployees) was got into closed trucks and the long convoy set out for Emmel.

At this moment Hadolaris' brain began to re-register the conceleration situation. About half a minute must have passed since his departure from Oluluetang, he supposed, in the Time of his top bunker. The journey to Emmel might take up another two minutes. The route from Emmel to that bunker might take a further two and a half minutes there, as far as one could work out the calculus. Add the twenty-years' (and south-ward journey's) sixteen to seventeen minutes, and he would find himself in that bunker not more than some twenty-two minutes after he had left it. (Mihan, Deres and the other two would all be nearly ten years older and the children would have begun to forget him.) The blitz was unprecedentedly intense when he had left, and he could recall (indeed it had figured in several nightmares since) his prophecy to XN 1 that a break-through might be expected within the hour. If he survived the blitz, he was unlikely to survive a breakthrough; and a break-through of what? No one had ever seen the Enemy, this Enemy that for Time immemorial had been striving to get across the Frontier. If it got right over, the twilight of the race was at hand. No horror, it was believed at the Front, could equal the horror of that moment. After a hundred miles or so he slept, from pure exhaustion, sitting up in a cramped position, wedged against the next man. Stops and starts and swerves woke him at intervals. The convoy was driving at maximum speeds.

At Emmel he stumbled out to find a storm lashing down. The river was in spate. The column was marched to the depot. Hadolar was separated out and taken in to the terminal building where he was given inoculations, issued with walker, quick-gun, em-kit, prot-suit and other impedimenta, and in a quarter of an hour (perhaps seven or eight seconds up at the top bunker) found himself entering a polyheli with thirty other men. This had barely topped the first rise and into sunlight when explosions and flarings were visible on all sides. The machine forged on, the sight-curtains gradually closing up behind and retreating grudgingly before it. The old Northern vertigo and somnambulism re-engulfed Had. To think of Kar and their offspring now was to tap the agony of a ghost who shared his brain and body. After twenty-five minutes they landed close to the foot of a mag-lev train line. The top-bunker lapse of twenty-two minutes was going, Had saw, to be something less. He was the third to be bundled into the mag-lev train compartments, and 190 seconds saw him emerging at the top and heading for bunker VV. XN 1 greeted his salute merely with a curt command to proceed by rocket to the top bunker. A few moments more and he was facing XN 2.

'Ah, here you are. Your Relief was killed so we sent back for you. You'd only left a few seconds.' A ragged hole in the bunker wall testified to the incident. The relief's cadaver, stripped, was being carted off to the disposal machine.

'XN 2. Things are livelier than ever. They certainly are hot stuff. Every new offensive from here is pitched back at us in the same style within minutes, I notice. That new cannon had only just started up when back came the same shells – I never knew They had them. Tit for that.'

Into H's brain, seemingly clarified by hunger and exhaustion and much emotion, flashed an unspeakable suspicion, one that he could never prove or disprove, having too little knowledge and experience, too little overall view. No one had ever seen the Enemy. No one knew how or when the War had begun. Information and communication were paralysingly difficult up here. No one knew what really happened to Time as one came close to the Frontier, or beyond it. Could it be that the conceleration there became infinite and that there was nothing beyond the Frontier? Could all the supposed missiles of the Enemy be their own, somehow returning? Perhaps the war had started with a peasant explorer lightheartedly flinging a stone northwards, which returned and struck him? Perhaps there was, then, no Enemy?

'XN 3. Couldn't that gun's own shells be reflected back from the Frontier, then?'

'XN 2. Impossible. Now you are to try to reach that forward missile post by the surface – our tunnel is destroyed – at 15° 40' east – you can just see the hump near the edge of the I/R viewer's limit – with this message; and tell him verbally to treble output.'

The ragged hole was too small. H left by the forward port. He ran, on his walker, into a ribbon of landscape which became a thicket of fire, a porcupine of fire, a Nessus-shirt to the Earth, as in a dream. Into an unbelievable supercrescendo of sound, light, heat, pressure and impacts he ran, on and on up the now almost invisible slope . . .

A Two-Timer

. . . I was standing, as it chanc'd, within the shade of a low Arch-way, where I could not easily be seen by any who shou'd pass that way, when I saw as it were a kind of Dazzle betwixt my Eyes and a Barn, that stood across the Street. Anon this Appearance seem'd as 'twere to Thicken, and there stood a little space before the Barn a kind of a clos'd Chair, but without Poles, and of a Whiteish Colouring, and One that sate within it, peering out upon the World as if he fear'd for his life. Presently this Fellow turns to some thing before him in the Chair and moves his Hands about, then peeps he forth again as tho' he fear'd a Plot was afoot to committ Murther upon his Person, and anon steps gingerly out of one Side, and creeps away down the Alley, looking much to right and to left. He had on him the most Outlandish Cloathes that ever I saw. Thinks I, 'tis maybe he, that filch'd my Goods last Night, when I had an ill Dream.

I came out of my Arch and onto the Street and follow'd him down the Alley a little way, not looking straight upon him, but making as to cut my self a Stick, that he might have no thought specially of me, if he shou'd turn round, and espy me. Then when I saw he was gone a good Furlong off from his Chair, and look'd not to turn about, I slacken'd my steps, and presently ran back to that Chair. No Body was abroad.

I look'd stedfastly in this Chair and I must tell you, I never saw the like of it before. A Top Peice it had, four Walls, four Windows of thick Glass, two little Doors with Glass to them, and a Floor, and all of a kind of Silver, but never so lustrous as

21

that Metal, nor so Cold. Within was a hard silvery Seat, but cunningly fashion'd to the Buttocks of a Sitter; and before the Seat as 'twere a Lectern or Bench, on which I saw many Circles with Figures, like so many Clocks or Marriners Dials, and within them Handles with Pointers. I came softly in by one Door, and look'd narrowly on them. One Circle bore Writing, or rather some some kind of Engraving, in a stiff Roman Print, with Words, which I cou'd not understand: GEODETIC-COSMIC RENORMALIZER: SEALED IN WORKSHOP. Another had Words across it engrav'd: HEIGHT CONTROL. Another was a great Dial with YEAR ($0 = 1$), engrav'd below it, a Pointer and Handle within, and round its Circle, Numbers running from the Top clock-wise round, from Nought to Nine and Ninety. Another Dial like that Dial had engrav'd below it YEAR x 10^2, and Numbers from Nought to Nine; and a Third Dial had, YEAR x 10^3, and Numbers from near the Bottom of the Circle from 49 to Nought at the Top, clockwise upon the Left hand, and again to 49 clockwise down on the Right hand. Another, a small Dial, had, MONTH, engrav'd below it, and twelve Numbers like an Hours Clock. Another Dial had, DAY, and one and thirty Numbers. Another had, HOUR, and four and twenty Numbers. In the midst of all these was a Knob of Red colour, smooth and a little hollow, as big as my Thumb.

Thinks I, this is Witchcraft indeed; but I fell to studying the Dials for the Years. I had learnt something in the Mathematicks, and I understood that 10^3 cou'd be the same with One Thousand, while 10^2 might by that token be the same with One Hundred. When I had puzzled these Dials and their Pointers out, methought the Pointers stood not at this present year 1683, but at the year One Thousand Nine Hundred and Sixty Four, with the Pointer for the Thousands of years touching the Number, 1, on the Right-hand side. The Day and Hour (and the Month) were the same as that Day's in April was in truth. Thinks I to my self, This Necromancer wou'd find him self Two Hundred and Eighty One years after this Time, when he is tir'd of seeing how 'tis with this Year of 1683. But you must understand that I was all of a maze, even while I thought these things so cooly.

With that my Foot slips on the strange smooth Silver of the Floor, and I stumbles, and I puts forth my Hands to save my Body from falling, and with this comes down my Left Hand full upon the Red Knob, and in goes that Knob with a sudden push and a small sound. I felt as it might be in a Faint-ness, and the Street went out of my sight, but the Chair stood still. In the place of the Street and the Barn was a new and strange Place, like to a Chamber, and there fell a terrible Clangour about me.

The Chamber was high and smooth. I cou'd not discover, whether it were Built of Wood, or Stone, or Bricks, for all was cover'd with a manner of smooth Plaster and painted over. The Windows were uncommon great and let in much light, and gave upon a great Road, whereon stood great Buildings of Stone. In the Ceiling of this Chamber I saw long Lines or Rods of some Substance, that were Glowing as if they were of Iron heated in a Furnace, for from them came much Light of a Whiteish Hue. I was afear'd they wou'd fall down upon me and burn me. There stood some Tables and Chairs, of a strange kind of design, and some were of Metal.

The Clangour I thought came from without. It chang'd every minute, with a dreadful Thundring and Moaning. I crouch'd me down in my Sorcerer's Chair and commended my Soul to ALMIGHTY GOD, for I thought, that some fearful Disaster was nigh, War or Earthquake mayhap, and that I shou'd soon perish. Before many minutes had past, the Thundring grew more lowd, and a manner of Chariot or Coach came Rowling down the Road without, with a swiftness that no Coach cou'd ever have (as I thought). No horse drew it, and so swiftly went it by, that I cou'd not perceive, whether any Body were within. As it went it Rumbled and Moan'd, 'till the Soul had like to leave my Body for meer Terror. I was still shaking from the Fear of it, when by there came another such, going the other way, making a like Noise, and Snarling besides. Within it methought I saw a Face, that look'd ever forward,

23

and took no mind of me or of the Buildings round about. It seem'd to me then, that all this Thundring and Moaning that continually assail'd my Ears, must come from a sort of Chariots, that came and went in the neighbourhood, but for the most part out of sight.

Now (thinks I) the Boot is on the other Foot, for if that Sorcerer was afraid for his Life, so now am I. And am I (I says to my self) to take leave of this Machine wherein I now sit, and suffer it to be spirited away by the first Comer, even as he did? So (after offering up a short Prayer to the LORD GOD) I fell to examining my Chair more searchingly and narrowly, then I had yet done. And I perceiv'd, low down by my Feet, a Black Rod, that seem'd as it were meant to slide to and fro in a Hole or Slot. It stood out to the Right hand, and by that side was writ (but in Metal), OPERATING. On the other side was writ, LOCKED. In a great Trembling I slid that Rod towards the Left. Then, to make sure that it wou'd indeed return, I slid it back to the Right. I cou'd not well understand the Words, but it seem'd to me, that with the Rod to the Left, the Machine might be safe, so that no Body cou'd do any thing with it, untill he had slid the Rod back again to the Right. Mr Sorcerer, for all his fears, was so secure, as to let alone that precaution.

So, finally, and with another Prayer, I slid the Rod toward the Left again, and stole out of my Machine. The Chamber was warm, and wonderful clean, but there was a mighty strange Odour in the Air, somewhat as of Burning; I suppos'd, it might come from the Hot Bars in the Ceiling, and I perceiv'd that there were great Marks of Soot or Dust upon the Walls and Ceiling, tho' there was no Hearth in the whole place. The Floor was made, or cover'd, with some singular Stuff, which was smooth like Wood or Stone, but resembled more some manner of Linnen-cloth or Carpet to the sight. On a great Bench stood a Row of Books, bound, not in Leather, but in some kind of Cloth (as it seem'd to me), each one in a different colour. Their Paper was more fine and white than I cou'd have thought possible, but thin and frail. The Letters were wonderful black and fine, and they dazzled my Eyes. Tho' the Words were (it's certain) English, yet I cou'd scarce comprehend the meaning of any two or three together. They us'd not our tall s, but throughout only the little one. Their printing was in London, but one, that I took up, seem'd to be printed in some place call'd Chicago (which put me in mind of my Spanish Travells). Yet was this writ in the same English as the rest. As to their theams, as I cou'd not understand the Words, I can tell you little about 'em. Many of 'em seem'd to have much Mathematicks in them, but I found I cou'd not understand that either. The Title of one was, Diamagnetism, which I suppos'd, shou'd be some kind of Magnetick Operation, but it was full of Diagrams and Numbers, and I cou'd find no Loadstone or Compass pictur'd therein. Another Book was entitul'd, Thermistors, but what those might be, I cou'd not discover, tho' herein there were a sort of Plates, such as I can give you little idea of; beyond saying, that they were smooth beyond belief so that they resembled less an Engraving, than a real vision of the Eyes, tho' without colour beyond Black, and White. I cou'd not recognize any thing in them, for all was strange, except a Finger and Thumb in one Picture, that appear'd very large, and a Pin in another, that was also very big. Thinks I, am I come among Gyants? But I remember'd the Face in the Chariot, that was of an ordinary middle size; and the Chairs wou'd not have taken a Gyant, nor the Door.

There was a heap of Papers on the Bench, all printed, but of a marvellous smoothness and lustre. I cou'd not imagine, who wou'd desire to see so many Words in print in a lifetime, and all concern'd with such strange matters withall. On the Wall, hanging from a kind of Pin, was a great Table, as if engrav'd upon a kind of Parchment, but lustrous, that prov'd to be a Calendar or Almanack of the days of one month, that Month of April. But the days of the week had chang'd, so that they did not fit. I saw that the year was indeed that of 1964, Anno Domini, so that my Machine had brought me, where it was appointed. And I thank'd ALMIGHTY GOD for that, and pray'd once more with all my heart, that all shou'd be well.

By this time, I had become in a manner accustom'd to the Clamour without. I was now so Bold, that I thought I cou'd safely go out of this Chamber and out of sight of my Machine. So I softly open'd the Door of the Chamber (and a mighty strange fashion of Door that was), and listen'd (as well as I cou'd for the Chariots) and look'd into the part beyond it. This was a Passage like a huge Hall or Court (but all roof'd), naked and smooth however, and lit by these strange White-hot Bars over-head, that yet seem'd to cast no Heat. No Body was to be seen there, but there were many Doors that open'd out of this Court. I turn'd round to see the Door of the Chamber, that I might know it again, and saw that it bore the Number, Thirteen, high upon it, made of solid Peices of some substance that was Black. Thinks I, may no ill luck attend this Number. Then I closes this Door, opens it again, and closes it finally, and steals along the Hall or Passage where day light came round an Angle.

Here was a great Door, that led perhaps to the Road without, for the Noise of the Chariots was now much more lowd. On the Wall hung great Tables, bearing Papers, and Charts, and solid Numbers, and Knobs, and more things, then I cou'd take note of. Then (before I cou'd vanish) a Door opens, and out comes a Fellow in a mighty strange manner of Cloathing, that I wou'd have burst out laughing at, if I had not been so much in fear. He had long slender Breeches, or Trowzers, of a light-coloured Cloth; a short Coat of smooth Stuff, that came down to his Waist or little lower, but open at the front, with Linnen within and some thing ty'd at the Neck. The fashion of his Hair was mighty strange. He look'd on me, open'd his Mouth, and spoke, what I took to be some forren Tongue, for I cou'd make nothing of it. And here was all our Discourse.

He: Lowgh. Naugh dwenthing foyoo? (With a kind of Questioning voice.)

Myself: Prithee, Sir, do you converse in English?

26

At this he frown'd, and turn'd back thro' his Door, but left it open, for I heard him in speech with another, as follows.

He: Chappea lux lau ikthtauon crauea. Now enthing bau ootim? Caun honstan zaklay wottee sez.

The Other: Nowoulman. Nopmaugh pidgen enwaya. Prapseez thatfla caimea mon thcow. Breezdin breezdaught. Weo tav moce curetay.

Now I thought, I must not stay, for I cannot explain my purpose or my being here, and these do not speak English (I suppose). I ran back to the Door number'd Thirteen, but making as little sound, as I cou'd, open'd it, clos'd it again, got me into my Machine, slid the Rod to rightwards, and, to make the least and safest change I cou'd think of; turn'd the Pointer for the Months to one less (that for March, as I suppos'd) and push'd on the Red Knob. After a short Faint-ness, in which the Chamber turn'd Clowdy in the middle parts, and darker, I found my self and the Machine in the same Chamber, slid the Rod to lock it, and came out to look to the Calendar. This indeed show'd the month of March, and I stole out of the Door (observing first, that the Papers were not in the same state in which I had seen 'em), and came down the Hall. Before I turn'd the Angle there comes past it another Body, cloath'd something like the first. I was thankful that I wear my own Hair, for neither of these Fellows had a Wig, and as I found, all Men in this People wear their own Hair. He turns his Head and looks at me. I bow'd to him, came towards the Tables on the Wall, star'd on them, turn'd round, and stept slowly back to the Room from which I was come. At the Door I turn'd me round, but the Fellow was not to be seen. Back in I went and once more into my Machine, slid the Rod back, and debated within my self; where shou'd I go now. At length I resolv'd, to try a Time a few months ahead, and so I set the Months Dial to August, and shortly found my self there.

Now I still heard the Clamour, but less lowd, and when I got me out of the Chamber I found no Persons without, tho' I waited for the space of above half an hour. When I try'd the great Door to the Road I found it fast, and 'twou'd not by any means be open'd. I concluded, I must have lit upon some Holiday. When I came to look more closely upon one of these Tables of Calendars, I found that the Day of the Machine was a Sunday that month of that year. I thought, I had brought my self into some Colledge, tho' the matters discours'd upon in the Books therein, must have puzzled the very Virtuosi of our Royal Society. I found in some Chambers a number of Books writ in High-Dutch, and two in French, but never a one in Latin, and the tongue of nearly every one was, English. I had a clowdy notion, that the strange speech of the Men that I had met with heretofore, might be a kind of English, not-withstanding it's sounding so uncouth, and these Discoverys made me encline the more to that supposition. But this but made me fear the more, for my chances of coming alive out of such a Predicament, when I cou'd not even play a false part, such as to be some Traveller, that I might be let alone. If I cou'd but find some of the simpler sort of Books, I might learn some news from 'em, but how was I to Interpret their Outlandish expressions?

'Twas while I ponder'd on these matters, that I came upon a great mass of Broad-sheets, folded together, in one of the Chambers. I fell to perusing them and soon saw, that I had a manner of Courant before me, wherein was printed all News, that might concern this People. The Print was shut up in many Columns with long Lines between 'em and huge Words at the head of each Column. But here again, I cou'd make out little, and what I cou'd, 'twas all Robberies and Murthers, with some Warlike Entertainment. There was besides a subtle sort of Engraving, mighty life-like, such as I saw in that Book before, that shew'd Men running hither and thither, and single Faces that look'd sadly upon me, and Wenches half-nak'd. On one Sheet was a Chariot, such as I had seen in the Road, with no Horses, all clos'd in with glass Windows. I saw News that seem'd to be come from India, from China, from Moscovy, and from the America's, with a date but one day before the day of the Sheet (which was that Saturday), as't had been in the next Shire. At this I began to Tremble anew, for I wonder'd to think, what Wizards I was come among, and what a People, that wou'd know what went about across the World, as well as what lay at their own Door Steps.

Now I crept back to my Machine like a Dog to it's Kennel, and debated with my self, what I was to do. I desir'd mightily to know more of this World, but I cou'd not see, how I was to get by in it. Now my Eyes fell upon a Peice of the Lectern in that Machine, whereon 'twas writ across, HORIZONTAL MOVEMENT. Thinks I, here is the means, that I can Journey by, or that will at least bring me out of this Building, without a Soul troubling me. The whole Peice cou'd be mov'd, 'till it slipp'd down along-side, and underneath there lay a number of little shining Crystalline Plats, like Windows in the Metal, each one mark'd out in Squares, and each with two Buttons along-side to right and left. Below the first Plat was a Subscription, METRES; by the second, DM, HM; by the third, KM X 1, 10. The Squares of the second and third Plat were each laid across with ten Lines each way, that made finer Squares. Lastly were two small Half-Globes, or Hemi-Spheres, with Lines of Longitude and Latitude clearly mark'd upon 'em, and faint lines, that shew'd the Continents. The Hemi-Sphere on the left hand had below it the Letter, N, the other, the Letter S, so that I could well see, that they meant the World to north and south of the Equator. These Spheres had the same two Buttons each beside 'em. By every place, the Button on the left hand was mark'd with a Bent Arrow to right-ward, and a Letter N, whilst the other had a like Arrow and the Letter E. I thought, it must be, that the first Plat is for the smallest movement, and the Globes for the greatest, across the World. The left-hand Buttons, are to move north-wards, if you turn 'em clockwise, or south, the other way, and the right-hand Buttons, are to move east, and west. Now will I make a Tryal of the first Plat, with this Green Knob (for there was one, like the Red Knob, but amongst the Plats).

I pray'd once more, then I turn'd the left-hand Button with

what Care I cou'd. I saw a little black Line begin to grow straight up along on the Plat. When it had grown to the extent of half a Square, as I thought, I stopt my Turning, and the Line grew no more. Then I push'd on the Green Knob. And behold, some thing struck my Shoulder, and I found, the Machine was come about two foot to one side, so that the Wall of it on one quarter was vanish'd within the Wall of the Room. Then, too, I saw a kind of Needle within a little Dial amongst the Plats, and one end was mark'd N, so I thinks this must be a Compass, that will tell me, where is North. The Road is to the north-east of where I stand. The breadth of a Metres Square, I now saw, must be three, or four foot, and since there were ten of these Squares each way, it cou'd be, that the smallest Square in the next Plat was the same as ten Metres, whatever these might be in truth. Then I mov'd carefully one Metre to east-wards, and it was so, and I had the fourth Side of my Machine safe and sound once more, for which I gave hearty thanks. A Metre, I concluded, was a Yard or an Ell in this People's speech, that is, if 'twas indeed among this People that the Machine was made, but of that I had no certain knowledge. The ways that I had turn'd lay all mark'd out in black upon the first Plat.

Now I consider'd if this Machine is to move Horizontally, and it come within a Hill, I shall Choak, or if it come over a Valley, I shall fall within it to the ground, and be kill'd. So I look'd again at the Circle where 'twas writ of Height, and I saw it had two Dials, one within the other, the outer Dial mark'd COARSE, the inner, FINE. Above them was a slender Tube, with a shining Green Glow, or Spark, floating in it, and writ alongside, METRES, SURFACE INDEX, BLUE = CAR; and even Marks all the way up the Tube. I thought long on these things, and in the end I thought that I knew what they must mean. The Fine Dial wou'd send me gently up, or down, the Coarse one far. If I saw a Blew Spark, I shou'd know it was to shew, where the Machine wou'd be, and how far from the Green, before I push'd on the Red or the Green Knob. So shou'd I be sav'd from Death.

Now, says I to my self, I see no Body in the Road, and the Chariots have not come on it for these many minutes. I will bring my Machine beyond this Building, but so near, that a Chariot is not like to strike against it. And this I did, moving three Metres east and two north.

Here the Clangour was twice as terrible, and the Smell of Burning far stronger, mix'd with some thing sweet, that caught my Breath. I saw no Persons about, but I judg'd it prudent, to place my Machine close by a Wall, and this I presently did, with a little Manage. No sooner had I contriv'd this, than a Host of Children came by. One had a Stick, with which he Rattled upon the Wall and on my Machine. Another stopt and cry'd, as I thought, Luk, his a new found Keost (or somewhat of this nature) na Man putting git op na Saun-day. I was in fear once more, but another Child calls to him, Horriop, wa lay it! and they all runs on. Then I saw three Chariots standing idle further down the Road. The Buildings that were near me were vast Edifices of Stone, but where the Chariots stood, was a low sort of Brick-made Houses, standing each in a little Park or Plot, with a few Trees. One Chariot, I saw anon, was standing in a Side-Road in such a little Park, and a Fellow was rubbing it down like one, that wou'd Curry a Horse. He had a Pail on the Ground by him, of a light Blew colour. On each side of the Road, and evenly sett apart from each other, were tall Masts, like so many Gyants Pikes, but of Stone, and crook'd at the Top, with a little Cage of Glass at the Crook. I found later, that they were publick Lanthorns, as you shall hear. The Borders of the Road were wonderful neat and trim, with Grass, shut in by Pygmaean Walls of Stone, and beside these Flaggs, to make a firm Path. The Sky above was dim and smoaky, for all that there was no Clowd in it. Tho' I seem'd to be in the midst of a great Town, there was no Ditch in the Street, but it bent up towards the middle part, and was smooth and black. At the Sides, under the little Walls of the Grass, were Holes with a broad sort of Grate, as if to let the Water down, but no Water ran there.

Now I wax'd very Bold, and wou'd see, what the Fellow was doing with the Chariot. I saw him empty the Pail he had, at a place by the House, and while he was thus busy'd, I mov'd my Machine as many Metres as I thought shou'd bring me on t'other side of the Road by him. I found my self in the middle of the Road with the Ground of it over one side of the Floor of my Machine, and a Chariot was Rowling up to me as if the Devil rode it. I gave my self up for lost, but the Chariot made as to stop, with a Fearful Sound, and swerv'd round me, with a Devils Countenance in deed within it. At that the Fellow that had the Pail look'd round, and saw me, and came out upon the Road Edge, and call'd out, Wot you doing with that Contrapshen? I took the Sence, of what he was saying, and open'd one Door, and cry'd softly to him, If you will go back a Fathom or two, I'l bring it safe to the side. He seem'd to know, what I meant, for he ran backwards to his Chariot, and stood staring at me, while I mov'd the Machine two Metres in his way and (with the Fine Dial for the Height) enough upward to bring my Floor clear out. Hahaughdgea do that? says he, and 'twas his turn, to be frightned. Then I thought, this Machine is not known to this People, its either a Mystery of some Virtuosi, or 'tis come from some other Time. My Fellow had a soft open kind of Countenance, that made me put some trust in him, so I slid the black Rod across, that lock'd the Machine, and came out, and told him, I was come by strange chance from another Time, where I had found this Machine, that I had learnt to manage, that cou'd send a Man from one Place to another, or from one Time to another. I told him, I cou'd not easily understand his Speech, but that if he spake slowly, I wou'd make shift to follow, what I cou'd. Can you put that Thing ouva Ther in the Shayid clouce ptha Hauooce? he says, and points. So I brought my Machine little by little, where he wou'd have it, and lock'd it again. Comm insauid, he says, so I went into his House with him.

Every thing in this House was smooth, and for the most part very clean, and almost all the Doors and Walls were painted over. There was a savour of Soap and Spice about. He set me down in a great Chair, and star'd on me, then he moves his Hand to a little Button on the Wall, and of a sudden a Light shone out of a Bowl, that hung from the Ceiling. There was no Flame to it, and it was perfectly steady, but I cou'd perceive no cause, why it shou'd begin to shine. I can see (he seem'd to say) that ye're not from this Time. I suppose (but he said Tauim and suppowze) you come from the Seventeenth or Eighteenth Century? I told him, it was even now the Year 1683. He ask'd me a deal of questions, but some I cou'd not understand, and others I made not to understand, for I had no mind to give him too much instruction. But I told him, I wish'd to lie here for a time, for I fear'd a Reckoning with the Sorcerer that had brought the Machine to my Village, and knew, that if I left it there for long, he shou'd find it again anon, and I shou'd have lost all chance, of further enterprize. Then says he, You must meet my Wife (in his odd Speech), and he goes out to call her in, from her Garden. While he was gone, I looks out at my Machine, which was safe by the Wall, and observ'd what I cou'd about the Chamber. He brings in his Wife (a mighty pretty Woman, as I saw when I had got accustom'd to her sawcy fashion of Cloathing) and presently we three set to't to find, how I was to live there. I found, they had no Children. Says she, Of course you must stay with us, and, looking on her Countenance, I found it easie to agree. But how am I to repay you, and how am I to go unnotic'd in these Cloathes, that are so unlike your's? Says I. Have you nothing of Value with you, says he, then we can buy you some Cloathes and so on? I have nought, that shou'd get me a Suit of Cloathes, says I. Have you any Books, or Clocks, or Silver at home? for they wou'd fetch high enough Prices today, says he (but he says howm, hauy, prowesses); you see, a thing like that, two or three hundred years old, will be quite costly today. And, as it happens, I know how to place this kind of Antique. 'Tis agreed, said I, I'll go back and bring some Fine Things. But let me wait, 'till to-morrow, for by then it may be, that my Sorcerer will have

33

given over searching for my Machine, or that he will have journey'd far off. To this he agrees, and his Wife said, she wou'd bring in some Tea. While she was gone, he said, he wou'd shew me round the House, but all he did, was to bring me up the Stairs to a Closet or Privy, which he told me, was wash'd by Water, that I shou'd pour on, by pressing on a kind of Handle. Next by it was a Chamber for Washing your Person, that had a Bason, with two Taps, from which Water came. One brought forth Water very hot, that I was like to have Scalded my self, if I had not seen the Steam rising from it. By this Bason was a great Trough with two other Taps, and a Dish full of Holes in the Ceiling above it.

Besides a Dish of Tea, they had some Bread and some Jellie and a deal of little Cakes. After this the Husband goes to a Box, that stood on a Table at the side, and of a sudden a lowd Noise comes from the Box, and it was some kind of wild Musick. Thinks I, this is a new sort of Toy, but presently the Musick ceas'd, and the Voice of a Man came forth, that I quak'd for sudden fear. Then another Voice discours'd for some time, and presently ceas'd again, and the wild Musick began once more. They gave me an explanation, it was Musick from many Miles away, but how it came into their Box, they cou'd not make clear. This Box they call, a Raydeow. After that the Man remember'd his Chariot, which he call'd, his Car, and went out to conclude with his cleaning it. He shew'd it to me, and said, that it went by Burning within. When he had done with the cleaning it, he lit the Furnace in it's Bowels, by no more then the turn of a little Key, and, seating him self in it, conducted it into it's Stable, which he call'd, a Garraudge. He said, my Machine shou'd be more safe, within the House, and after we had measur'd it with a Measure he had of Steel, that bent round, and had measur'd the distance too, I mov'd it once again, within a commodious Porch he had.

Over a good Supper of cold Mutton, wash'd down with some bitter Ale from a glass Bottle, he assures me again, I shou'd be able to get a good Price, for a Book or a Peice of

Silver. Several Pounds, says he, enough to buy you a Shirt or two. My Spirits shot up to the Heavens with the First part of his Sentence, and were blown half way back, with the Second. That a Book, purchas'd for a Shilling, cou'd be so priz'd, as to command several Pounds; and that such a vast Sum, cou'd buy no more, then a Shirt, I cou'd scarce credit. But he made me know, that a Pound was nothing today. I saw, I shou'd have to furnish my self well, upon my Excursion to my own Time. But in the mean while we fell to talking of the state of England. They took me for an Irish Man, it seems, which put me out of countenance, 'till I saw they meant no harm by it, but were puzzled by my Speech, which indeed they found near as hard, as I theirs. So I told them, I came from a Village, where now stood his Town. And I found, the name of my Village, was now the name of a Sobbub of his Town (which is their name, for a part of a Town) and that was the part all around us. I thought his Town must be a very great City, but he says, 'twas of but a middle size, with only fifty thousand Souls in't. You may suppose, I open'd my Eyes at that. But it seems, they do not reckon a City is great, unless it reach above two hundred thousand; and of that reckoning they have a good number, while a few of the greatest have above a Million. How the Land cou'd support so many, I cannot tell, but where we have one Body, they have ten or twelve. Whilst we were speaking, the Lanthorns in the Road all came alight in one instant, and no Body lit 'em. He said, 'twas by Electricity, which they make in great Buildings from turning Wheels by Steam, or (in other places) from an Esoterick sort of Chymistry, and send many miles along Wires.

I was drowzy long before my Hosts, and they had me a Bed made in a spare Chamber above Stairs. But before I went to Rest, my Host perswaded me, to wash my self over in that Trough they had. The Dish with Holes, that hung from the Ceiling, was for Water to Rain down upon you, but I lik'd it not. They wash them selves in these Baths nigh every day, for that the Water is kept so hot with this same Electricity (by

35

which they can accomplish well nigh every thing they wou'd), that they may keep them selves sweet-smelling (for they set great store by that), and in order to the cleansing off a kind of Soot or Dirt, that fly's every where in the Air, and from whence comes this odour of Burning, that was about.

I had an uneasie Rest at first by reason of the many lowd Sounds without, but never-the-less I woke at the usual hour with me. My Host and his Wife made no sound, and neither within the House nor without was any Body stirring, which appear'd mighty strange to me. I thought, now 'twill be safe, may hap, to return impuned to my House and Time, to gather what I will and bring all back here. I stole down, and after a while found how to open the Fastnings of the Door out to their Porch. There stood my Machine. I unlock'd it's Rod, and remember'd, that I shou'd return to April, and so mov'd the Months Dial, besides the Years Dials, which I set back to my own Year. Then I saw the Green Spark rise in the Tube, that shew'd the Height, some three Metres on it's Scale, and leave below it a Blew one. So I knew, I shou'd come out from here under the high Meadow at home, or there abouts. I study'd the Plats for moving your place narrowly, and mov'd their Buttons, untill I brought the Lines on 'em back, to whence I begun, and the Green Spark sank down to swallow up the Blew. Now I try'd the Red Knob, letting alone the Green, and all was well, for I found my self in the Machine in the Lane at home near to the Barn, whence I had come. But I felt as if I had been in this Moment before, and a great Dizzyness and Clowdy-ness in my Head. Then I saw, that it was no dim Morning that I beheld, but a bright After-noon; and a Bird, that I had left perch'd upon a Bough close by, sate there exactly as't had been. At length I knew, that I was back at the very Instant, when I had first mov'd the Machine, and that my Sorcerer shou'd be but now gone down the Alley, and might at once return. I had forgot my Hours and Days Dials. I mov'd 'em straightway back eleven hours, to that day's Sun-rise, before he had come. All my tarrying the night before was to no end, for I cou'd chuse any Time.

When I press'd upon the Red Knob there was I in a grey half-light. No Body was yet about, and step by step I mov'd my Machine down the Street, 'till I came before my House, which (of course) was bolted and barr'd. Then I mov'd it inside in the great Chamber, and in the Gloom search'd about for my Hanger, a tall Jugg of Silver, a Snuff-box, a fine Time-peice that I had, a glass Bowl, two Books of Sermons and three Broad-sheets of Satyricall Verses, and the Volume of Mr Sympkins his Travells of a dozen years heretofore. Then I thought, I will need to Shave my self, so I found my best Razour. And I now knew, who 'twas had these Things from my House, that Night, and not the Sorcerer. I took up an old Sack, in which to carry my Goods, but the Bowl and the Snuff-Box I wrapp'd in soft Cloth, and plac'd in a little Coffer I had. I plac'd all with some labour within the Machine, and was about to take my leave, when I bethought me of the time, and how at that hour I had been in Bed asleep. Am I then there in my Bed, or am I here? thinks I, and I stole into my Bed-Chamber to see. The Day-Light was coming in now, and there in the Bed was my Body asleep, my Face being turn'd half to the Wall. But there was a kind of Shimmering Motion in it. The Hair lifted on my Head and I turn'd Cold as Ice, my Mouth parch'd and my Heart knocking fit to burst it's House. And I felt my Body (my own that I was in, so to speak) pull'd as it were a Grain of Iron by a Loadstone, towards the Body that lay on the Bed. That Body stirr'd and turn'd, and cry's out, Ish (or some thing such). I flung out of the Chamber, and it was like straining against Ropes, and I crept Quaking into my Machine, mov'd it beyond the House, and in the Light manag'd it to the morning of the next day in August of the Year 1964, and before the House of my Hosts. Then I brought it within their Porch, and knock'd a Box over there, but woke no Body by good chance. And I fell on my Knees in my Machine (bruising my Shins and scraping my Elbow in the doing it) and humbly sought Pardon

37

of ALMIGHTY GOD, if I had offended against His Laws in the making such an Unnatural Journey, and besought Him to keep me, from the Snares of the Devil.

It was the hour, when I had gone from the Porch; but I had no Stomach to remain alone 'till these Late-risers shou'd awaken, so I mov'd the Hours Dial forward two hours. And what shou'd I find, but that they were up, and had miss'd me, and were running hither and thither in Gowns, which they wore at Night, thinking that I had gone for ever. And so, methinks, was I nearly so gone. But No, says I, I have been back to my own Time, to bring back where-withall to trade, but do not ask me to do't again. I wou'd not, for all the Gold in the Indies, untill I depart for good. Says the Wife, You look as if you had seen a Ghost. And I, Why so I have: I have seen my Self. I wou'd say no more, but I thought, If I had been Drawn into my other Body then, who knows the End of't?

After a time I shav'd my self with my Razour, and the Husband lent me some Cloathes of his, that I might escape Notice, which I got into, and laid aside my own. He wou'd not look into my Sack or my Coffer at the present, for said he, he must to work, where he cou'd tell me more, what might be got for my Merchandize. We three took a great Breakfast. There was some golden Biscuits, but very fine and small and broken, we ate with Milk, which they call'd, Sere-ills; there was a great Potfull of Coffee, but made too thick, and mix'd with warm Milk from a Flask; there was Bacon fry'd and Eggs fry'd, and slic'd pieces of Bread lightly brown'd, with Butter, and a Marmalade made from Oranges to spread on 'em.

Then the Husband bade me climb into his Chariot beside him, and fastned me in with a Harness, that I might not be tost about, and him self in too, with my Sack and Coffer in the back part, and he rode this Chariot with me, to the middle part of the Town. I had new terrors, with the Noise, and all the other Chariots (which were scores, nay hundreds) and a Throng of Folk, and all rushing hither and thither like a People possess'd of Devils. I shou'd have been more frightned, if I had not been

38

full of strange Feelings in my Body, that put me in mind of a Sea-voyage, for I seem'd to be push'd to one side and then to another, and anon back into my Seat; which made my Stomach very uneasie, the more because of several thick Odours in the Chariot. We were going the slowest of almost all the Chariots, or Cars, that I saw, for all hurtled past us. There were great Wagons, like Hulks full of Slaves, two Tiers of them, all painted Red. My Host said (as well as I cou'd hear him, for the Noise), they were publick Coaches, which he call'd, Busses (as tho' they were Boats), and that you pay'd to be carry'd so far. From the Cars issu'd flashing Lights, to shew, said he, what they meant to do. I saw great Pictures (when we were brought to a stop for several minutes together) as high as a House, in many Colours, by the Road side, but got no chance, to ask him what they meant. He leaves his Car in a great Place full of others, and taking me by the Arm, marches me a fair way round past tall Windows where were all manner of Wares shewn for Sale, and at length into his Shop, where he and others sold, for the one part House-Furniture, for the rest Books (but bound in Leather, not like those I had seen in the Colledge) and a great many sorts of Baubles and Silver Ware. He left me for a time, and spoke with another, then brings me into an inner Chamber, and bids me open my Sack and Coffer. First he looks in my Books. The first he took was that Volume of Travells, and his Eye lit up, and he reads it's Title Page, and looks quickly thro' it, and goes to some cloth-bound Volumes he has in a Corner, and reads in various of 'em, and comes back, muttering to himself, Not in Wing either (what ever he meant by that). Then he looks at me, and says, I'l give you fifty Pound for that. I was ready to swallow his Offer, but I saw his Tongue licking his Lips, and his Hand shook a little, so I took counsel with my self, and I says, It grieves me, but I cou'd never part from my old Companion in many Lands, unless for three hundred Pound (for I knew now, these Pounds here wou'd not go far). He laugh'd at that, scornfully, but we fell to chaffering, and in the end, we agreed upon one hundred and seventy five

Pound, against a Bottle of good Wine, which I forgot to tell you, I had snatch'd up and put in the Sack. And, says he, I cou'd yet have the Words of Sympkins, for he had in his Shop at the back a wonderful Engine, that wou'd take Pictures of what ever was put before it, that were perfect Likenesses, and that in the twinckling of an Eye each. He calls this Engine, a Zerrocks. But, said he, with so many Pages, 'twill take time. Then I cou'd bring these Likenesses, but on loose Sheets, back with me to my own Time.

For the rest of the Books and Tracts he settled upon some tens of Pounds each, but more for the Silver and Glass, and especially for the Snuff-Box, which surpriz'd me not a little. The Hanger too, which had a good Blade, pleas'd him mightily. In the end I was rich enough for a long Stay, as he assur'd me, as soon as he cou'd draw out his Money, from a House, where he had lent it, and that he wou'd do at the middle of the day. Then he told me, I shou'd do best, to stay quietly in his Inner Room for that morning, while he did much Business in his Shop. But first he takes me to the Zerrocks, which was like a Vat cover'd with Glass, with nothing in it, but great Coyls, and Peices of Metal, and a Green Light, which came and went. He gives my Book to another, and bids him take much care with it, and begin to copy it therewith. The Light goes to and fro like a Loom, and after a time Sheets of Paper come down at one Side, with (as I saw) a very perfect Picture, of what was turn'd towards the Light.

My Host gave me a Dictionarie, printed very small on thin Paper, a Duodecimo Atlas of the World, and the Courant he had had that morning, but had not read. There was much, that I cou'd not understand, but I learnt, that there was now a great Nation in America, many Nations in Africa and in the West and East Indies, an Antipodaean Continent call'd Australia betwixt India and the Southern Pole, and a barren Continent about that Pole. Ships ply'd betwixt these Continents, and all knew each others business. Terra Incognita there was none, for the whole Globe was mapp'd out, or well-nigh so. Men, and

Women too, were trying to cross the Seas from Dover to Calais by Swimming, for the meer Sport of't; if there were no Gyants, they were Gyants in strength.

About Noon, as he knew by a marvellous small Watch, that was held to his left Wrist by a close Chain of metallick Peices, my Host carry'd me to an Ordinary, which he call'd, Launsh. Men and Women together, and even Children, came up behind each other in a long Line, and waited, to take from a long Bench, what ever Meats wou'd take their fancy, with Knives and Forks, and pay'd at last, when they sought a small Table, whereat to sit and eat. I cou'd understand little yet, but what my Host (or his Wife at home) spoke to me slowly, so I sate like one abroad in a far Countrey. Afterwards he brought me to his Bank, the House where he had his Money in loan. He told them, he wou'd draw an extraordinary Fund out of his Moneys, which he was pleas'd to name, the Antiquitys Account, and before me he paid into this Fund, all the Moneys he had agreed to pay me for my Goods, but all was done meerly upon Paper, with much writing and signing. He told me privatly, he durst not make me a Customer of this House, for fear, too many Questions shou'd be ask'd, but I stood by and they were to think, I was a Man of his. Then he draws out twenty Pound for smaller Expences, which he gives to me, some of it Coyn, but what they call Pounds, are nothing but Scraps of Paper, with green Pictures on 'em; yet he assures me, they shou'd buy a Pounds worth of Goods, and indeed 'twas so, as I found (except that a Pound goes such a little way with them). He takes me to the Taylors, and buys me a Suit of Cloathes, with all kind of Linnen, and pays for all out of a new Book of Papers, that he calls Checks, subscrib'd for this new Account, and shews me, how much it comes to, which was a great number of Pounds, that I was still not us'd to.

When at length we were got back, to his Shop, 'twas half an hour after Three. I spent the next three hours studying, but got little further. He carries me back to his Home in his Car. I was standing by it near to the House, when I saw in the Heavens a

Meteor, like a shining Thread, growing ever at one end. I was astonish'd but he told me, 'twas a Plentrail, or a Plaintrail, or some such thing, which I did not understand. But anon there came a Rumbling, and in another Part of the Sky a Thing like a huge Bird, but that mov'd not it's Parts. Says he, that was another Plain. He gave me to understand, that Men may travell in these Plains, which are like Shipps that go in the Air, but driven like his Car by a manner of Burning. In truth, they also call 'em Air-Craft.

When we were come in, where his Wife had a Welcome for us, she gives us a Glass full (but very small) of a Sherry Wine, but the Tast was strange to me. While she prepares a Meal, he turns to a Box with a Window in't, and there Shines in it's Window a Picture, that mov'd and chang'd continually, and Sounds withall, like as it had been a Comedy play'd within the Box by Dwarfs, but the Colour was but Black, and White, with a Blew Cast to't. Some part was News, but chiefly Folly. This too they have in every House, and from this great Servant Electricity. I fetch'd now my old Cloathes and Shoes and ty'd them in a Bundle, which I left on the Floor of the Machine. My Host took a great Cloth, and cover'd the Machine, that it be not try'd of curious Fingers, or set too many Tongues wagging.

At the Meal and after it (when they were not staring upon this Box with the Window, which they call a Tellie) they talk'd with me, upon the State of the World. I shou'd make too great an Excursion, if I shou'd take upon me to Communicate every Thing that befell me in this Adventure. You will wonder especially, what sort of People they were indeed, that I was fallen among; and tho' it took many Weeks in the Learning, yet I shall make bold to take only as many Minutes, in the Telling it. They spoke much then, of the Insolence of Youth, which they thought new, but it seem'd to me, that there was nothing new but Wealth and Idleness, that feed this Insolence. There are no poor unruly Apprentices here, but good Money is to be earn'd easily by a Stripling. If these live too easily, so too in a manner do the Children (for all their Schooling is so hard, as I shall tell you later); which is the Seed of the other Trouble. They are not brought up to Obedience and Godliness, but (as I found) to Rail upon their Parents, when they are scarce five year old, and make Sport with them. But the Spring of this, is in the Wives, for these own no Man's Controul, not even in Law, but manage all things equally with 'em, and take all manner of Work, as bold as Men (for they are as well school'd), and High and Low dress them selves in Finery, and leave their Children to bring them selves up (so that many run wild), and are fix'd upon Folly and Man-catching, as I saw from a Journal, made in Colours (and more like a great Quarto, then a Journal) that is printed for Women alone. They go bare-legg'd or with Legs cover'd in bright Stockings but marvellous fine, and close-fitting; and their Legs shewing immodestly above the Knee. In this Journal I saw all manner of sawcy Pictures. (But some Journals for Men, are full of Lewdness and Filth, both in Pictures and Writing.) As to Man-catching, Marriages are made every where, not as the Parents shall agree, but as a Young Man and Girl shall fancy each other, and Divided as lightly, by an easie Divorce. Religion has little to say to all this, for our Tollerance, is become their Indifference, and tho' there be Churches, few go to 'em, and of Enthusiasts there are scarce any. They have for this cause nought to live for, but to get as much as they can, whether it be Pleasure, or Money.

Yet do they have a sweeter and a quieter Living, than any we see. I saw few Persons diseas'd or distemper'd, or even crippled. The King's Evil, Agues, Plagues and Small Pox, are all but gone. Not one of a Man's Children die before they come of age, if you can believe me; and yet his House is never crowded, for they have found means, that their Women shall not Conceive, but when they will. This seem'd to me an Atheistical Invention, and one like to Ruin the People; yet they regard it as nothing, save only the Papists and a few others. Every Man and Woman can read, tho' the use the Generality make of't, is only to Wager by Letter, which they call Pulls, and in Assemblys, which they call Bingow, and to

43

read the Notices, that are every where planted, like Texts, but prophane ones, to tell 'em where they may go, and what Business is in hand. They have great Safety, in the Streets and in the Fields, so that Thefts and Violence to the meanest Person are the cause of News in the Courants; but they slaughter one another with their Cars for that they rowl by so fast, and altho' they are safe from Invasion, by their Neighbour Nations in Europe, yet they are ever under the Sword of Damocles from a Destruction, out of the other End of the Earth, by these same Air-Craft, or from a kind of Artillery, that can shoot many Thousands of Leagues, and lay wast half a Countrey, where it's Shot comes to ground, or so they wou'd have me believe.

They have a sovran Queen, yet is the Power of the Crown so diminish'd, that they have rather a Common-Wealth, then a Monarchy. They have a Parliament, with what they call the Torys, I know not why, for they are nothing for a Papist Succession, but for Wealth; and against 'em no Excluding Whiggs, but a Party, that wou'd have all the business of the Kingdom (or Queendom) in the hands of them that govern. One third of what a Man earns, goes in Taxes, such as England never heard the like of in my Time. Every Man however lowly, and, what is worse, every Woman, has a power of Vote for who they shall have in Parliament, yet the Members do little, but Vote in Parliament again the way their Leaders tell 'em. But Money is King of half England, for the great Merchants and Heads of Business Houses can do pretty much what they will. The King of the other half, is the Labourer, for if he like not his Lot, he engages his Guild to command all the Men to lay down their Tools and depart, it may be 'till months are gone by, untill he has it his own way; his Guild will give 'em Moneys to provide for 'em. In the mean time the Customers suffer, from both Sides: the one sending Prices up; and the other taking labour away, so that nothing is done.

But for all this they live fine enough. They are grown so nice, that they make great outcry, at the least Dirt or Violence. In

44

their Punishments they have no Burnings, no Quarterings, no Whippings, Pilloryings, or Brandings, and they put up no Heads of Ill-doers. Their Hangings are but few, and are perform'd in secret; and there are those in the Government that wou'd bring in a Bill, to put a stop even to that, so that the worst Felon, shou'd escape with nothing worse, then a long Imprisonment. Tho' they are in fear, of what will come of it, and trouble them selves much about Ill-doers in the Land, I never saw a Brawl, or a Rabble, or the least Insult offer'd to any Body, the whole time I was there, nor any Man taken in Drink, beyond a little Exaltation. Altho' my Cloathes were so strange to them, yet I verily believe, I cou'd have walk'd abroad in 'em, without meeting any untoward entertainment in the Streets. They are so many, those who wou'd get a Place, at a Play-house, or in one of their Busses, must wait in a Throng; but in stead of Jostling, they stand orderly in a long Line, without the need of enforcement. I saw not one Man begging, and but few that seem'd poor, or wasted by Sickness.

Yet in truth they are a Staid, and Phlegmatick Folk, that will not easily laugh, or weep, or fly in a passion, and whether it be from their being so press'd together, or from the Sootyness of the Air, or from their great Hurrying to and from work, their Faces shew much Uncontent and Sowerness, and they regard little their Neighbours. All their Love, is reserv'd to those at Home, or their Mercy, to those far off; they receive many Pleas, for Money and Goods, that they may send, for ailing Persons, that they never knew, and for Creatures in Africa and the Indies, whom they never will see. Every Saturday little Children stand in the Streets, to give little Flags an Inch across, made of Paper, in return for Coyns, for such a Charity. As for their Hatred, 'tis altogether disarm'd, for none may carry a Sword, or Knife, a Pistol, or a Musquet, under Penalty, tho' indeed there be Ruffians here and there, that do so in secret, but only that they may committ a Robbery impunedly upon a Bank, or a great Store of Goods, and so gain thousands of Pounds in a moment. (As for my Hanger, 'twere only an

45

Ornament to them.) So is there no Point of Honour with them, but what may be settled by Law and so line the Lawyers pockets, if the matter be grave enough.

That their ways are so soft and peaceable, comes perhaps from the being so well supply'd. They have Light, or Heat to cook with, or to keep their Chambers warm withall, at the meer touch upon a Button; tho' for these they must pay, when the Reckoning is brought to 'em. In the very Heat of Summer, they keep their Meat sweet, in a Chest, which is ever so cold that Frost and Rime encrust the inside parts of it; and this comes, as their Light and much of their Heat, from this same Electricity. If they wou'd have discourse with a Friend, or wou'd buy or sell any thing, without a Journey, they have an Engine that they call a Found, or a Tellie-found, in their Houses, where they can both speak, and hear, any other Person that they chuse, by the turning a Dial with Numbers writ upon it. And this too is from Electricity. They may listen to Musick on their Raydeow Boxes, or see Plays in their Tellie Windows, any week, more then you cou'd meet with in London in a season in our Time. They have all manner of Things, both for work, and sport, and Meats too, that I can scarce describe to you. In their Shops I saw a vast number, both of sorts of things, and of different fashions of the same, and of single examples of each fashion. Some of these, are so Costly, that only the richest can buy 'em; but many may be purchas'd by any but the poorest. With all this High-living, every Man is thus like a great Prince; and tho' he have not Servants (for few of 'em will serve another) Electricity is his Servant. Yet are they no more content, then a great Prince might be, or less, for they know no better, then to conceive this soft Life is their Birthright, and that if they live not as well as, or better then their Neighbour, the State is to blame.

For that they buy and sell at such a rate, and keep them selves so mighty well supply'd with all manner of Engines, and Stuffs, the different Houses, that supply 'em, are in great rivalry one with another. From this comes a great Shew that they make every where, with Words and Pictures, with bright Colours, like those of some Painter at Court, but in thousands of Copys for all to see, in their Journals and on huge Placards, that stand by the Roads, especially in the Towns. This they call meerly, Advertisement, as who shou'd call a Shout, a Murmur.

This brings me to their Words. Tho' they have many Words, that I never heard or saw before, I was quite as much in a quandary at learning their Tongue, by reason of Words that I knew well, but that they us'd otherwise then with us. Many, as I found in the end, had sunk (where Advertisement had flown up). So when they say, Terrible, they mean Great; when they say, Fabulous, they mean Goodly. Enthusiasm, is a meer Zeal, or pleasure in doing. But other Words, are much twisted in their Sence. Sex, which with us is the being Male, or Female, with them is the Coupling of Man and Woman. Romance is no Fantasticall Tale, but an Affair of the Heart; and so too with Romantick. A Buss, which with us (in that meaning) is a kind of Sea-vessel, with them is a Publick Carriage, as I have said. To Want, is not to lack, but to have a wish for some thing. One who is Nice, do's not turn his Nose up, he is not Delicat, but meerly pleasing to the speaker. One who is Sensible, is not keenly perceiving of some thing, but a Man of good sence. They interlace their sentences with absolute Cant, that with us is heard from Cut-purses and Ruffians, but with them is perfectly gentle. On the other hand, they abound in long learned expressions, that their very Children use, and wrap their Notions up in Bundles, as to confound the listener. As for their manner of Uttering, 'tis altogether odd, as I have shewn it, but not without a smack of the low speech of a Cockney from London. After a time my Ears grew accustom'd to it, so that I heard, what was meant.

The Nation that dwells in America, and they that dwell in Moscovy, they say are the Arbiters of the World, for they have that Artillery, that I wrote of before, in the greatest quantity. Besides this, from these two Nations, come the Inventions, of Machines that they have fired off toward the Moon, and the

47

Planets Mars, and Venus, as if they had been Cannon Shot; which send back News of their Journeys, and (in some manner) Pictures, of what they meet; and so methinks, it is to take nigh on three hundred years, and an Enterprize from abroad, not from England, to fulfill these Flattring Verses of Mr Dryden,

> Then we upon our Globes last verge shall go
> And view the Ocean leaning on the Sky:
> From thence our rowling Neighbours we shall know,
> And on the Lunar world securely pry.

And besides, these two Nations, have sent Machines round the Earth, some hundreds of leagues above it, with Men in 'em, and at last fetch'd 'em down in their Machines safe and sound. And yet was my Machine unknown.

As for Moscow, they look upon it in their England, much as we look upon Rome; and as we look upon Papists, and Dissenters, so do they a kind of Levellers, that they call, Communists, that wou'd overthrow the State, if they cou'd, and yet are suffer'd to come and go every where without let or hindrance, save only that they may not get employment, where they can learn Secrets of State. For the meer Papists and Dissenters among them, they make no distinction against 'em, and hardly know, what Religion a Man professes, or what they profess them selves.

They have in the Land another sort of Stranger. For they have many Indians, both from West and East, who are come to make their livelihood in England. Their Neighbours are afear'd, the great numbers of these shou'd take their Wages from 'em, or bring new Plagues, or that their way of living shou'd be too Nasty, for the Publick Good; and some English Men (they say) have rais'd up Brawls against 'em. But the generality of English Natives are so mealy-mouth'd, that they dare not speak these Fears alowd, lest they have a foul Name of Racialist clapp'd on 'em, of which they are in mortal terror, from the thought of some Massacres perform'd a score of years before in Germany, and Oppressions committed thousands of leagues away in Africa and America.

For this they have some Colour, seeing that they are so much, as they call it, One World, that notions travell fast in their Time. But I think it partly but one case of a ready Superstition of Opinion among 'em which comes, as I ghess, from their singular prospect, whereby all can read, and vote for Parliament, as if they were equal, while most regard neither the Word of Religion nor fair Argument, but are blown this way and that by the least Gale or Breath of Censure from their fellows. They have a vast Esteem for Sophistries; they are very easie in believing such things as they wou'd have to be so, and are not forward to entertain a solid Reasoning. He that can fasten a Good, or a Bad name, howso ever ill-conceiv'd, upon any thing that is done, or made, or worn, or said, is scarce question'd, but straight his word is taken up. So they are blown hither and thither, by the Writers in the Courants, and the Speakers in the Tellies, and the Devizers of the Advertisements, the Blind leading the Blind.

Another cause of their being so biddable and so quiet, is perhaps that from the Hurry of the Day, they have little stomach for Trouble, and little room, in which to think for them selves. For tho' they live so well, yet they are also in a continual Coursing, and if their leisure is long, yet even there the World presses on 'em from all sides. Between their Running after every Notion, and their perpetual Hast, you wou'd say, that Ants had been mated with Munkies, to breed 'em.

All these matters, as I have said, I learnt not at once, but during many weeks. I spent my mornings in the back parts of the Shop. For my Dinner (always at the early hour of Noon) I went to a number of Eating Houses with my Host, or return'd with him to his House. If we came home, I often stay'd there afterwards, and try'd some Husbandry in their Garden, or walk'd abroad untill I knew the Neighbourhood well. The Wife, who also controul'd the Chariot, sometimes kept it by her after Dinner, while the Husband return'd to his Shop in one of their Busses. If the day were bright, she wou'd then bring me out in this Car, and over the Countrey-side. I suffer'd a Surprize, when I saw our Range of Hills, not much chang'd, tho' with single Houses here and there built over 'em, and Poles of Metal to carry their Electricity over the Land. But every where was a Vapour or Smoak on the brightest of days. A Stream, where I am wont to fish, was become a Sluice between Walls of Stone, and black besides, in the midst of another Town, where is nothing today but a Farm (after which this Town was nam'd, as I found). The great part of the Land about is cover'd with their Houses, and where our Farm-tracks wind, are hard Roads, where-on their Chariots continually rush by and roar. Their Towns are for the most part built of red Bricks, but blacken'd by their Smoaks, of which a great amount comes from Factorys as wide as Villages and as populous as Towns, where they make their many Goods.

On fair Saturdays, or Sundays (for they went to no Church, which much troubled me) my Host and his Wife wou'd bring their Car further abroad, and on occasion to the Sea. There I had another Surprize, for there hundreds, yea thousands of Men, Women and Children sate upon the Beaches (and many with lowd Raydeows whose Clamour assail'd my Ears); and a few score even walk'd into the shallow Sea; but all cloath'd, tho' in such small Garments, that hid scarce any thing, of bright Colours. My Hosts wou'd likewise Bathe (as they call'd it) in the Sea, and had with them these Garments, and one for me, but I wou'd not, and contented my self with watching. What they thought to enjoy by this stay, I cannot tell, unless it were the sight of so many bare Bodys, for there was nothing but Sand blown in your Face, and Wind too cold, Sun too hot, and a clamorous Multitude of Persons and Dogs.

Their Inns are places, where you may be very well entertain'd, at least for Food; for Drink, 'tis only at certain hours that their Law allows it. Their Ale is thin and has little Smack, and their Wines want strength. They have much liking for a strong Spirit out of Scotland and Ireland, that I took for Uskebaugh, a harsh Drink fit for Bogg-bred Savages. They call'd it Wiskay. Two Fruits which I cou'd not well stomach, but of which they eat a vast deal, are a Red Juicy Fruit, but very sower, that they call, Tomautows (I suppose the Tomate from the America's), and which they eat with Flesh, and the Shaddock, or Pomple-moose, which they call, Grape-Fruit, tho' (for the many that know it not) it is like a great yellow sower Orange, and no Grape. But of other Fruits they get a Multitude, Apples, Pears, Bananas, Oranges, Peaches, Straw-berries, Rasp-berries, and many more from the ends of the Earth, in season and out of season, both fresh, and preserv'd, some in sweet Sirop in clos'd Jars of Metal, that they call, Cans. 'Tis also so with many other Meats, Fish, Cheeses, Butter, Honey, Preserves and Marma-lades, that come from the America's, from many Lands in Europe, from Africa, from the Indies, and from the Anti-podaean Continent.

Besides their Food and Drink, I must tell you, many of the younger sort, and especially the Girls, have a foul custom, of smoking Tobaco in little Rowl'd Peices of Paper, which they call, Sick-Rates, because in the end they Corrupt the Lungs of many, tho' many years after. These Sick-Rates they smoak on the Top Tiers of the Busses, in the Eating-Houses, when they drink at home with Friends, and when they are at Work. In their Tellie Play-houses (of which more anon) the Air is full of their Smoak.

Altho' the Towns were so crowded, that you cou'd scarce stand for the press, yet they told me, a great part of the People were from home at this time. (And by October, the press was ten times worse, altho' I was by then somewhat accustom'd to it.) For every Man that is not a Pauper, takes his whole Family with him nigh once a year, for a week, or even for a fortnight, to rest from their Labours. My Host and his Wife had taken their Excursion in May, and that but for a week. These Retreats they call Holidays, for they have but few of our Holidays, only at Christmas and Easter and by Whit Sunday, and for two or three days beside in the year. Some go to the

Coasts (whence that great Throng I saw on the Sands), some to wild Countrey and horrid Mountains (to flee the Crowd), but many to other Lands, so that the humblest Merchant makes his Tour like the finest Nobleman's Son, and not once in a Life-time, but every year, tho' for a meer two weeks. My Travells, that I thought some thing to be remember'd, were to them a trifling Excursion. But this comes from the great Ease of their Journeys, in Air-Craft or in their Cars, on Shipps that are sent thro' the Water by a Furnace of Oyl in their Bellies, and in great Caravans or Trains of Coaches (but each Coach as long as a Barn) that are drawn along Rails of Metal by a Machine, that burns Oyl likewise, or goes by Electricity. The Hostelrys every where are so commodious and clean, that a Traveller wants nothing and may lie easie where ever he may pass in Europe, or (indeed) in some parts of Africa and America.

The young Men and Women of Fifteen years upwards often travell in Partys together to other Countreys. Some of 'em go to Norway or to Swisserland in the Winter, in order to the enjoying a Sport, that they call Skeeing. This is nothing but to climb a great Mountain of Snow (or to be drawn up to the Summit on Wires) and to Slide down it very swiftly upon Boards that are strapp'd to your Feet. So soft is their Life become, that many of the bolder sort are uneasie, without they risk their Limbs and tire their Bodys this way. They have made for them selves all manner of such Sports. Some take Sticks with flat Peices of Metal at their Ends, that they call (forsooth) Clubs, and strike a little Ball from place to place up and down a great Park. Others joyn together in two Crews or Partys that are Enemys one to the other, and strive to kick a Ball as big as your Head between two Masts in their Enemys Ground; thousands of Men and Boys sit round on Benches to watch the outcome, and this Rabble rages like Enthusiasts out of a Bedlam. In the Summer they strike a Ball of the bigness of a Fist, with a Club of Wood that has a flat Face, while others endeavour to catch the Ball. These (and the others after Summer) send Crews from Land to Land to try which

Countrey shall come off best; and all the world and the Courants, talk continually of their progress. Other Men again strike such a Ball, but more soft, from end to end of a Plot of ground across a Net, and to discomfit one the other, and this they call Tennis, but it resembles nothing our Tennis, as I have seen it in London. Others rowl heavy Balls along an Alley within doors, to knock down ten Pins, and this Sport is much like our Nine-Pins, but hundreds play at it, and thro' the whole Night. Others run on Skates, like the Dutch, but for Sport, and besides Running, do Dance wonderfully upon 'em, as I saw, in great Halls where the Ice is kept ever cold, even in Summer, tho' how I cou'd not understand. Others swim in Lakes or the Sea, but under the Water, for they have found a way, to carry Air with them, and to breathe it, as far as ten or twenty fathoms down; and these go also to take Fish with Spears. Others clamber down into Caverns and Holes in the Rocks, and walk (they say) in these many miles under the ground, for the Pleasure (if there be any). Others climb the highest of Mountains and the steepest of Cliffs. Others (but few) ride Air-Craft that have no Machine to drive them, and sail but with the Wind and Air. And others (but fewer still) leap from Air-Craft, and fall thousands of fathoms, for the meer Feeling of it, but save themselves at last with a great Bag, folded at their Back, that they open out, so that it fills with the Air, and holds 'em up, and so they come gently to ground. In all those Sports Women strive as well as the Men. In the month of October the Nations over all the World sent Crews of both Men and Women, to run, or leap, or to toss Weights, in a friendly Strife or Concurrence, in a place in Japan; and this Sport all saw in the Windows of their Tellies. (My Host told me, that what I saw came thro' a Ball, that hung hundreds of miles above the Pacifick Ocean, but this I scarce credited.)

For most take no part in these Strivings, but look on their Tellies, to see what the rest do; or to hear a sort of Musick (from little Raydeows) that shou'd make you cover your Ears, but which they wou'd surround themselves with all day, if they cou'd; or they wager, as I said before, in great Assemblys, upon the meer Chance of some Numbers shewn upon a Table. Or if they find their Life too becalm'd, they go to a kind of Play-houses, but without a Company, where (for Heroick Plays) they may witness Tortures, Ravishings, Sorcery, and Murther, with in between (for Comedys) some crazy Folly or other, all enacted in a Gigantick sort of Tellie, but often with Colours, so that it seem the more real.

Besides their Cars, on which they love to drive furiously, they have a kind of metallick Pony, but driven by this same Burning, which they call a Mowtasoikle. This makes a worse Roaring even than their Cars; it is much favour'd of Striplings. Another such has no Furnace in it, but you must drive it onward by pushing round with your Feet on two Pieces, that go round. This they call a Boique, and it goes only as fast as a Man may run. Of Horses I scarce saw any, but they use them for Sport.

For that they use so much written Words, to send far, they have perfected a kind of Pencil, that writes with Ink, which it holds within it, and very Black, or Blew, or (indeed) Red or Green. But the Merchants and Houses of Trade (and some Men at Home) have a Machine, that prints Letters upon a Sheet of Paper, when you shall play upon little Keys on it, each mark'd with a different Letter; but it's Musick is a sad Rattling. And what amaz'd me, they give this work, to young Wenches. So you may read the Word of any Body, without troubling, how hard or easie is his Hand. And I may tell you, their Hand-writing is so strange, I cou'd make near nothing of it not above one Letter in twenty, altho' their Printing is very like ours. A few Persons write, however, in a kind of Italick Hand, very formal, that I cou'd read pretty well. They use little Civility in their Epistles, but affect a strange careless Friendliness, calling all Dear, even those they have never met and hope never to meet. But in their Speech as in their Writing, all their Address is abrupt and careless, so that like Children they use their First Names almost upon first acquaintance, Men with Women too, married or single; yet do they seldom salute each other with the least Gesture, unless it be (upon first Presentation) to clasp Hands.

My Host had Friends some times invited to Supper, and I found, that as this People had so little Civility, they cou'd meerly murmur, And this is Jow (for so they call'd me), and the Company wou'd seek to know no more, so that I cou'd sit and listen, without venturing a word. As I became more bold, I wou'd go out alone, to their Tellie Play-houses as it might be, and pay my Fee at the Door; or make a Sally to a great Shop, where I cou'd chuse all sorts of Wares, and carry 'em about in a Basket made of Metal, to the Door, where a Good-wife fetch'd 'em out and made the Reckoning. So I grew us'd to purchasing my Hostess her Provisions, which mightily pleas'd her. The Sheets of Copys, by the way, from Mr Sympkins his Travells, by the Zerrocks, I kept in a Parcel within my Machine.

Some of my Hosts Visitors had Children, that they left at home, and I learnt, that the Children here, for all they make so much sport of their Elders, must work hard, for they suffer their Schooling from Five years of age, to Fifteen, or some more, so that they are grown Men. And the Girls are so school'd likewise. If they wou'd have a good place in Life hereafter, they must do well, before Examiners, for whom they write many times long Discourses and Answers to hard Questions. The elder ones learn even some Natural Philosophy, that some of them may practice to controul those Marvels, by which their World runs. They learn Languages, but little Latin, and many other matters besides.

In September my Host had Business in London, and carry'd me thither in his Car. And here I had another and over-whelming Surprize. For the London that we know was all but gone, save a few Monuments, much blacken'd and almost beyond recognizing, smother'd in the Bellie of a Town, that was more like a whole Countrey, compos'd all of Houses and other Buildings. I cannot begin to give you an Idaea, of the Extent of it, and you will not believe me, when I say, it is about

Fifteen Leagues across, and all Buildings, for the most part begrim'd with Smoak. At Night, however, 'tis much lit up with wonderful Lights of many Colours. (Another cause, they have so little Murthers and Robberies, is, that their Citys are lit near as bright as day.) But when I saw Paul's, that was in building in my day, and since, they say, finish'd; but now 'twas half bury'd in the midst of great Buildings hundreds of feet high; I was glad, to come away.

That October, besides the great Sport in Japan, there was in Britain a great Election, when all in England and her Neighbours voted, for a new Government. I thought, there shou'd be Riots, but tho' the Courants had much to say, Folk round me took't very coolly. In the end the Tory's, that had been in more then a dozen years, were out, and t'other Party in. They said, there shou'd be some great Changes, tho' their numbers were scarce over those of the Tory Members.

It happen'd that one afternoon late in September, my Host's Wife and I were looking out at the Rain. The Day was a Friday and she said, she wish'd she knew, whether 'twou'd be fair Weather on the Saturday, or no, for an Excursion. Then she says to me, Why not travel to tomorrow in that Contrapshen, and see? At first I put her off, for I made her see, that if I mov'd to tomorrow, I shou'd meet my self, and that I wou'd by no means do. Then she says, Try the early morning, and keep out of the way of your Bed-room. So at last I agrees, to try early on Saturday morning, and again early on Sunday morning, but to stay below stairs. And to this she says Yes, but nothing wou'd satisfy her, but that she must come with me, to try this manner of Journey. For a long time I sought to disswade her, but in the end I submitted. We pull'd off it's Cloth, then in we goes into the Machine (mighty press'd together) and I mov'd the Rod and Dial. Seeing that she took little Notice, of how they went, I was the more secure. Then I press'd the Red Knob and she cries out and clasps me for Fear, but I comforted her. We listen'd for a time, but all was still and dark. So then out we crept and softly into the Chamber, where the Tellie was. The

Night was something Windy, but we cou'd hear no Rain. At last she and I crept back to the Porch, and gently unlock'd the Door, and so out into their little Park, or Front Garden. Under foot the ground was damp, but there was no Rain falling. A few Stars were in the Heavens, and a Half Moon thro' the Clowds. Then we stole hand in hand into the Porch again, and made all fast, and so within the Machine. Here I found all the Numbers and Pointers, and other Letters, glowing in the Dark. So I found it easie, to turn the Machine to the Sunday morning. This time 'twas strong Moon-Light, and no Clowds in the Sky, but the Air was very warm, and the Ground dry. So we thought, 'twou'd be a fair Week-end. When we were come within again, she wou'd bring me into their Living-Chamber again, that we might enjoy the sight of the Moon, without danger of Surprize from the Watch without. This we did for some time, and I found her more kind, then I had expected. But at length (and I something uneasie with my self) we return'd to the Friday after-noon, and cover'd my Machine again with their great Cloth.

Our Fore-cast was a true one and a fine Journey we had of it all three, but said nothing of our Auguries, to her Husband. From that time she and I often made Tryal of the next Day's or of the next Week's weather, but always by Night. As we knew, we were lying both above-stairs in two other Bodys, we had a kind of delight-ful Terror at the thought. In the day-time we were at first Discreet, because many Persons came ever to the House, to bring Provisions, or to reckon for the Electricity, or to sell somewhat at the Door. But at length we grew too secure, and fell to travelling much in the Car to places, where she was little known, and at last, began to snatch Hours, above stairs.

One after-noon towards November, we were but then back from a Sortie into the Night before (for now we were grown so bold, as to do this too, but we took care, not to make three Pair of us that Night) and without covering my Machine again I had follow'd her up to their Bed-Chamber, where we fell a Kissing once more, when her Husband appear'd (who must have come home early, and up the Stairs, but cou'd not be heard). He threw me down the Stairs, which was like to break my Neck. In my Confusion, I stumbled into the Porch, and into the Machine, and mov'd it, without taking breath, two or three furlongs up the Road.

And here I made an Errour, for I found within my Machine the Pole of a Stopping-Place for Busses, and an Old Wife, that screech'd for mortal Fear. I push'd her out, and she went down the Road crying Murther, Help, Murther, and spilling her Merchandize out of her Basket as she went. Then I took counsel with my self, and looking carefully upon the Plats, prepar'd to move within that Colledge, where I first came, but back to my own Time, by the Barn. I set the Dials to the exact Hour, when I first left our Village, for I thought, the earlier Time is perilous, for I shall meet my self, and a later Time is dangerous, for the Villagers will have mark'd my being away, and will press me with Questions; besides if my Machine is seen, I am like to stand Tryal for Witchcraft. I had little Breathing space, for as I turn'd the Dials, I saw a Buss coming up the Road.

When I push'd the Red Knob my Faint-ness nearly overcame me, and a fearful Clowdy-ness beset me, worse then before. I had the Wit to remember, that I had been twice in this Place and Moment, and that if I cou'd wait, my other two selves, and their Machine, shou'd both be gone, the one into the Future, the other into that Early Morning, eleven hours before. At last the Clowdy-ness pass'd. I lock'd the Rod (which at least is some safeguard, I thought), hastily cast off my new Cloathes (one of several Suits I now had) and pull'd on my old; and leaving the others within, as well as Sympkins his Travells from the Zerrocks, I crept forth into the empty Street. Now I sped home as fast as I might, for I had a Plan, to try other Times in the Future, or even in the Past, but first to furnish my self with more Goods (what I had left) to purchase a living there. Unhappily I encounter'd an Old Man that knew me well, who held speech with me, talking I know not what

58

Nonsense, for the better part of ten minutes. At length I escap'd, and took a Wheel-Barrow, and fill'd it with fine Cloathes, and three Pistols, and an Abridgement of Janssonius his Atlas, and a quantity of jewells, and a Mirrour besides. I went back with all to the place, but my Machine was gone. Since 'twas lock'd, I concluded, the Sorcerer was come back, and had gone off in't. And so I had nought to do, but to bring my Barrow back, and sadly unload my Gear. I was the poorer by some hundreds of Pounds (1964), the Sheets of Sympkins Travells, and several changes of Cloathing, but the richer by some Memories, a Wrist-Watch, and the Knowledge of an unghessable Future.

Not So Certain

The Shm'qh, or Sshm-qh, or Sshmeqh (which sounds like 'shmukh', only breathier) were getting more unsatisfactory every day. In private, Jacobs cursed them and the whole business of his mission. All had seemed auspicious at first. Here on this planet was an intelligent race with a learnable language, and, all things considered, an almost pronounceable one. The labour of establishing communication had at last begun to bear fruit. Questions could be asked, co-operation could be sought, explanations could be given, propaganda could be made. The human interpreters with the expedition had mastered enough of the language to be able to express almost anything the administration demanded of them, and to follow most of what was said; eventually most of the crew could get along in varying degrees, and Jacobs became himself quite fluent. It was rather like conversing with moths in moth language: no vowels to speak of – except that now and again a surprising clatter of vowelage broke out among the Shm'qh themselves, no one knew why; a lot of feathery, sneezy consonants that no one could quite master. Yet the Shm'qh had tongues, mouths, even teeth (of sorts), a soft enfolding muscle that took the place of lips, and something that passed for a voice-box and lungs. It had proved possible to imitate their words near enough to make oneself understood, with occasional repetitions. The grammar was very unusual, but could be digested after practice. The absence of plurals, except in what passed for pronouns, was a stumbling-block, but one that could be got round.

The natives seemed friendly and surprisingly unalarmed by the human invaders, who were careful to avoid any behaviour that might have been construed as a sign of desire to dominate. They were not inconveniently curious. They had no machinery, but their intelligence was evidently high. They had everything in abundance on their planet: perhaps their intelligence was insufficiently exercised. They were in some competition with the non-intelligent species, but not seriously menaced by disease, parasites, plant or animal predators, or starvation. They did not seem to be trying to conceal anything or deceive the humans. Yet their co-operation seemed to reach a reserve somewhere. There was a barrier, an evasion.

The interpreter of a team would ask 'Can we return this way?' (*Tsh'ny lh'ly wh'ng 'zhny' bv'w w'gh'pf 'w*, literally 'Pass shown reverse open eh? self-and-others relevance': it had been established conclusively that 'open' was equivalent to 'possible' and 'shut' to 'impossible', and the order of words in a sentence was now well understood.) The Shm'qh spoken to would answer with a sort of sneeze meaning 'No' (*Shny'wh*) and the party would go home the long way round. Weeks later it would be discovered that the track avoided, though difficult, was by no means impassable to either species; yet no evidence was ever unearthed of secret activity there which the Shm'qh might have wished to keep inviolate. A man fell down a gully once and when brought back, bones broken, developed a type of pneumonia which did not respond to drugs. 'Will he live?' (*Ny'p'lw gh'qhty bv'w 'pf'lh 'w*, literally 'Activity continuation eh? the-other relevance') produced a slow '*Shnyauwh*' which was taken to mean 'No', since the rare vowels apparently meant nothing. The man recovered in a fortnight, after a crisis. Need the Shm'qh have been so brutally pessimistic? In the middle of a native feast two men passing humping an unwieldy generator were much annoyed to hear one of the two nearest natives say to the other, quite loudly and with amusement-posture slanted in their direction, '*Tyiwhdyim ipf*', which means 'Folly the-others' (that is, 'They're crazy!'). The posture, the equivalent of a broad grin, involved the wide whipping of the tail, the rocking up and down on out-bent elbows, and the spread of the ear-tufts, with the head turned towards them. Perhaps this was friendly guying, but *ty'whdy'm* was an exceedingly offensive word, as Scatterthwaite had discovered to his cost when he had used it on a native who got too close to a high-tension coil. An abject ceremonial apology had had to be made by Scatterthwaite and Jacobs to the head official and the offended native, before all the tribe, to avert a complete withdrawal of all contact. All the crew were warned never to use the word again. That was three months before the feast incident.

Finally, when Jacobs asked if his mission might take back to Earth a few native ornaments, utensils, and cultivated plants (without mentioning the elaborate decontamination and quarantine that these, and the team, would have to undergo before release), he met with a flat no, delivered with the Shm'qh equivalent of an inscrutable smile, the tail switching gently, the ear-tufts slightly displayed, and the elbows spread out. Jacobs tried persuasion as eloquent as he could make it. All to no effect, except that '*Shny'wh*' turned to '*Shnyiwh*' and finally to '*Shnyeewh*' and the elbows spread wider and wider.

The doctor doubled as ethnologist because of his experience in physiographic measurements. He was unable to help. 'Why don't you try Jimmy Anson? He's better on the psycho side than I am. I've a lot on my hands just now. I'm much more worried about our leucocyte counts than you are over your precious relics.'

'Why's that?'

'Oh, no cause for immediate alarm. But they indicate we're adjusting to something, some foreign body or bodies; I don't suppose it's one so much as a whole host of different alien entities. It isn't doing us any real harm – but how would Earth react?'

Jacob sought out Anson, the linguistician. 'You have the advantage over us, old man; you can at least take back all those analyses and recordings. All we've got is photographs and film.

I can't think why they're so down on letting us have specimens. I shall be darned unpopular with the powers at home. Never happened to me before.'

The linguistician had been added to the expedition almost as an afterthought, together with a great deal of equipment which had caused some bad language among those who were working out loads and logistics. Pitied by the interpreters at first, he was later regarded with envious tolerance as he took, with their only too necessary assistance, recording after recording, from cubs and adults of both sexes and all ages, often using thumbnail sketches to get his or their meaning across, or to keep the victims amused. He had a battery of results which seemed to keep him perfectly happy working on day after day, only now and again breaking surface to get the interpreters to arrange a new test interview. The Shm'qh let him torment them with palatograms, pharyngoscopes, torches, and X-ray photography, uncomplaining. Eventually he took to wandering in the settlements with a pocket recorder, sometimes sketching the vegetation to distract attention.

'Are they adamant about it then?'

'A flat refusal every time I ask – quite cheerful, but always No. I think we must have offended them more deeply over Scatterthwaite's gaffe than we realized. You know two of them threw it back at Simons and Harte the other day?'

'Really? I can't believe it! What were they doing?'

'Doing no harm, simply carrying the genny up to Blue Knoll the day the beano was on. Two Shmur' – Jacobs usually called the race that to his crew – 'did the grin gesture at them and called out – you know – *tchuffim* or whatever it is.'

'You mean *ty-whdy-m*, I suppose?'

'That's it. Only they used the short-*i* vowel. Could there be anything in that? Does that take the sting out of it, do you think?'

A slow smile spread over Anson's face, then became a grin. 'In a way, yes, but not the way you suppose. I think I have the answer to that problem.'

'Do you indeed? well let's have it, for God's sake, man. We might be on the edge of a volcano – they *could* be working up to attack us!'

'No, it's all right, I think. There's no malice and no guile in this race, as far as I can see. But first about that vowel. These vowels aren't phonemes in the strict sense—'

'What's a phoneme, for heaven's sake?'

'Take too long to explain properly. But roughly speaking, it's a class of sound, like say *t* or *d* or short *o*, recognized by a particular language, which makes a brick you can build meaningful words out of. Now these Sshm-qh vowels aren't like that at all. They're more like the intonation in an English sentence. They carry feeling-tones. If I say *Sshm-qh* by itself, with a sort of murmur-vowel – we'd call it schwa – in the middle, it means I am just mentioning the Sshm-qh without any special feeling. (By the way, if you can't use a phonetic schwa-symbol when you're writing the language, why not write an ordinary e, instead of that ambiguous apostrophe, or the hyphen?) Now, if I say *Sshmiqh* or *Sshmeeqh* (or in this case, probably *Sshmüqh*) with an *i*-type vowel, I'm amused, or specially cheerful. If I say *Sshmooqh* with that *u*-sound, it means I love them, or I'm feeling sentimental or something. If I say *Sshmahqh* with that *a*-sound, it means I'm angry, or frightened, or that some sort of emergency is on. If I say *Sshmauqh* with that *o*-sound, it means I'm sad, or depressed, or awed about something.'

'Would you use these vowels just for key words, or a whole sentence?'

'A whole sentence or a whole speech. They're supra-segmental phonemes in the American sense, really – they carry over the whole utterance. The Sshmeqh mouth returns to the *i*-position, or the *a*-position, or whatever it is, whenever it gets the chance. In fact they're an unconscious reaction, more or less.'

'Is that why their speech is so monotonous in tone?'

'Yes, you've got it. They've no function for pitch variation.'

'So those two villains were amused at the idiocy of the men carrying a heavy genny?'

'Not necessarily. No, I don't think so. They were in a cheerful mood, or joking, but I don't think they were jibing at Simons and – was it Harte you said?'

'Yes. *They've* kept clear of the blighters ever since. Say they hate their guts.'

'Quite unnecessary. I wish they'd called me in. You see, I don't think you quite realize the sound structure of this language. How many different consonant sounds do you think there are?'

'Well, there's *b*, *d*, *f*, *g*, a sort of *gh*-sound, *j*, at least two kinds of *l*-sound, *m*, *n*, and I suppose linguists call *ng* another? Then there's *p*, *q*, a *qh*-sound, *sh*, *t*, *v*, at least one kind of *w*, a separate *wh*- or *hw*-sound, that ubiquitous *y*-sound, and a kind of *zh*-sound – or is that the same as *j*? That makes, say, twenty-one?'

Anson sighed, just perceptibly. 'Of distinguishable consonants there are at least thirty-six; not that that's high for a language, that is considering there are no vowels properly speaking. And these consonants are not as haphazard as you seem to think.'

'You mean, we may have got a consonant wrong in that *tchuffjim* word – it may mean something else?'

'Just that – and a little bit more. Come and look at my charts.' Anson rolled down a cylinder on a wall. Three columns of twelve symbols (six pairs) each, were printed on it in his clear hand.

'I can't follow these phoney – phonee – phonemes, do you call them?'

'No, these are not phonemic symbols. They are my shot at a structure of broad *phonetic* symbols in accordance with Sshmeqh phonology; or rather according to *this* Sshmeqh language: there are others further round the planet, I'm told, quite different, and what's more many of them are full of true vowels too. In fact I've been going to ask you if I could have a month away at the nearest language frontier – it's supposed to be the equivalent of only 2,500 kilometres south-south-east – and take a tape machine. *That* one's a tone language, more-over, like Chinese as it were. I could test whether the Sshmeqh pictograms were interlingual too. I'd use one of the short-hop craft. I'd like to take one of the interpreters and a native friend of mine who knows the way and could help with the other language. We'd need some hot-climate clothing and so on. I would have to leave all the possible analyses till I got back. It should provide enough material to give the elements of a second language for any future expedition, eh?'

'What would you do about your stuff here? You'd be out of effective radio range, too.'

'I'd leave it sealed and labelled, in case anything happened to me, with all my notes. I could leave instructions about what native to contact in case we never turned up again and you thought it worth sending a second machine with a search party.'

'I think maybe we could manage it, if you set out within a week and come back within four weeks after that. That gives us a week or two's margin for search in case. Sound the inter-preters and see who would best like to go with you . . . Well now, what do these columns of symbols stand for?'

'Thanks, Chief. Well, the left-hand column here is what with us would be labials – lip-sounds. Actually they use the orifice-mantle and outer teeth. There are two kinds of *p*-sound, two *b*'s, no *f* or *v* by itself at all, two *w*-sounds, two *wh*-like sounds above them there, two *m*'s, and two labial laterals (rather a strange bird linguistically).'

Jacobs snorted.

'Similarly with these palatals, or what with us would be palatalized gingivals and such. They use the inner rows of teeth and the tongue. There are two *ty*-like sounds, two *sh*-like sounds, and so on, all corresponding to the labial examples in the first column . . . Then on the right are the quasi-velar, quasi-uvular sounds – two *q*'s, two *qh*'s and so on. They use the retro-tongue for these, not the main tongue at all. All these thirty-six are not counting collocational variants. What the retrolingual *l* does to a neighbouring orifice-*l*, for instance, is nobody's business.'

Jacobs ground his teeth silently.

'Well, the word these two men thought was *tyewhdyem* (but I spell it with only four consonant symbols to your seven, and two schwas) was, I'm pretty certain, *tchewhdyemm* – look, I'll write it here, though I'd spell it professionally with only five consonants at most; and the first consonant, you see here, is a different one.'

'And that means?'

'Tough, brave, stout-hearted; or courage, guts, if you like: that's what they were calling them, tough guys. The *i*-vowel and the grin posture, in so far as they were conscious at all, were complimentary, a slap on the back, I expect.'

'My God! . . . How do the words come to be so much alike?'

'They're only alike to you because you aren't used to Sshmeqh phonology. Also, we don't know for certain what really reaches their aural centres in their brains. Listen to this –' and he switched on a machine. It was saying over and over again, '*Tch-mb-, tch-mb-, tch-mb-* . . .'

'Now this.'

'*Ty-mm-ny, ty-mm-ny, ty-mm-ny* . . .'

'Can't hear much difference except at the end.'

'Wait. Listen to this. This is word number one.'

Depressing another switch, Anson produced from the same machine something in a deep yawning tone that sounded like '*Ttthawmhwbbah . . . ttthawmhwbbah* . . .'

'That's quarter-speed or so. Now the second word.'

This time the machine produced '*Ttrrhhohmwwawhnn . . . ttrrhhohmwwawhnn* . . .'

'Yes, I begin to see. You think that's what they really hear?'

'Who's to say? We can't dissect them, and even if we could! And as they have no true writing, only a kind of pictography, there are no graphic clues. All I'm saying is, there is a difference which quartering the speed brings out, and maybe their auditory chain can pick up this difference easier than ours can. Now I have another surprise for you. These thirty-six consonants aren't true phonemes. There are only about eighteen phonemes. A pretty meagre equipment by human standards, particularly as there aren't any true vowels, but quite adequate to furnish a language. Anyway, about half of the thirty-six consonants are the manifestations, I'm pretty sure, of *combinations* of phonemes. You know how some men'll say "Canh say" instead of "Can't say." Well, that voiceless *n* at the end of "Canh" may be regarded as a combination, in *their* speech, of an *n*-phoneme and a *t*-phoneme. Same here, only all over. Look, here's my battery of phonemes.'

Anson unrolled another chart in which the three columns now contained six symbols each.

'I won't bother you with details, but that sound *tch*, for instance, in the word meaning brave, is a compound of two *ty*-phonemes. I have a suspicion that in that particular case the first *ty* comes from a word *ety* meaning very, which you can hear quite a lot of. And the long *m*-sound at the end is undoubtedly two *m*'s, only I haven't disentangled their meanings. One of the two *b*-sounds in the language is really a combination of *p* and *b*, and so with all the other pairs of voiced stops and fricatives.'

Jacobs groaned softly. 'I'd give a lot to be dealing with Earth!'

'Oh, I could show you far worse things in a lot of human languages. This lot is child's play. Now, I have another little surprise. You say you're always meeting a no, especially when you ask if you can take some specimens home – right?'

'If only I could crack that! It's wrecking all my programme!'

Anson regarded his chief with a calm but guarded gaze, like an experienced mother considering a fractious child.

'You think there's one word *shnyewh*, don't you? and so, I'm afraid, do the interpreters; they're very helpful, but they can't know everything. But there isn't one word: there are two. Neither of them starts with the same sound as the word

Sshmeqh, by the way – that's another compound, a double *sh*-sound. Both of them begin with a simple *sh*. Listen to this.'

After some fiddling, Anson got his machine intoning '*Shny-wh, shny-wh, shny-wh* . . .'

'That's the word I got whenever I pitched my informants a question I knew had a negative answer. Now listen to this; this was a response I got when I asked certain carefully chosen questions.'

Again a repeated '*Shny-wh, shny-wh, shny-wh* . . .'

'There is a difference somewhere.'

'Well, try the slow speed. Here's number one.'

Jacobs heard '*Thkhhnnauhhwh* . . . *thkhhnnauhhwh* . . .'

'Now number two.' '*Thkhhnnohfhgh* . . . *thkhhnnohfhgh* . . .'

'The *vowel* sounds different!'

'Only because of the influence of the final consonant. In the first word it was *that* one, the second symbol of the second pair on my first chart; in the second word it was the *first* of the second pair. If you can't stomach my symbols, you could write the end of the second word with *ph* instead of *wh*. It's tenser, tighter if you like. But let's try the sound-spectrograph.'

Anson switched on a small illuminated screen, on which he presently conjured up two versions of a figure resembling an out-of-focus black-and-white photograph, marred by movement, of the ruins of a rope-bridge in a dense jungle gorge, during a thick fog.

'Now here's your *no*-word, *shnyewh*. Left to right is time. Upwards for higher pitch. Compare the other word, alongside, *shnyeph*. This time we get this odd transient up there near the end (which you never get in our own attempts – may be something to do with the tensing of the mantle round the outer teeth) and the second pseudo-formant' (pointing to a sagging strand of the rope-bridge) 'drops quite a bit, compared to its level in your first word, here . . . Now here instead are my synthetic versions. They are the minimal freehand drawings that I could get a 95 per cent "correct" response to when I played them back as sound to natives. They are, if you like, the skeleton, the basic structure; all the rest are adventitious trimmings.'

Anson lit up a chastely futuristic piece of abstract art in which the rope-bridge and jungle had been replaced by smooth blips and snakes, and the fog had gone. Then he 'played' it back. It was recognizable, if rather clipped and twangy, as the two original sneezes. The second came to a perceptibly harder end.

'Now, this *ph*-sound turns out to be a compound of two *wh*-phonemes. I happen to have succeeded in dissecting these two words, so to speak. The first, which means, roughly, no, is a kind of agglutination of *esh*, which means indeed, in fact, or something like that; *nye*, which means not, or negative; and *ewh*, which means thus, or so, or in that way. So their no means, etymologically, "Indeed not so."'

'"Indeed not so!" What about the second word, for heaven's sake!'

Again that considering gaze.

'Well, the second word is *esh* plus *nye* plus *ewh* all over again, plus another *wh* which comes, I'm virtually certain (but it'd take months to prove) from *whe*.'

'And what the hell does *whuh* mean?' snarled Jacobs.

'*Whe* means definitely, certainly, or definite, certain, known, or certainty. They use it to indicate the exact spot on a plant or a picture, the known place of an event, an agreed shade of colour – their colours, that is, not the ones we distinguish.'

'And what the – for God's sake cut the cackle and tell me what all that means!'

'In literal order, it means, "Indeed not so certain;" or, as we might say, "Indeed not definitely or certainly so."'

'"Indeed not so certain" – what does that mean?'

'It's *their* equivalent of our word perhaps.'

'"Perhaps": then all they've done is refused to make their minds up about the specimens. And, my God, that ravine that wasn't supposed to be crossable – they only meant *perhaps* it was crossable?'

'Very likely.'

'And poor old Jackson: they only meant *perhaps* he'd survive?'

'Yes, I should imagine so. I ought to have cottoned on to that myself – I heard about it.'

'My God, you should. Maybe I ought to have thought sooner about asking you, but you could have thought about our practical problems too, Jimmy . . . By the way, surely when two words are so alike one of them is going to drop out sooner or later. I mean, it could be risky even to a Shmur?'

'Remember we don't know how their aural set-up works Or even their syntactical consciousness. Their grammar must bring about some queer verbal thinking. You know, so far I can only distinguish two classes of word, Dependants and Independants, and two functions, Absolute and Modifier; the Independants can act as Absolutes, but need not do so . . . But still, there is something in what you say. It could solve itself by an extra consonant creeping into the perhaps word through the shoving on of yet another Modifier. But as a matter of fact it wouldn't surprise me if the *perhaps* word were to die out presently in favour of some other less ambiguous expression. Language never stays still. They have produced such an expression in my hearing which may gain ground, although at the moment it has a rather contemptuous overtone. It's *bheng elyeny*, or *phonemically*' (he wrote on the pad) '*you* might write it *wweng elyeny*, which of course means chance equal.'

'So they can't make up their minds whether to let us have specimens or not. How am I going to persuade them to say yes? It's vital to our programme to get at least some artefacts back, and the geneticists and so on will want to take the cell structure of crop specimens apart.'

'No, I think there's something else here. Don't tell me, let me guess . . . I don't think the interpreters would have slipped up on this one, but you were going it alone, weren't you?'

'Yes, I was.'

'Well . . . what those fellows may have *thought* you were

71

asking was, I suggest, whether you could, physically, succeed in getting their specimens safely from here to Earth. The syntax is a bit tricky, but you should have requested permission –*qhedyep geph* if you like – instead of inquiring about possibility –*ezhnye bvew*. So, if I'm right, they thought you thought they might know how tough these specimens'd be. And naturally they said perhaps. Am I right?'

'My God, I believe you are! All they meant was, they didn't know whether the things would survive the journey! I'll start begging specimens off them right away . . . Well, Jimmy, I'll give you a dinner at Savoni's for that, when we get back to Earth; after we get out of quarantine, that is.'

'Do you think' (Anson dropped his voice) 'they'll ever let us out of quarantine, Chief?'

'Indeed . . . not . . . so . . . certain.'

The Transfinite Choice

Something went wrong with the five-mile linear accelerator. The public were no wiser when the press, radio, and TV had given their impressions of what the official spokesman's interpretation of what the atomic experts' version of their own suspicions was. By 1980 they were still arguing about it.

All Naverson Builth knew about it was that one moment he was standing by at the first of a new series of experiments and the next moment he was lying on his back and that the hall was completely deserted. Moreover, it seemed to have acquired a number of new gadgets and machines, and a different coat of paint. There was dead silence. The hall was lit, but rather dimly.

Naverson tried shouting. He discovered that he was all right and eventually got to the doors. They were locked. He went round to the communication phone. The phone was not there. There was no trace of it or its connections.

He was still shouting and banging on the doors when a huge metal arm came out of nowhere and picked him up. About twenty feet up it pulled him through a hinged opening and deposited him on a floor which he could not recall existing at that height and place. A long jointed prong approached him and felt all round him, while his arms and legs were held back by clamps. It clicked disapprovingly and folded up. A metallic voice spoke from the roof. It said: 'Namplize.'

'Who the hell are you, and what the hell do you think you're doing with me?' shouted Naverson. 'I was working in the hall and suddenly I find myself all alone. What've you done with the phone, and what are these machines pulling me about for? How long have I been here, anyway?'

'Namplize.'

'Don't you speak English, then? Who the hell are you?'

'Namplize.'

'*Parlez-vous français? Qu'est-ce que l'on fait alors dans cette galère?*'

'Namplize.'

'*Govorítye li vy po russki? . . . Türkiyizce konushurmusunuz?*'

'Namplize-urnlay.'

'*¿Habla Usted español? . . . Parla italiano?*'

'Namplize-farce.'

'*Sprechen sie Deutsch? Um Gottes Willen, was ist hier los?*'

'Namnadrissplize.'

'To hell with you. I can't understand a word you say.'

Silence.

The clamps tightened on his limbs and another long prong approached. It had a tiny mirror or window near its end, and an opposing pincer-pair alongside. It felt its way into his over-all-pockets and pulled out and appeared to inspect various objects from them. Finally it got hold of a typed envelope addressed to him. It scanned this slowly all over, both sides, upside-down and sideways as well as right way up, including the postmark (which for once was legible). Then it returned the envelope to the pocket, and folded up. The big arm, still clutching him firmly, swung him up into a recess in the wall, tidied his feet in, and a door slid shut. The recess shot up like a lift, stopped, a door slid open on the other side, and he was blinking at a small room dazzlingly lit. In it was a little old man with shaven poll, in a pale blue tunic, apparently seated at a console with stops and levers. He was facing the recess, and just taking a swig from a curiously shaped flask, which he set down on the floor. Naverson clambered stiffly out, feeling his legs and arms.

'Now what the hell is all this? Who are you, and what are

you doing in this plant? I've never seen you before here and you seem to have been monkeying about with the machinery.'

'Suzzdummuvspightchplize,' said the little old man gently but firmly, staring at Naverson. It was the same voice.

'I don't understand you. *Ne comprends pas. Verstehe nicht. Ya ne ponimáyu. Anlamiyorum. No capisco. No entiendo.*'

'W-atplize.' The old man pressed a switch and called downwards: 'Undrowda, hooh srigh. Nannriggig. Paarurwclurz. Paarurwimvlup, nammprax navverrazawn boughillut un paarurw-rawtung, prundatt prax wennawnsimtaow! Nattgurwuzzuzdum . . . Sregjunzplize.'

A metallic voice cackled up at him. He pressed a button. Metal arms gripped Naverson. A little pang on one earlobe. Unconsciousness.

Naverson woke up in a swirl of mental confusion. Clamps were being peeled from his skull, which had been shaved. He was naked, lying on a couch. A few attendants, about half of whom (to his horror) appeared to be women, were studying charts and manipulating knobs. The room was even smaller than the last, and brighter. The temperature was about 80° F. He found that he was able to understand the speech of those about him, on the whole, though some of their nouns and even verbs were strange. The attendants were dressed in one-piece translucent suits which covered most of their faces, but were transparent at the eyes.

'Where am I?' he said, or rather he said 'Waayaa?' (*Where here?*) in the speech of those around him, but the intention was the same and we can transpose from now on. *But let no one suppose that ours is more than a free translation . . .*

'In glossopsychic centre,' said a voice behind his head, which proved to be that of a young man standing there. 'You seem from year approximately one, nine, seven, two. Trouble in sub-quark domain probably switched you here, linear accelerator, year two, three, four, six. Linguistic shunt achieved. Skill, please.'

'Skill? Elementary particle analysis.'

'Perhaps try utilize . . . Suit ready here, on please.'

Naverson slipped into the translucent suit, which was evidently made to measure.

'Hungry,' he said.

Ten months later, months of intensive education, found him in a post with the new world-government department of Direct Parameter Control ('Drik Premda Kindrurw'). Naverson thanked his stars. The world population was now some four millions of millions and the lot of most persons under the relentless pressure of their own increasing numbers was unenviable. Confined to a small cabin (with every mod con) in continent-wide multi-storey warrens, which only stopped at the sea and the mountains, they and their children 'educated', supervised and entertained by giant television screens, compulsorily sterilized after their second child, fed on piped algal infusions, never seeing natural daylight except when drafted for their one year's open-air hard labour in every five of their first thirty adult years, the great majority had little to live for and nothing to die for. When children grew up (at twenty-four, owing to the low diet) they had to find a new home, and the population computers assigned them one in a new block built at a new level above the old flat roofs, or in a marginal section nudging the nearest foothills. Roof blocks, however, were few, being difficult to construct because so many interfered with the air-transport and interplanetary roof-termini and the solar energy collectors. Such colonies as Mars and Venus and Luna could support were negligible.

Only the more active and enterprising workers such as the sea-farmers, and the higher brainworkers, had more freedom of movement, space, and occupation, and more choice of food. Naverson, at Direct Parameter Control, was one of those. Whether it was the undoubted genius with which he had started (he was a postgraduate of dazzling promise in the late 1960s) or the stimulating effect of the accident, or that of the cerebral pummelling he had sustained at the glossopsychic centre where they had imprinted in him understanding of the language, or all three, his examiners found him really capable of appreciating all the relevant advances from AD 1972 to 2346 in subatomic, subelemparticle (quarkic), subquark and hypo-subquark physics. He discovered that the glossopsychophysi-ologist (who naturally knew nothing outside his own sphere) had been wrong in attributing his time-shunt merely to sub-quark events – it could not be due to anything grosser than hyposubquark phenomena . . . The little old man he never saw again; he was, in effect, nightwatchman at the old accelerator, nowadays automated.

Most of Naverson's new colleagues, in any case, came equally fresh to the ideas of Direct Parameter Control, or DPC as it was coming to be known. A formal introductory oration, or Pip (i.e. *Pep*) as it was called, ran somewhat as follows:

'Now, sports, DPC takes over where complex gross physical control too costly or too imperfect. Momently we feel our way, but expect expand into many subdepartments. Statistical as-semblages normally poor fields, molecular operations good, genetic material best; organisms and small living groups fair. Usual attack via subquark domain. "Direct" misnomer. Shunt-ing quarkwise, subquarkwise, affects parameters. Each sub-department to have four hyposubdeps: Parameter Assessment, Research, Application, Public Relations. In practice many of you will work in several. General questions?'

In a few months Naverson found himself assigned to the budding subdep. of Ageing Control (AC, 'Adjung Kindrurw'). His role finally settled into that of a researcher, with excursions into Application and PR.

'See,' he was explaining to a friendly pubhealth man two years later, 'geriatrics failed, unable increase life expectancy over 18 per cent, active life over 12 per cent. Direct parameters now target. Relevant parameters in ageing show in three quasi-dimensions as variety of helix. Organism enters at conception on broad base, spirals upward on time axis at constant gradient, and inward as on a cone/dome towards literal *point* of death, on slope peculiar to itself.'

'Why spiral, why not straight line?'

'Straight line no end. Cyclic returns of the spiral correspond cyclic effects of internal/external environment, for instance annual. Comparative circumference-length corresponds comparative subjective and physiological time.'

'You mean, long long hours of infancy?'

'Exact. Childhood hours pass like adult weeks, years flash by more and more swift towards old age, healing-times meanwhile lengthen; hence spiral inward, circumference shortens. At zero diameter zero circumference, healing infinitely slow, subjective time infinitely swift, death . . . Width of individual's life's base and general slope of cone go with genus, species, variety, genes. Also affected by conception-environment, gestation, radiation, disease, accident. Mild radiation shrinks diameter, disease tilts cone in domewise, accident pushes dome in flattish; recovery swells it out. Cylinder up time-axis would mean immortality!'

'How 22nd Century would have welcomed this!'

'Yes, you mean when computers assessed individuals' health factors yearly, produced graphs and per-cent chances different death-causes different years ahead?'

'Exact. Tense cigarette-smoker aged twenty, for instance, given choice 5 per cent chance die senility at age eighty, 25 per cent death lung-cancer age sixty, 30 per cent bronchial fifty, 25 per cent coronary forty, 10 per cent gastric cancer thirty-five, or 5 per cent vehicle accident twenty-five. Panics, suicides, druggery.'

'Now seek directly affect viability, prolong life, cheat computer!'

'What classes personnel?'

'Managers, directors, government chiefs. Later top brain-workers?'

'How attack?'

'Three possible: widen cone-base, steepen cone-side, flatten spiral pitch. First trying widen cone-base (conception); small animals. Subquark-wise. Subradiate parental gonads. Hope ready selected managerial-caste parents in year.'

'What percentage time-increase?'

'First 10 per cent age increase? Hope later cumulative 5 per cent increase each generation from single dose, if trick find-able.'

'Useless *general* population, longer life unendurable!'

In any case it was not to be. Research on the cone-base method produced feeble flies, overgrown tadpoles, foetus-like mice, sub-infantile baby monkeys after long gestations. The mouse-mothers and monkey parents that survived the preg-nancies neglected their offspring; those grew up socially twisted, and lived their 110 per cent life-spans a misery to themselves and a torment to their mates.

Builth, now head of the subdep's Research branch, was switched to cone-angle steepening, on which the Parameter-Assessment boys had now a full picture. Five years later he had the answer in the subquark domain: a tiny transmitter of subquarkons embedded in the pituitary as early as convenient, which would send its infinitesimal products through the organ-ism and in a few weeks, it was expected, would affect genes and somatic plasm of every cell in the body, after which the trans-mitter was left in to function for life. No cumulative effect on later generations was possible this way, however.

Unfortunately they found that in 40 per cent of higher-animal experiments a psychopathic personality was induced if the transmitter was implanted in infancy. Implantation in adult life gave rise to mosaic effects, so that some cells persisted in ageing normally, and in up to 30 per cent of higher-animal individuals tried, these mosaics reduced the organism by its middle age to a distressing degree of malfunctioning, of which fits and cancers were only two of many manifestations.

'Sports,' said Naverson Builth formally to his research team, 'now must try parameter three: helix gradient. DPC's Director agreed switch our PA sports to gradient month ago.'

'But this means hypo-sub!' called out Eck.

'Exact! hypo-subquark transoscillation necessary basis . . . No harm start these lines now, sharpen our tools against Parameter-Assessment verdict day.'

Two years later the PA boys came up with the answer: all the known physical world was subject to the same pitch or 'gradient', the natural rate of time. Its connexion with entropy was complex, but the basic rate was fixed.

It took eleven more years, years in which Naverson lived, slept, and ate helix-gradientry, before his hypo-subdep found their answer: *infra*-hypo-subquark shunts were the only hope, for the fundamental structure of time lay in the i-h-s-q domain. Some amazing things came to light as a result of their researches. Mank Showk (Domenico Zhukov) was chatting to Naverson one day.

'Sole reason we cannot see/hear Past is, recession-velocity c, therefore its signals undergo transfinite redshift, arrive with zero energy.'

'What about Future?'

'Not in being. Continuous creation of Time, expansion from zero-volume Present. Or conversely, Present advances into Future with velocity c.'

'Explain: whither?'

'Fourth space dimension. A moment eight and a half minutes ago is one astro-unit away along fourth dimension. A moment one year ago is one light year away along it.'

'Then we shall never explore Future or Past?'

'Not on supra-i-h-s-q levels. Not on any practical level probably, and not at all without fifty years' grind.'

'And no professional motive or money in present world conditions.'

In fourteen further years, with Naverson now in greying middle age, the solution was found, after a fashion: the experimental rats, surrounded by the palladium coils, were pushed into a 0.01 per cent flatter gradient, as assessed by computer . . . They simply vanished; they ceased to intersect with the rest of the known universe except instantaneously, and therefore imperceptibly . . .

'Flatch!' called the Director on the visiphone to his opposite number in Population. 'Our AC sports have hit a Wunkun for you.' A Wunkun was the current term for a rewarding disaster, an ill wind that blew somebody good, an ugly duckling that was somebody's golden-egg-laying swan. The name derived from the name of the head of the century-old expedition round Venus that had shattered half the planet's surface, destroying itself in the process, and in so doing had made the planet landable-on and ultimately habitable.

'Out with; I'm suicidal now: Earth's only three generations from standing room. Riots, virus-epidemics increasing monthly. Like the 21st-century crash, but no solution this time.'

'Visit, please: security.'

'Right; in fifteen minutes till forty-five minutes convenient?'

'Make twenty till sixty.'

'Non-poss. Twenty till fifty?'

'Right.'

When Flatch Bemp (i.e. Flotsham Bassompied) landed from Sahara, the DPC Director, Kulf (pronounced Kulluf) Gren (i.e. Kinloch Grattan) had a shot of lysergibenzedrine ready for him. 'Now,' said he, 'I call Nevzen Bewce, dedicated man – he explains quick.'

Naverson Builth appeared in the secure internal visiphone screen.

'Nev, this Flatch Bemp, Director Population.'

Naverson nodded, a subservient greeting in those days. Flatch twitched his left eyebrow.

'Population may have use, your gimmick. Explain it.'

Naverson explained that, depending on the degree of shunt, any gradient desired could be given to the organism.

'Steeper, too?' asked Flatch.

'Steeper too – ages *quicker*, flatter slower.'

'How many gradients total?'

81

'Infinite. Only limitations precision of infra-hypo-subquark gadgetry operation.'

'In practice?'

'Say 105 flatterwise, 108 steeperwise. Technically possible also produce zero gradient or negative gradient, respectively eternal life and regression to infancy (backward time), humanly pointless. 105 flatter but positive.'

Flatch spread his hands outwards, an outrageously extravagant gesture in that crammed and pressed world, but warranted by the moment and encouraged by his boost from the 1-b shot.

'Eureka! How apply shunt?'

'Chamber of coils. Any age.'

'Size limit? Get in several together?'

'Say 70 metres cube; 34 times 104 cubic metres.'

'Get crowd in then?'

'Possibly. Tell you in year perhaps.'

'Eurekest! Select families from volunteers, promise lebensraum, shunt off; divide world population by 105 at least! Extend top privileges to all here, heaven on earth!'

A vast grin spread round his face . . .

'Understand, moment security, silence, death penalty.'

'Rest of team?'

'Temporary silence to lower echelons. Eh, Kulf?'

'Right. You are Project X now. To remain here, Flatch?'

'Exact, best remain here, channel to me via you, Kulf.'

'Right.'

It took two years to establish the intra-coil limits. They worked on elephants and on sequoias (complete with roots), also on families of zoo bears, and goats (most land animals were in zoos or labs, except farm animals too precious to waste). The practical limit proved to be a 97-metre-diameter sphere. The gradient-density limit worked out at 10^5 x 2 channels for the flatter gradients, and over 10^7 for the steeper ones. Flatch Bemp found ethical objections to sending people into a gradient with a shorter life-span, and again to extending the life-span beyond 300 years (besides, how many would ever volunteer for outside these limits?). So he was obliged to be content with the least flat of the flatter gradients, which meant under 10^4 channels. Still, to propose to divide the world's present population by nearly ten thousand was to give it a glimpse of hope.

'If we can take them at that rate!' murmured Naverson.

'Does Flatch know what we'll send into?' twanged Mank.

'Fowp's best theoretician. He and Eck say each gradient manifestation same multigrade reality, gross physical world same in each. Just ensure good population density shot in, enough specialists, hydroponic equipment, soil bacteria cultures, ultrasonic crumblers, algae, fish-spawn – build up civilization in three generations.'

'Fully voluntary basis, Kulf,' said Flatch two rooms away; 'we'll appeal world-wide time-gradient emigration. Plenty volunteers, tough pioneers, independents, claustrophobes, crowd-haters. Ask full details. Computers assess potentialities, eliminate misfits, compose suitable shunt-manifolds, balanced gradient-populations. Details to include preferred life-span – of juveniles: parents to fit in or stay behind. Can't give a tenner, a twentier and a fiftier same gradient and expect all three live same length!' He chuckled fatuously.

Linked batteries of computer complexes worked out time-logistics and densities so as to give the minimum of hardship. Meantime Naverson's boys (he was now in charge of the whole subdep X) had built a series of Shunters, one for each desired gradient. Human bulk transport was easy and they preferred not to disperse the project at this stage; besides, the emergent migrants were best concentrated in one spot whence they could fan outward and where they could hold pioneer councils.

The emigrants were duly selected and shot off into the unknown. A rate of 10,000 a day was achieved, which exceeded Flatch's own logistics researchers' forecast by a factor of ten, but was still an insignificant offset to the birthrate. Four years later, years of intense negotiation and effort, one thousand batteries of Shunters were up and the rate (improved for each) now totalled thirty world-million a day. Eventually Naverson, a prematurely elderly man at seventy, had 7,000 million leave each day through 30,000 batteries, dispersed over the margins of the habitable globe, a rate which might be expected to drain off nearly the current birthrate-excess. It was a real achievement to have reached this plateau, thought Naverson.

The Shunter complexes were nearly all sited on poorly populated highlands away from the warren-edges, where vast reception camps could be set up and where the migrants, when they passed through, would be able to survey the lowlands as they held their first councils. The scenes in the gigantic Reception Areas – as each accepted family with its minimal goods was admitted, documented, inoculated, made up on basic rations, weapons, tools, camped on its bench for two days, was re-checked for infection, was herded on, passed through, was corralled in the polygonal eight-storey intra-coil chamber, and, with some 20,000 other individuals, a herd of goats, and a lot of equipment, shot off into the unknown – would have electrified an Eichmann, at such an *Endlösung* to end all *Endlösungen*. But it was a *Dies Irae* minus the wrath. The countless hosts arrived, if not actually singing, at any rate chattering, to stream through their gates, not of pearl, but of palladium; and if they held hands as they saw the last of this continuum, that was only to be expected.

Naverson, on whom the strain of the great operation was telling, had a curious dream about this time. He was talking to Flatch (who was already dead in fact) and saying, 'We are attenuating local world-line reality, riddling it, fractionating it. Previously 104 gradients dense, so to speak. Now only one. Emigrant populations burrowing structure. Won't survive 1/10,000 rarefaction much longer.'

'Nonsense!' said Flatch and at that moment the whole inhabited surface-region of Terra comploded, like a termite-infested building. Naverson woke up with pounding heart, sweating, dry-tongued, to hear the visiphone alarm calling. It was 'morning', but he had slept in.

'Nev!' said the figure of Misk Howla (Flatch's successor; today he would have been Méthexis Ulvelæj). 'Nev! Something up. Unexplained population figures, not down enough. A lot of illegal squatting empty marginal dwelling spaces. Have they all come back?'

'Impossible,' said Naverson, then he paused. 'Check births, origins, genes if necessary, computerwise.'

'Why?'

'Check first.'

Ten days later the computer complexes gave up their answer: up to 15 per cent of the world population (concentrated near the new dwelling spaces on the warren margins) were unexplained, with no known origin. Their gene-type percentages gave a picture which was partly identical with that of the local population, but partly composed of puzzling variants which, or in proportions which, the computers were quite unable to match.

'Know why, Misk?' whispered old Naverson to the young Population Director in the dazzling privacy of the Directorial office, lit by real sunlight through real glass on the edge of a warren by the Ahaggar Mountains. 'Know why? The other gradients aren't void or uninhabited; they are full! Just like us, more or less, probably. Our time-universe is only one among millions, perhaps infinite number. They've hit on our method approximately same time-point.'

Misk, an impulsive man, jumped through the window, 278 storeys up.

Naverson, who knew Misk's staff well now, took over Population's end of the problem and in another week had further details: the immigrant-sending gradients were all steeper; there were several thousands of them known to be sending at the moment, though rates and numbers were likely to increase. The sending chambers were not identical with his own, or in the same places, but created new populations in similar

85

marginal areas. The immigrants had found themselves in a populous world where they had been expecting an empty one; however, they had made the best of a bad job and, being enterprising, broke up their chamber-storeys, scattered, infiltrated the mass, occupied vacant cells in the warren-margins, and had evaded detection for some years.

Three months later a series of strange short-lived virus epidemics, beginning near the Alpine and Rocky Mountains margins, seized 60 per cent of the American and European population, and killed 25 per cent of those they struck. In spite of the television propaganda, the survivors blamed the 'invaders', and any unvouched newcomers to a warren district were butchered from then on, including the children. Later, actual Shuntee batches were found by out-labour gangs, sometimes still in their multi-storey capsules, and a fight to the death would ensue with such weapons as came to hand. Naverson pictured the same fate fallen and befalling, and to befall, his own shuntees . . . At seventy-five, he had reached retiring age. Worn out, he died, a disappointed man, in the grey winter of 2395 a few months later, leaving the Worlds to struggle with their monstrous burden.

In February AD 2021 in the same continuum, just before the Second World Famine, the newscasts were full of the death of Naverson Builth, the brilliant young researcher struck down by a once-famous accident at the great accelerator, who had lived on in a permanent coma for forty-nine years, kept alive by modern medical science . . . It was *his* reality which had been fractionated by infra-hypo-subquark shunt.

Psychosmosis

'One has succumbed in the house by Thorn Thicket, Little Ness,' said Tan, rapidly and shamefacedly, meeting the chunky fellow on the edge of the swamp where Ness had been trapping for some days.

'One of their old ones?'

'No, no, it is the one who was the wife of Kemm; she had a sudden illness.'

'Ah,' breathed Ness, 'then we shall have two new namings – or are the wife of Nant and the second daughter of Big Ness already named again?'

'No – it happened an hour ago. You are in time to hear.'

'This was a troublesome death, then – but we shall have fun at the naming-feasts.'

Little Ness found that he was breathing rather quickly. It had been on the tip of his tongue to ask Tan casually 'And how is –?', for he was interested in Big Ness's nubile younger daughter. A narrow escape.

The house of Kemm and his parents and old aunts was carefully bypassed by everyone. It had a black cloth stuck on two stakes across its entrance. Nant and Big Ness had seen the way things were going for a day or two and held secret councils in their houses, so they were ready when the black cloth appeared. Since Nant's wife and Big Ness's second daughter had the same name as Kemm's second wife, they must be renamed at once. As a precaution, Nant had taken to addressing his wife as 'wife' at first. She had settled finally for Mara, which faintly recalled her old name, and Big Ness had persuaded his daughter that Nura (which was even closer) would do for her; though he shunned saying or even daring to think so, it recalled his dead wife's name too, which had the same *u*-vowel as well as all the other sounds. A quarter of an hour after Little Ness had heard the news from Tan, Nant and his wife paraded round the settlements banging an old dish and calling out 'Nant's wife is Mara. Come to the feast tonight!' Everyone began to mutter 'Mara, Mara, Mara' to themselves to memorize the name. Ten minutes behind them Big Ness and his family came hitting two spoons together and shouting 'Big Ness's second daughter is Nura – come and see us tonight.' The hearers muttered 'Nu-*u*ra, Nu-*u*ra.' and debated which house to visit first. They thought there would be more amusement to be had at Nant's house later, on the whole.

Little Ness, however, decided to call first on Nant, so as to have the rest of the evening with the girl whom he must now, with some distaste, think of as Nura. What a name! There he found Nura herself paying a token visit and sliding down her first drink of the evening. They greeted each other self-consciously and remained rather ill at ease. Little Ness did not like to criticize the name directly, but Nura knew instinctively what was wrong. Kemm, walking like a man in a dream, came in on the arm of the doctor, hoarsely greeted Mara by name and touched the proffered (and nearly empty) cup with his lips. Then he and the doctor walked off to Big Ness's, and the company breathed more freely. Presently the doctor, Sull, came in again alone. Everyone knew he had taken Kemm back home. (Parents and aunts were bedridden.) Sull downed several drinks quickly and began to tell one bawdy story after another. Mara and Nura nodded at one another and, escorted by Little Ness (who would now rather have heard the stories) made their way in the bat-haunted dusk to Big Ness's house. As they entered, the dark beauty, Forna, arm entwined with that of Heft (her husband Freth was safely off at Nant's house) was saying loudly 'Don't know *how* we managed in the dull old days.' After a drink, Mara went back on the arm of Big Ness, while Tark, his eldest son, played host for the time being.

Little Ness, in whom the drinks were beginning to work, would have liked to get Nura on her own, but it was impossible tonight. He stayed to the end, to keep an eye on her, and somewhere in the early morning bade her an amorous farewell outside and lurched homeward. His father was snoring, having got away before midnight from the party.

The doctor, Sull, woken an hour or two later by the owls and a rumbling stomach, squinted at the moon, mixed himself a strong tonic, and crept out without waking Skenna. He made his way in the moonlight with a second draught to Kemm's house, stole in without disturbing the old folk, shook Kemm by the shoulder but found him rigidly awake, made him drink the draught, and with him laid the body on the cart at the back. In two hours, during which neither spoke, they reached the lip of the volcano. The grey dawn was touching the summit as they tipped up the cart and shot the body down the hot cindery slope. Sull, after returning the cart, brought Kemm on to his own house, where Skenna gave both men breakfast in silence. Then, as Sull had his rounds to make, she started to take Kemm home. They had not gone far before a confused outcry broke out. Presently a youth came running up. 'Mara's husband is gone!' he shouted and sped on.

Nant had spent an uneasy night (or rather, early morning), his brain muddied with alcohol and vague disquiet caused by the too-eager manner of Surt towards Mara that evening. As they stirred in the early rays of the sun he groaned and, out of half-sleep, began:

'I say, Nira –'

Mara shuddered fully awake to find her husband gone. She knew what had happened. A scream formed in her throat. She staggered up, snatching at a cloth. Half a dozen frowzy heads appeared at house doors and windows. 'He's gone! He's gone! He said it!' and she collapsed on the ground, beginning a continuously fluctuating moan.

No one came near, but disturbing news was carried frantically from house to house. Fortunately no one had been awake enough to comment on last night's party. Surt, whose interest in Mara was indeed active, decided to keep out of the way, to bide his time. He went fishing for the day.

The sobbing, writhing girl was ignored, with revulsion, by everyone in the community, except, after half an hour, by the doctor. Sull came striding down, sat her up, slapped her vigorously across both cheeks, forced a drink down her throat, and then tried to take her to her parents' house. She shook free and stumbled inside her own door. An hour later her mother, on her way to market, peered inside but did not speak or go in.

That night, exhausted, Mara drifted asleep, only to meet her husband in vivid dreams. He was smiling at her, pulling her along by the arms, leading her down imaginary valleys, up imaginary hillsides. In the morning she woke to the empty reality and in ultimate desperation, as one who falls on a sword, spoke his name. Sull on his rounds found a silent house and, guessing what had happened, warned the community that 'The wife who was named but was unlucky is now gone too: a double vanishment.'

As the syllable 'Nant!' closed in her mouth, Mara felt as it were an edge cleave her brain, a white pang, then she found herself without transition lying on a steeply falling fern-clad slope, facing the morning sun. The slope was like nothing she knew in waking life: the only hilly country in the Land had been the bare sides of the volcano. Woods and great folded hillsides spread below and across from her. The air was brisk. A wind was pouring down the slope. Gulls called. A squirrel chittered at her from a tree behind her, one of several dotted about the hillside. Voices singing and chattering sounded faintly to south.

After a minute Mara clambered unsteadily towards the voices. Among some trees she came across a group of people, several of whom she knew. There was a middle-aged man who had vanished three years ago, at a feast, shortly after one of his friends had died. There was a girl whose lover had vanished after his brother's death, and who herself vanished shortly thereafter. With the girl was her lover. All nameless now to the People.

'Nira!' called the three joyfully. It was her first name, changed yesterday. But *they* did not vanish. The three left the group and surrounded her.

'You have crossed!' said the girl. 'Nant is here. He has been calling you all day and all night. You are here at last; you are one of the Invokers now. Yes, he is waiting for you. Let us take you down to him – it is only a mile or so.'

'Are we all dead, then?'

'No, we are not the Faded; we are the Invokers, we are Inside. We spoke the names, in carelessness or defiance, so we crossed.'

'They – they know nothing about this world where I was.'

'No, but we try. We call. And at night we dream of them, as we dream of the Faded. But they are too circumspect, the Hard of Hearing. Few of them leave the Outside.'

'Is he well?'

'He is half-wild, but still hopeful of your coming.'

'How do you live here?'

'Just as the Outsiders do. We hunt, we fish, we grow plants, we harvest fruits. It is another land, simply, only Inside. There is nothing all round but the seas, the great waters; you can hear them roar far off. We have never got far out in them. There is no way back. Few of us regret it long.'

'We shall not . . . How did those children cross over?' added Nira, seeing a bunch of small ones on a track below them. 'They look too young to have bandied the names of adults about – or did they say a dead brother's name?'

'They didn't cross over – these were born here.'

'What are those mounds over there?'

'Burial mounds.' And, seeing Nira did not understand: 'Mounds built to cover the bodies of the Faded.'

'Do we not live for ever here, then? Or were those people killed by accident?'

'No, no, we simply live a normal life-span. We put the bodies of our Faded in these mounds. Those flowers you see are their birthday flowers for those who were born here, or crossing-day flowers for those that crossed here.'

'Do you not remember the days of their deaths, since you think so steadily of the dead?'

'What would be the sense of that? We want to recall the lucky day they came among us, not the sad day they faded from us . . . Let us try calling Nant now.' And the girl began shouting downhill through the forest. The others joined in. Presently there was an answer. In a few minutes someone came running uphill, dodging the boles and tussocks. It was Nant. The others melted away.

When the first ecstasy was over Nant and Nira – he insisted on calling her by her old name – walked hand in hand to the valley, where they meant to build a home not far from one of the clusters of houses. On the way they passed a small grouping of burial mounds. Several were decorated.

'You and I will have crossing-day flowers like these one day – you on one day, I on the next.'

'May that be long hence. Our children's children will be there with the first to lay them, I hope. Now we must find something to eat to restore you, pale thing. Then we must get some help to fell the timber for a start. And tonight they will have a guest-house for us. Tonight, too, will be held a specially joyful celebration for you and me together.'

'What shall you do for a living?'

'What should I do but hunt, as I always did?'

A day before the great boar hunt, and a week after the burning of the vanished couple's house and goods, Sull told the community, 'The man that was Heft's father has died.' No one was surprised – Heft's father had been doddering for some time. Heft had stuck up the black cloth. That evening he and Sull pitched the corpse into the volcano. Heft was avoided for a few weeks, though he was already learning to say 'The man that was my father' by the time the boar hunt was over. People had become nervous, especially the mothers and fathers of families.

One of the heroes of the hunt was Little Ness's friend Tan. This was because exasperation and self-contempt had made him foolhardy, and he speared and shoved among the ravening beasts like a madman. The fact was, Tan had quarrelled bitterly with Danna, his girl, about half an hour before. She had spoken warmly of 'our two friends who were unlucky after naming, and vanished', and Tan, who always felt an irrational dislike of the attractive Nant, accused her of thinking too much of 'the man'. The colder Danna grew the more blindly enraged Tan became, and they parted as if for good. Once the hunt was on, Tan felt himself to have been insanely and pointlessly jealous, and doubted if he could ever patch matters up. Hence his 'heroism'.

Three others would have been heroes of that hunt, but of them only Keth survived. One man died speedily, and his corpse was slung on a pole to be committed to the volcano as soon as convenient. Another, after ten minutes' agony (he had been extensively trampled and gored) bethought himself of a way out and groaned out 'Nant'. He disappeared as the bystanders scattered in horror.

The procession, with Tan and Keth carried shoulder-high among the inverted hanging carcasses, arrived home to a wildly excited mob of women, children and old men. For a tense moment these, who had studiously avoided mentioning names of those away on the dangerous enterprise, heard the news that the first son of Pemf and the second of Rann were gone, then the joyful uproar recommenced.

It was only to be expected that Danna should keep away from the crowd until she heard of Tan's prowess, but he hoped she would come round presently. As the feast developed without sign of her, however, an icy clamp seemed to fasten slowly on his bowels. He fought his way towards an old woman at the back of the green and murmured in her ear, 'Tell me, please, is the daughter of Ban and Daaba anywhere to be seen?'

'Why no. I have not seen her today at all.'

'Would *they* have seen her, then?'

'Perhaps. Wait.' And the old crone ambled over to where Daaba sat balancing a large beaker. Tan saw Daaba shake her head and call across to Ban two rows in front. The huge man rose and lumbered towards her. Daaba whispered to him. Ban stared back at her. Then he shuffled towards Tan, threading his way through the half-drunken feasters.

'No.' he said unsteadily, meeting the youth's eyes (his own shatteringly like those of the missing girl). 'No, our daughter spoke to us after the hunt moved off. She was upset over something. Then she walked off down the path.'

'Could she have wandered far?'

'I don't think she did. Someone would have seen her. And although she was upset, she was not – you know what I mean – she could not have . . . I am sure . . . Besides there was nothing she could have used, unless a knife. And we missed nothing.'

'Or an accident – a wild animal?'

'Let us speak to Forna.'

They made their way to where the couple sat, arms round each other's necks, cackling and swaying, not far off.

'Forna!' shouted Tan in the dark one's ear. 'Was your old friend that was my friend, my girl, was she in the place all day? Tell me, I must know.'

'Eh – oh it's you, you are a hero now, you know. Oh yes, it's odd she isn't here. No; I remember, she was sitting down grumbling to herself about something down by your hut all afternoon. About an hour before the hunt came back I saw her last. Next time I looked, she was gone. Freth – did you see her?'

'No-o!' said her husband.

Tan, followed by Forna and Ban, escaped from the assembly and went round, through and all over his own hut and its neighbourhood. Nothing disturbed within. Nothing gone. A smoky torch showed the ground scuffed up in front of his hut, but there were no obvious recent footmarks. They looked at one another.

'She that was my daughter must have met vanishment. Perhaps she spoke a name of those two – she knew them well,' said Ban heavily. 'I must warn the rest. Let us go back to the feast.'

Tan spent the rest of the night wandering alone round the settlement. He dare not call her name. In the morning he began a search throughout the land, even wandering among the dust-devils as far as the encircling desert, but to no avail. In his heart he could hear the girl uttering the names of her vanished friends. Estranged from Forna when Forna married the frivolous Freth, ill at ease with most of the community, too tender-hearted, too thoughtful, she must have felt herself deserted by Tan, and in desperation called on that unlucky pair, and so like them was swept away. Now Tan dare not even think her name. Yet when on the third night he slept he dreamt repeatedly of her, sad, reproachful, hungrily staring at him, calling him, calling.

Of this he could speak to no one. As a hero of the hunt he continued to rate an uneasy slap on the back from men like Heft and Little Ness. In the end he drifted back for form's sake to the good cheer and the drinkings of nights, but Ban if they met would stare at him grimly for an instant and turn aside; perhaps he suspected, thought Tan, that there was a quarrel at the back of it; but neither man could even mention the vanished girl now. (In truth, Ban was merely avoiding the embarrassment and risk of an encounter that must remind him of his former daughter.)

The recently vanished couple had made many friends, indeed, whom wine and meat and good company could not entirely distract. Thus it was that impulsive Valla, one day at dinner with her husband (they had married very young more than a dozen years ago) said of a basket she had seen in Sull's house: 'You know, it was exactly like the one Mara—'

Vol stood up shouting, scattering platters as he did. The

place opposite was empty. Vek was away from home; but he had to be told, and the whole community. No one had to change their name. Vol tried to forget, busying himself with Vek's coming of age, and as for Vek, he was wholly taken up with himself.

It was about a week after that Tan was found standing staring silently at nothing, near the house of Little Ness, one arm half-extended, one heel slightly raised. He stood thus like wood for two hours and then consented to be led away. They penned him up behind Sull's house, where an eye could be kept on him, and used to fling him scraps of meat whenever they went by. He raised a few laughs, but most preferred to look aside. In two months he was dead. But his name had long ceased to be spoken.

Vol had successfully outlived his dreams of the woman who had been his wife, but in waking he found her memory growing rather than diminishing. Five months after her disappearance, with Vek safely launched, he found himself sleepless one night and in agony called Valla's name.

A cold slice cut through his brain and he felt a gravelly bank about him, while the stars (different stars) twinkled. This is death, he thought, but by the time morning came and his stiffness made him all too aware of his body, he knew it was no death. He was on the bare neck of a long drumlin, grass-covered, in the midst of a rolling vale. Above him on both sides rose ferny and foresty slopes, the nearest a couple of miles away. Far behind and about them there gleamed mysterious white shapes which Vol could not interpret. Water chattered over stones not far off. The birds skimmed and screamed overhead. A continuous faint murmuring roar rose and fell far off downhill. Movement glimpsed upstream showed him where the settlement was.

When he had hobbled up to it, there was Mara, there was Nant, there was Danna, with a new darkness in her eyes, but a new boy; there was even Vaata, whom he remembered as a lass, much older now but still recognizable. There were many

96

others he had once known, but somehow different. He realized the truth almost at once.

'Where is Valla?' he shouted at them. 'I have come through! Where is Valla?'

'They are at the flower ceremony for poor old Somm,' called a young girl, anxious to show off her knowledge.

'Come, Vol, you are going to have some trouble; come, dear boy,' said an old woman he had forgotten or had never seen, taking his hand firmly; 'come with me and listen carefully; steel yourself; you have been too long among the Hard of Hearing.'

At this moment, in a grave group of people advancing down the hill, Vol saw Valla. She was hand in hand with a tall man, a stranger. The truth burst upon him. With a cry he sprang forward.

The people encircled the three, who stood, as though of stone, face to face a few paces from each other.

'Yes, Vol, you would not come. So few come anyway from the Hard of Hearing. I married Tel here. I am sorry. It is too late. I am going to bear his child.'

Wheeling round, Vol broke through the group and fled upriver. Eventually he found the gorge, where he threw himself over. They found his body on the rocks beneath the sombre crags, and carried it back and buried it. On the anniversary of his crossing Valla and her husband (and half the settlement) used to load his mound with rich flowers and chant their saddest songs. On this first occasion the whole community, singing, escorted them back to their house, and with a long chant bidding Valla think of the future and of her coming child and seeking to reconcile her to herself, took farewell of them for that day.

'That is the most terrible crossing I have ever known or heard of,' said Losp to Mek as they were walking away.

'Yes indeed. Though all crossings are painful at first. The careless-mouthed children are the most difficult: I saw two – long ago. But they have grown up all right among us.'

'Kush is a pretty unsatisfactory fellow, all the same.'

'Well, yes; he is hard and moody. But one of the worst crossings till now was poor Gal's, wounded in the boar hunt Outside. He'd expected a quick release, but he came Inside only to die in pain.'

'Still, he had Doctor Lann to help him. But it was a bitter end.'

'We have had rather many crossings lately, but in general they are getting fewer, don't you think?'

'Yes, the Hard of Hearing are getting harder. But we Invokers have more children than they have, according to report: our numbers are growing steadily that way. Look at us two: at least third-generation Invokers.'

'Fourth-generation: the latest of my ancestors to cross over was a great-grandmother of mine. And Menga knows of none of her ancestors that were not born Inside . . . Where *is* that woman? Still gossiping with the other wives back there . . . By the way' (with a wry smile) 'our burial mounds are becoming too thick on the ground, as the old fade out. We shall have to build them further off, and on barren ground. I must raise the matter next Council . . . But here is your house. I shall try and pluck Menga from the old wives' party! Good day to you, and fine hunting.'

'And a good crop to you!'

In the Outside, the Hard of Hearing heard the volcano begin to rumble for the first time in living memory.

The Show Must Go On

I wander through each [censored] street
Past which the [censored] times do flow,
And at my back satanic hear
Marx' millions grind exceeding slow.

On the first stroke the little procession of gilded figures stepped out, strutted round the silver circle and disappeared on the final stroke of thirteen. The tourists gazed; one man took a film sequence. Some of them moved off, others started idly chatting or consulting charts. The Down's syndrome case tried to sell matches at the corner; no one was interested. Piitasan, who had glanced up at the figures on the tower, now went on with his argument. 'It's all a matter of statistics, Eitshi. If their quota isn't up, there have to be redundancies here.'

'There'll be trouble, Piit,' said Eitshisun, picking his way over a meths drinker who was lying half in the gutter.

'Well, we just can't carry the labour force if we can't produce. Our margin isn't that safe.' Piit paused to admire a set of figurines in tinted crystal, set on glass shelves and lit from concealed sources below, in a shop window. 'Exquisite, but at half a doz each they're too dear.'

Further conversation was blotted out by a brass band which swept down the street. Behind it came a gear-grumbling cortège of held-up vehicles. As these thinned out, Piit began to speak again but his words were cut short by two shots. From a high window opposite a man pitched down into the crowd. He fell onto a well-upholstered elderly lady who was knocked to the ground, sustaining a badly sprained shoulder and extensive bruises to her face and body. A little boy made off with her handbag, but, making too hasty a getaway, ran slap under the wheel of a long-distance bus. The passengers in the grounded bus went on discussing in pairs their symptoms, their home neighbours, and the outrageous price of meat. The handbag remained under the bus.

'Noisy here,' said Piit.

Eitshisun looked at his watch, a reflex gesture really since thirteen had so recently struck. 'Must be off now,' he said. 'So long. Thanks for the lunch.'

He turned a couple of corners, passing Maadj, who was discussing with Younis how to cook rinsettes. Younis prided herself on her cuisine and Maadj was really angling for tips. She found time, however, to flash Eitshisun a brilliant smile, and watching this rather than his step, he knocked into Benkt, who was propelling a middle-aged spastic in a wheeled chair. Benkt spent all his spare time and half his small income taking human wrecks for an outing, or otherwise relieving their lot. 'Sorry!' called Eitshisun and swept on. Benkt just saved the spastic from being tipped out, but twisted his own arms so severely in doing this that he had, reluctantly, to call off good deeds for a week, and barely managed to propel the poor man back. However, he felt sure he would be well enough to look forward to spending his holiday in three weeks' time redecorating the homes of some aged widows who were bedridden. Younis, who was meeting her husband Kevn for lunch, parted from Maadj. She found him at the Brushnish, and did his arteries a bad turn by being catty about the menu. Kevn had already had a trying day at the office. However, the balance was nearly restored when she let him buy her two of the crystal figurines at Frassy's. This was by way of being an anniversary present. At the counter alongside two elderly women were complaining to each other about the new numerical system. 'All this duodecimal nonsense is quite unnecessary, Maatheh,' said one. 'Just gives them a chance to rook you right and left. And measurements! I can never remember that one point six is one-and-a-half span.'

'I know, dear. And those weights. I got a shock when I weighed myself, I thought I'd have to go on a diet.'

Outside the shop a group of youths was kicking a boy in the stomach. The noise he made swelled to an unpleasant volume as the pair with their parcel of figurines came out of the shop door. He began vomiting blood and Kevn had to steer Younis carefully past to avoid soiling her tights. A sandwich man passed down the road bearing a placard announcing 'Dance at Mazy's'. The Down's syndrome case was still trying to sell matches. Younis slipped him a half, but declined the matches. He was still gaping disconsolately after her when the youths, who had got tired of kicking the boy (who was now unconscious), came by, knocked his tray of matches over his head and pranced on roaring with laughter.

Stepping over the unconscious boy, Vall and Matte were discussing the decatonic piece they had heard last night. A pair of acrobats advertising next week's nude circus came down the pavement on their hands, not naked, however, but dressed in luminous psychedelic scarlet and green.

Maadj stopped at a stationers' to pick up a woman's magazine with a large section on beauticare, two moralistic and one etiquette-wise advice columns, a celebrity interview and three sentimental stories. She was about to turn up the alley but heard screams and saw that two thugs were raping a girl there, so instead walked on down the main street where a queue of stolid middle-aged women in their best furs were waiting, perspiring in the sun, outside a Stingo hall. Next door a boy on a motorbike had just flung a Lermontov cocktail into a fish-fry place kept by a coloured family, and roared off as the shop went up in flames. 'Serve 'em right,' one of the prospective Stingo players was saying: 'It's a shame,' said another; nobody moved. Down the road came a little procession carrying banners saying SOLIDARITY WITH THE MIATVEN LIBERATION

FRONT. One banner was held by a toddler in a pushchair. Further down, the college was in a state of siege, from one per cent of its students, who had proclaimed in large letters splattered over its walls that they wanted abolition of exams, total control of the syllabus and free contraceptives on the premises. Below its steps, a child of seven was selling flags for Poxfam. Just beyond, a girl of eight, hesitating, was being invited persistently into a car by a stranger with an ingratiating leer. A traffic warden, who had at first suspected him of being about to park illegally, tramped on reassured. Maadj, who was thinking about her beauticare, walked steadily round the corner and past the green, noting idly that building was going on at lightning speed there, no doubt with the object of forestalling legal objections. The art museum, hung about with mobiles, wrecked machines and chopped-up posters, was round the second bend. Finally she got to the local bus stop and queued up. The queue was very long and after twenty minutes someone in the queue suggested that another lightning strike must have broken out. The queue dispersed and after a long hunt Maadj found a taxi which she had to share with two other occupants, one of whom was going three miles east, the other some four miles south. As Maadj's home was five miles west and she was the last to get in, this delayed her considerably. Moreover, the taxi had to dodge a couple of minor riots and two corpses. Its radio produced a soothing line in cool jazz, interrupted by some rather spastic observations on the firm's intercom. During the last three miles the driver regaled her through all this with his (until recently) unprintable opinion of immigrants. Maadj, however, paid little attention – she was peeping at her magazine's beauticare section.

Paying off the driver at the chemist's to buy some of the products she had just read about, she was treated to a long discussion on the weather, which was wet and cold, according to the chemist, though Maadj privately thought it was muggy but on the whole dry. Eventually she got away and turned into her drive, stepping over the pile of cartons and sweet papers discarded by passers-by.

The telephone was ringing as she let herself in but it was only an obscene caller. It had occurred to her that it might have been Vall ringing, so when she had replaced the phone she rang up Vall herself.

They had a long talk about curtains, cats, Vall's children's latest sayings, the garden and the guinea-pigs. 'What on earth's that noise?' said Vall at one point.

'Hold on, I'll see.' It certainly had been ear-shattering. Maadj put down the phone and walked over to look up and down the street out of the room windows. Presently she came back to the phone. 'Only a crash, dear; I hope they get it cleared up before Henn comes home – it's on the corner. Go on about your mower, darling.'

The driver with his chest stove in was slowly dying. The motorcyclist, his neck broken, lay twenty yards away against a lamp post. The lady from the back of the car was vomiting over the cuts on her face, which was dangling out of the door window. The child of five, on the car floor, was screaming thinly and continuously. The car engine was a total wreck, the bike a tangled mess half wrapped round it. Eventually an ambulance showed up.

Vall, reminded of the guinea-pigs by the conversation, went out into her garden to see how they were getting on. She found them lying dismembered on top of their cage, which had been broken into. After some reflection she buried them herself, with much trouble, in the bed behind the shrubbery, so as not to upset the children too much when they came home. Then she tried the TV.

Programme 5 was showing the football match at Blovno. The ruined buildings gutted in last week's invasion could clearly be seen in the screen, and tanks ringed the stadium. Our team appeared to be winning, and the commentator remarked that it was hard luck on the Blovno team, who had had to find three substitutes in a hurry for three of their best men, shot two days ago by the invaders. Vall, who was not interested in football, switched to Programme 6, which had a fascinating critical discussion on the anti-literature 'poems' of Mikfursan. Unluckily the children burst in just before this finished, and had to be told something of the guinea-pigs' fate. *The Exploits of Pinpin* on the screen consoled them somewhat, after which they switched to *Treble Loot*.

Matte left his store and walked to the multi-storey car park, found his car intact, and started down the ramp in it. His car radio was announcing two more hijacked planes. In front of him on the ramp was a little Angula; Makisun, the driver, was thinking about the model of St Polters at home that he had been constructing for three years out of used matches. Behind Matte, on the other hand, was a Minima driven by Boruz. Boruz was sweating a little because he had just carefully set fire to five wastepaper baskets in Matte's store before closing it. In the next car behind, Tommis was promising himself a fortnight studying the habits of a family of foxes in the Old Forest. Behind him again drove Abut, a lecturer who was in the middle of writing a history of tithes. The exit bar rose successively before them and they drove their several ways. Opposite the exit, heroin powder was being passed to a little group of schoolchildren by a middle-aged man.

Next morning Maadj, cooking the breakfast. heard the usual religious broadcast. A fervent voice was extolling the beauty of God's handiwork in Nature and the tenderness of mother love in birds and animals. While he was speaking, millions of parasitic wasps were laying eggs in live caterpillars, millions of spiders and mantises were devouring their mates, millions of tapeworms were growing segments in human and animal guts, millions of living beings were infected, infested or otherwise overcome with degrading and bestializing diseases, millions of elderly humans were declining in various degrees of long drawn-out indignity and stupor, and millions of travesties of humanity were being born. Of course there were other human wrecks, from car crashes, from boy racers, from heroin and other drugs, and there were other deaths in varying agony from the tanks of Bluntville SA, the tanks of Kingiz Camp, the tanks of Bedapusht, the tanks of Blovno, the bombs and petrol jelly of Miatven, the starvation in Polyafra and Infrasia, the riots, the fires.

Henn had a train journey to make that morning. As his train passed them, the sun shone on the car cemeteries. Henn was reminded of a film of Belschwitz, the piles of shrunken cadavers. His arrival platform was covered ankle-deep in debris, the excretion of the overcrowded human rat, human race, rat race, fouling its rat-runs. Matte, driving in by his car, heard more or less accurately on his radio the opening pseudo-Dies-Irae phrases of the Drum-Roll symphony give place to the confident optimism of the main body of the first movement. He parked in the multi-storey car park and took a bus to his store, to find it gutted. (His house telephone had been 'out of order' all last night, cut by a would-be cosh burglar who had been interrupted by the cars arriving next door for an orgy.) Boruz, ostensibly as concerned as the others, was gaping at the smoking shell.

Eitshisun went by train but never reached his destination. In his compartment he was writing notes for a vital conference of mid-morning, when he was hurled through the window as the train was derailed owing to the prank of six youngsters (who were watching the outcome of their handiwork from a bridge overhead). That was the end of his life and that of one hundred and twenty-six other passengers. (The conference, ill-balanced, went the wrong way, provoking a strike, putting thousands out of work and causing two suicides.) The youngsters, gleeful but scared, scattered before they were spotted and were never identified.

Piitasan read the newspapers over lunch. Their front pages had deployed all last week their most resounding rhetoric over the horrors of the invasion in Blovno; now they carried no less resounding rhetoric on their back pages over the fortunes of the Blovno match. The correspondence columns carried twenty incompatible confident 'solutions' to the international situation. Three liberal leaders had been assassinated in Usam, where ten cities and two penitentiaries were in uproar; three psychotics had shot down seventy people between them. Four more airliners had been hijacked. Shemites were still slaughtering Shemites across sand and water.

Coming out, Piit's eye was caught by an exquisite face, a girl in a million, crossing the road, but as she came over the light changed and he saw that the seemingly sculptured bone structure and the pellucid skin were a cosmetic trick, the hair a wig. The legs were passable. Sidestepping round a youth who was thrusting a jagged glass bottle-end into the face of another, he paused to buy a packet of cigarettes at a kiosk. (The owner, tired after a strainful night on the Good Samaritan Open Line, gave him the wrong brand at first.) He walked on, but was knocked down by a van which, doing forty, had cannoned off a little car without reversing lights that had shot back out of an archway into the main road past a stationary lorry, and whose vision (the car's) had been further obscured by a skeleton puppet, a toy lion on the backrest, six imitation bullet holes, a few stickers on the side windows and a boastful notice about cheetahs.

Piitasan's packet of cigarettes spilled and crushed in the road but most of the fragments were picked up later by a newspaper vendor, who thus succeeded in bringing his own suffocation by lung cancer a week nearer at no cost to himself. Piitasan did not survive the ambulance journey but the bottle-scarred youth did, though blinded. A minute later the Good Samaritan kiosk owner was also blinded, but only for fourteen months, by inexpertly flung ammonia from a snatch till-raider, who got away with the price of two packets and a half, but made half as much again out of a poor old woman's bag down the next street. Vall glanced out at the car accident from her window seat at a restaurant and went on with her conversation with Younis.

Henn ran into Abut, the tithe historian, in a mob that was

wrecking an embassy. 'Hello, fancy meeting you,' said Abut, pausing with a brick in his hand. 'Didn't I see you on the Fifth last night?'

'That discussion? Yes – what did you think of it?'

'A bit overweighted on the economic side of the argument, I thought.'

'Yes, but that chap Filipse wasn't high-powered enough, so naturally the whole thing tilted over on to our side.'

'I suppose –' and Abut paused a moment to hurl his brick – 'you know Dzhonsan's analysis?'

'That thing that came out last February?' Henn looked round for a missile, and tugged at a half-loose length of paling.

'Allow me.' Abut joined in and the two eventually got it loose. Henn fell over backwards and picked himself up, saying:

'Thanks; well I've only skimmed through it. Its arguments struck me as a trifle specious, but plainly it wants digesting.'

'I don't agree with you – about speciousness I mean – but perhaps if you were to look at it again?'

'Maybe you're right,' said Henn, grabbing a lump of documents tossed down from a window. Together they ran with them to the bonfire.

'How's Maadj?' said Abut, kicking a stray file into the flames.

'Fine, thanks. I say, we'd better make ourselves scarce, it's getting a bit too hot here – metaphorically I mean.' They slipped off. But when Henn reached his car a quarter of a mile off he found its tyres slashed, its aerial twisted off, and its side windows smashed, though there was nothing inside to rifle. He started to walk, tried the nearest phone box to warn Maadj, but found it disembowelled. Cutting across the square past the children playing hopscotch, he found a group of youths rocking a couple of cars and joined in, feeling sore remembering his own car. Soon they had one on its side, then the other. They smashed open the petrol caps, backed off and threw burning matches onto the gushing fluid. The result made a satisfactory spectacle. Looking at his watch, Henn slipped off to the nearest bus stop. The buses were running again, and he got home only a little late.

Abut, meanwhile, had taken a train. A stone struck his compartment window but he only got a cut face. He had to miss *Tomorrow's Gimmicks*, an entertaining programme about scientific gadgetry, and wait six hours in hospital while more urgent cases were dealt with, and finally was walking home at two in the morning when he was knifed in the ribs. The history of tithes never got published. (His widow later left their house unoccupied too long, and it was three months before the squatters were expelled, leaving slogans executed in excreta.)

Kevn and Younis next day, just back from a half-weekend celebrating the bicentenary of *Shiftem Trendy*, went for a walk in the park. The usual speakers were there, plus two they had never seen before. One, a flushed youth with the bulging forehead of an epileptic, was yelling, 'We are living in exciting times! A new morality is being worked out! A total revolution in thinking is under way! Bourgeois liberalism and bourgeois ethics are dead! A new dawn is rising!' His scanty audience ate ice creams and dropped the cartons and papers on the grass. The other, twitching, with tremulous limbs and dully glazed eyeballs bearing witness to the long-range toxic effects of too much continuous indignation, had lost his voice in catarrh, and his audience with it. His gaze fixed on a caravanserai of noble thunderheads sweeping and boiling above the horizon, he was hoarsely murmuring, 'Nature, unutterable muddle of elegance and horror, of micro-miniaturized precision and mega-waste, indefensible handiwork of Nobodaddy! Man, unspeakable paragon of presumption, who out-elegances Nature, who out-horrors Nature, who are so sure you are right in your casuistries and that others are wrong, who cannot spare a moment to imagine what your neighbour needs! Man, pleased with your most infantile follies and your most cynical manoeuvres, who – heckler, protester, terrorist, oppressor – in the name of freedom will obliterate freedom, in the name of peace plot war, in the name of right do wrong –

when will you make an end of yourself and give the illimitable messy universe a chance to start again clean?'

'Time for lunch,' said Younis. 'Something extra special I've run up. You'll never guess.'

Doctor Fausta

Plus ça change et plus c'est la petite différence.

I first met him when I was a year or two younger. Now I'm older and, perhaps, wiser, I know better what to think of that meeting. It was a day just like today. I was walking alone in the Peak District. The weather was fine (for the north of England, anyway) but not too hot; there was a fresh breeze blowing behind me, and I was climbing up a long gentle slope in the limestone-and-grass area when I saw him, a tall figure like myself, standing stock still, a mile ahead at the top. After a bit I saw that he was looking down towards me. He had his hands in his pockets, a rucksack like mine on his back, shorts, no cap. Gave me an uneasy feeling, having him waiting there staring at me. Looked casual enough, though, with those hands in his pockets. Lost, maybe, or just lonely. I slowed down a bit as I got near the top, and the wind seemed to drop. A few bird cries around. No one else in sight. Three hundred yards away now, he sat down by the track, still staring towards me.

As I came up I saw he was smiling tentatively at me, still silent. It was he who looked guarded. Then I saw why. My heart gave a great leap. He was very like a photo of me might be, only a bit more lined, a bit less hair perhaps, mouth tenser at the corners. Must have given him as much of a turn as me to see the resemblance. Then we both grinned at one another, like children who share a secret.

'Hello!' was all he said. Thin voice, but I had an idea I'd heard it before, somehow.

'Waiting for company?' I said.

'Thought I might as well wait, seeing you were coming this way.' His voice trembled oddly. A nervous chap. Kept watching my face. Hands still in pockets.

'I'm going over to the hostel down there,' I said. 'That your way too?'

'Yes; mind if I come with you?'

'Okay.'

After that we went along together, but he seemed to dry up. Let me do all the talking, didn't say much about himself, said his plans were vague, said he'd had a job abroad but it was good to get back. His voice lost its tremble and he seemed to relax, but he had the air of listening all the time, if you know what I mean. As if he expected pearls of wisdom to fall from my lips. None did, of course.

'Funny we look so alike – you might be my twin brother – only a bit older perhaps,' I remarked at one point.

He gave a snort of laughter. 'Doppelgängers, yes; we do.'

I asked if he knew my home town, and various places the family had come from. No, he said, but didn't go into details.

At the hostel he seemed to look around and get his bearings. We chatted about this and that – religion, sex, the government, students, food, drugs, TV, parties and so on. Except for a sort of reserve and vagueness here and there, his views were very close to my own, only a little more bitter at times in comparison. Next morning he went down the valley, while I went over the next ridge.

A couple of weeks later, when I was just rustling up tea after my first day back at work, who should turn up but this type again. There he stood at the door of my flat. He had a small case with him this time, and, a town suit. 'Thought I'd look you up,' he said. I must have given him my address, I supposed. I had to ask him in. Gave him tea. The fellow and I got talking. Pretty soon we were finishing each other's sentences, agreeing with each other like mad. It was late at night when we drew breath and I offered him a doss-down on the settee. We clashed in the bathroom next morning, but he presented me with a tinned ham and said he'd a day or two to kill; might he spend the evenings in my pad till then? This was all right by me. He said he'd browse around the shopping centre nearby, lunch out, and be back that night. Which he was, with some beer.

A couple of days later, early in the morning, we were deep in discussion of old Donne and Priestley and serial time. He was letting me do most of the talking this time. Suddenly he got up and began to pace to and fro.

'Ever hear a tape recording of yourself?' he said.

'No, why?'

'You'd be surprised at how different you might sound to yourself. So they say. Never heard one myself. Ever noticed your own mannerisms?'

'Now I come to think of it, *you've* got one that's rather like mine – rubbing your left ear when you're thinking. That's the only one I can think of. I suppose you made me notice it by having the same trick.'

'Ever studied your fingerprints?' And he came up close, seized my left hand in his right, swung round, and laid his own left hand alongside.

There was a long silence. Those left hands were twins. The lines on them were twins. The whorls and loops on their fingers were twins. Same thing with the right. I stared at his face. It had a mole on the right cheek, the spitting image of mine.

'We must be unique,' I said shakily. 'The only identical non-twins in the world.'

'You think so?'

'I'm sure so. Stands to reason. How—'

'Then what about this chickenpox mark?'

On his left temple was a little pit, in the same place (and with the same shape and size) as mine.

'Let me tell you a few things about yourself you never told

me, and haven't really told anyone. Your mother used to call you Bop when you were five or six – correct? . . . You were called Fits at school – spelt *f, i, t, s.* You pretended to like it, but secretly you hated it . . . You cried yourself to sleep the first day at boarding school, but no one knew – right? . . . A terrier frightened you by jumping at you, at the age of four, but no one saw – right? It was a sandy ginger thing with one black ear. And you never told anyone . . . You could never stand the way your father put his hand on your shoulder when he was trying to put something over on you – right? But you never said anything about it, you never let on . . . Have I said enough?'

I sat down and looked at him. I was rubbing my left shoulder resentfully.

'Your middle name is Absalom but you never told anyone. You changed your second initial to *I* because of the word that *A* makes, and you told that girl Katy two years ago that the *I* stood for Ian – right? . . . Now let me tell you who I am, and how I know.' (And he sat down.) '*My* second name was Absalom. *I* told that bird it was Ian. *I* was called Fits. *I* was frightened by that dog. *My* father put his hand on *my* shoulder. And so on. Yes, I am a doppelgänger: I've been buzzing you all this time, a real doppel. I knew you were going to come up that track up the moor just then. I knew you were back from your first day's work when I came to your flat. I knew where it was *and* where you work. I knew because I am you . . . only a little bit older . . . I don't expect you to believe it, not all at once. Let's have some coffee.' And he made the coffee. His hands were shaking a bit. As for me, *my* mind was whirling.

'Well now, let's begin at the beginning. You've heard of the idea that some of these elementary particles are particles going backwards in time? In fact I know you have. You read it about four months ago, or thereabouts . . . It's Saturday night, we may as well make a night of it and sleep in tomorrow . . . Someone said he thought there might be a reverse-time universe, what he called the Faustian universe, in which time went the other way, and all the particles would be anti-particles to ours. A silly name, Faustian – Faust was going the same way as the rest of us, only he got jumped back to a personally younger age at one point, that's all. The effect of spending time in the reverse universe ages you, it doesn't make you younger. For there is a reverse universe. The catacosm, the boys call it. This one we're in is the anacosm. The earth here is called the anageon, the other one is the catageon. Across there, only in the same spot, if you get me; only it can't really be the same spot, or the two universes would annihilate each other. But no one seems to know where it is, or even if the word where has any meaning in this context. Anyway, it's a nearly identical universe, with the same galaxies, clusters, novae, solar system, planets, earth, continents, seas, animals, plants, men, national groupings, events, and so on, broadly speaking; as long as you choose the same instant of time . . . But you can't choose, really. That's it. When you "print off" – that's passing from one "cosm" to the other – you print off onto the same point of time as you started in.'

'You mean, you mean, there's a lot of people switching from one universe to the other?'

'That's it. They are. As I was going to say, if you print off, as they call it, at, say, 1970, then 1970 is the year you find yourself in, or rather the anti-particle you that corresponds to you, what we call your edition. In fact you find yourself at the identical point of time, down to the identical attosecond, as it were. Only, when you "reprint", that is, when you come back here again, you reprint at the same old angle, so to speak. Suppose you print off at 1970, and then live on through the catageon for six years up till 1976, and decide to reprint back into this world; the year you come back to as a reissue as we call it, is 1964, six years earlier. You've been going backwards for six years. (For people who start off from the catacosm, it's just the other way round, they print off at the same time point, but reprint *n* units earlier.) Now meanwhile, you've perhaps met up with guys who printed off in 1973, say, and landed in 1973 in the cata-geon. Once you know the ropes, you can contact guys back here who maybe lived there as editions, say ten years, suppose from 1973 to 1983, then reprinted back to – 1963, it would be. If you play your cards right they tell you everything they know. Besides, you get a new slant on things just through living through them twice, as it were. One way or another, you get a sort of boosting effect; we call it the psychotron effect. The convertron boys – where you print off, you know – give you a bit of gen, of course, because everything's not quite the same, in that world. But it's near enough. History, current affairs, names – it's all pretty close to ours.'

'How long has all this been going on?'

'The primary convertron won't get built in this world till 1990. But a lot of scientists will go over then as first editions and stay twenty, thirty, forty years. Then they came back forty years older from the year 2030 in the catageon via the 1989 AD primary reconvertron there, into the year 1950 here. They lay low here and formed a gang of eggheads and built the secondary convertron here round about 1960. In some ways it's better than our primary will be. Most "printers" avoid doppels like the plague – doppels, that's "buzzes", I mean meeting your original self. But I thought I'd risk it and let you in on the secret (anyway I had to, because that's how it happened to us). You are me, only minus a year of experience as a cata, and another year working some things out as a psychotronized ana. You're going to print off, when you get used to the idea, and sample the catageon as a first edition, before reprinting as me. The secondary reconvertron went up about 1961 in the catageon, so we've been able to reprint as anageon reissues ever since.'

'How do I know I *will* go over?'

'Because I remember going over. I couldn't resist it. Don't forget, I am you, only a little older. Have some more coffee, it'll help you think.'

'Will it help me stay sane? Thanks – black, for God's sake, and no sugar this time. My God . . .'

'Pass us the biscuits. I remember I – you – did, they're in that cupboard, had to remind me – you – where they were.'

'Okay. Did you remember me dropping one like that?'

'I dropped one, yes. Well now, we've got the weekend to work out details and you can ask me questions. I think it's about 5 a.m. we get to bed, and we have brunch tomorrow about 11 . . . I get dizzy myself sometimes. They warned me about doppels . . . You get a touch of flu on Sunday night and recover about Tuesday, really a piece of luck, because *that* gives us time to make the switch before your office knows you're okay again.'

'Oh, I get flu, do I? Thanks!'

'Not at all! Delighted! Then we'll travel to the convertron and print you off.'

'What's all this print-off business?'

'Printing off is what happens to you in the convertron. Your particles here are all replicated by anti-particles in the cata-geon, the reverse-time earth, making another you, which we call an edition. Your own particles disappear in the machine. As the new edition is an exact copy of you, only going backwards in time, it's the same personal age as you. Of course it has the same memories and personality. Now, as I was saying, owing to some principle they haven't yet fathomed (or if they have I never picked it up) you always print off, from whichever world, onto the same point of time, every time you do it, even if you go round and round. But you always *reprint* from the other world into your original world, onto a point of time as far back from your point of view as you have lived through in the other world. There's a lack of time symmetry in this business, it seems. I spent about a year as an edition, then when I reprinted and became a reissue, as we call it, I found myself a year back in time from when I (or you) printed off, that is, from about now. I've been swanning around for a lot of that time, after working some things out with the convertron boys. Finally I came and did a doppel on you. Got it?'

'Dimly. What's the point of all this switching about? What's wrong with this world?'

'Plenty, when you think about it. Isn't there, now? Would

there be all these protest marches and unrest and so on, if there wasn't? A lot of people get fed up with this world, and when they get to hear about this conversion business, fancy trying the other. It's a brain drain in effect. Some of them decide to come back, like us. Some go round and round, gaining ideas all the time, each time round, more voltage, the psychotronic effect. Then again, some people are dumping unwanted goods by persuading the convertron squad to print them off – have to pay heavily for transport to dump, of course, or to market; and there is a tight limit to the volume you can print at a time. And they have to document your antecedents and addresses, in case an SOS of some sort comes up and a rescue operation has to be mounted from one universe to the other. (Messages are easily printed off, of course.) They did an Eichmann kidnapping once on an ex-Nazi who had got over.'

He spoke like a sleepwalker. Not like a sleep*talker*, no! Everything he said was crisp. But like an automaton. A kindly automaton. Easily, though, and with no suggestion of urgency. He seemed to wait for me. That was it. He knew what I was going to say and how long I was going to take over it, how long everything was going to take. He'd seen the play before – as me. At the moment when this thought hit me he opened his eyes (he had them lightly closed) and smiled at me. He knew what I was thinking. A goose goose-stepped on my grave and I shuddered, but a sort of relaxation communicated itself to me and from then on I floated easily along.

And so we went on. At one point I asked him, 'What'll you do for a living?'

'I'll have your job when you're gone. They won't notice – at first. Later they'll say "Fitch is a new man these days." I expect I shall look for a better job. Can't keep slogging on at the same ground – "Me that have been where I've been." '

About five in the morning it was, before we crawled into bed. After a late meal on Sunday morning we took things easy, especially as I was feeling groggy. By Monday morning I was lousy and the other fellow went to the call box to tip them off at work I had a spot of flu. It wasn't so much flu as shock. He nursed me a bit, and by Tuesday I was much better, though everything seemed a bit dreamy and unreal. I'd swallowed his talk hook, line and sinker by now, so when Wednesday came round and I felt okay he was able to get me packed up with a couple of cases, let me draw out fifty pounds from the bank to add to the notes he'd brought back from the other world – reprints with a vengeance! – and took me by rail to a town about fifty or a hundred miles off, which I am not going to name for obvious reasons. After that we took a taxi, then did some walking with the cases, and finished up by an old warehouse.

The entrance was dingy and unremarkable, but the inside must have been worked on a lot. Wooden panelling, probably three-ply, covered the walls and ceilings. The latter, however, were dotted with television cameras facing down the corridors. The floors were of cork tiles. Fluorescent lighting tubes ran continuously along the angle between ceiling and wall. The main warehouse rooms seemed to have been split into a lot of small rooms with soundproof dividing walls, aerated by an elaborate system of ducts and fans, and lit by more fluorescent tubes. The seats were of metal tubing, springy and nestable. Some sort of intercom murmured incomprehensible messages everywhere. Possibly they were in technical jargon. One hall of vast size (a large chop out of a warehouse space) was 'the gymnasium. Lots of the boys here never get out. They've got to keep fit. Next door's an indoor tennis court. Beyond, there's a squash court.'

Finally we stopped by a large door marked PRELIMS. The door opened silently as we stopped, a voice said, 'Come in,' and in we stepped. Opposite the door began an open corridor. A couch or soft bench made of unit seats backed against the right-hand wall of the room, facing a metal chair and desk on the left. On the desk were a pair of phones, an intercom grid, some switches and what looked like a desk notebook but grey and glassy. Behind the desk sat a stocky, smiling individual of about forty. My double called him George One. Somewhat to my surprise I took to him at once and was immediately at ease. I spoke to my double privately a little later about this. 'It's his professional charisma,' he said quietly, 'but all the same, he's a regular guy.'

'Well, you're going to sample the reverse-time world,' George One said. 'I hope you enjoy it. You have three hundred pounds with you, I believe, including your own fifty pounds?'

'What's your fare for the, er, switch?' I found myself saying.

'No fare at all. We are a non-profit-making organization; or rather, I should say, our profits come from another type of client. Besides, as a result of your loop, we have gained certain services from Fitch One here. In fact we are in a position to make you a small loan, which your reprint here will repay in his own time if necessary. We can let you have – now let us see –' and he flipped over a bunch of documents on the desk, which I now realized comprised my dossier, and wrote with a wired-up stylus on the notebook thing, which immediately turned his movements into luminous marks '– three hundred cata-pounds in five-pound notes, in return for your fifty ana-pounds. Yes, your reprint repaid us two hundred and fifty pounds here last year. The other two-fifty cata-pounds are out of his own – your own – earnings in the cata-future. Here's our contribution. Yes, quite genuine. No forgeries! Any little trifling difference in appearance is an ana–cata difference.' And he handed over a wad. 'You'll need it; or at least, you won't spend all of it, as we know now, but it'll give you more security. Pay it into – what bank was it, Fitch One?'

'Benchley's,' said my opposite number. 'There's a branch in this town in the Yonder. Mocklington Street, near the corner of Lime Square.' I noted it down. Funny, I'd never heard of Benchley's. But I supposed it was all right.

'What do I do for a job?'

'With that money you can make do for quite a bit, but still. What job, Fitch One?'

'Apply at Number 63 Godwick Avenue – the second floor.

The third week. They gave me a programming job. I stayed in the development side of the anaconvertron centre at first.'

'This buzzing has its compensations, *I* can see – for the buzzee, at any rate,' said the other man, smiling. 'But mind you don't try a "Steusöö"!'

'What's a shtoyzer when it's at home?'

'Oweh Steusöö did one a few years back. You may say he created the form. He belonged to the catacosm; he was, as we say, a catanthrope. He found himself confronted by a double doppel, *two* doppelgängers, when he'd never heard of reverse time or anything. He was on a bender at the time, so he took it in his stride. They all three got plastered, or so he thought, fell in with a joker who took them along to the reconvertron, that's the cataconvertron, and all four did a reprint together, or rather it was a print-off (what *they* call a print-out) because he was a catanthrope and so was the fourth fellow. Then all four of them went on another binge in *this* world, and this joker got them reprinting, except that one of them refused. The other joker must have stuck around, but no one knows whether he reprinted or stayed on in this world. Well, after Oweh had done the milk-round three times in three characters as it were, with them (it took an hour or so at a time, sobering up a little, because he drank less each time round) he stayed put in this world, in fact he was the edition that refused to reprint. Now he's Harvey Stoyce, the Centre's tame petrol attendant just round the corner, and quite happy except when dead sober. Better if you open the petrol cap yourself.'

'What sort of a name is Ovay Shtoyzer? Sounds German or something.'

'It *is* German, of a sort.' An indefinable expression appeared on his face. 'But he was naturalized English even as a cata. Well now, it's time to meet the boys and get on with it. First of all, let me assure you, you won't *notice* the switching process, so you can stop looking worried. It's all as easy as falling off a log, and a lot more pleasant.'

He led the way down the corridor.

'I thought there was a lot of preliminary screening?' I murmured to my double.

'Not in your case, thanks to me. I've prepared the ground, computer and all.'

A large hall with various consoles and panels round the perimeter opened out at the end of the corridor. About thirty men stood or sat around, some gazing into panels, some moving levers, some chatting. Most turned and looked at us. Here I had a shock. There were twins, triplets, quadruplets, multiplets. Hardly an untwinned face amongst them. A bunch of identicals standing together were distinguished, I noticed, by round scarlet plaques or badges about three inches across, on their lapels, each with a different number, 1, 2, 3, and so on, in white. A few had yellowish-green plaques of the same shape, with black numbers. Then I realized. These must be some of those reissues that my double had told me about. But why so many, and why all together?

'I thought you *disapproved* of doppels in general?'

'Only for the layman,' said our guide, 'because of the shock and the complications. For the con boys it's meat and drink. They reissue as much as possible, and team up here, after short runs in one world or the other. The psychotron effect makes for efficiency and know-how in convertronics *and* conversion sociology. So long as your runs aren't too long – it all adds to *anno domini*. The more reprints on this ana side, working together in teams (and ditto on the other side of course) the more efficiently they work and the more info we can pool. Five years back they'd have said we create a dialogue with the catageon. Now we call it a resonance. Yes, a resonance. It's quite a relevant term. Reprints together are like twins, multiple twins: they know without speaking what their other reps mean, except for really new info, something really negentropic, so they can get on faster. We don't talk of doppels and buzzes in here, as a matter of fact; we call them boings – impactions if you like. Impactions is the formal term. Every time a new reprint comes through it's a boing, or reboing. How many reppies do you make, Phils?'

'Twenty, it was. Only, six of them are out on a job, two went and re-edited into the Yonder, and five are somewhere round the works,' murmured four nearly identical men of about thirty years of age, in unison. The other three copies stayed silent.

'The "stock" Phil, what we call Phil Zero, is that quiet one in the corner – I think,' said our guide. 'Oh yes – that's him with Nought on a red badge. The rest are true reppies.'

'I don't see any women.'

'No, well, domesticated types don't print off. Families don't print off, much, at all. Too hippy a life. As for the other types of women, well, it'd be a bit disruptive for us. Especially with all those reppies about; who would pair off with who? They work well as agents in the field, do women, but not as convertron staff. So you don't see them around here, except for the occasional one printing-off, or reprinting. We have a resident nurse or two, of course.'

'How can I get along in the other world? It strikes me I still know next to nothing about it.'

'Oh it's all more or less like this one. We're printing off a carbon copy of your dossier now. The computer'll formulate optimum life ways, and the reception committee'll fix you up with info. You can't put a foot wrong. Anyway it's all happened, so you *won't* put a foot wrong, will he, Fitch One?'

'It was all right.'

'Still, I suppose I may as well say, better keep clear of your firm, in your home town. There'll be an analogue of your firm over there, probably, and very likely an analogue of you. We want to avoid these pseudo-doppels or transpactions as we call them, even more than ordinary doppels. They can be very dicey, very dicey indeed.'

'I'm still pretty vague about the whole set-up.'

'You mean the conversion business, or what?'

'The whole thing: the other world, the business of what time you get into which way, when they started this business, and so on.'

The man George sat me down again, pulled up a stool, and went into a long rehash, more or less like my double's talk on the previous Saturday, but in more detail. 'Suppose I refuse to come back? Suppose I like it there?'

'You won't stay on,' said Deutero-Fitch quietly. 'Remember, I *remember* what you did, because you were me. You'll be ready for reprinting at a certain moment. It all happened.'

'Time's up now,' said George One, the guide. 'Come on now. Sure you have everything? Yes, well, in here.' And he led the way into a central chamber made apparently of opaque plastic walls, but walls about three feet thick. A great chunk of clear glass or transparent plastic occupied the top half of a massive door which swung out. Three television cameras surveyed the scene from near the roof. The lighting was brilliant. I had expected all sorts of machinery, perhaps a sort of electric chair, but the place was bare except for grilles in the ceiling and floor, through which a fierce gale blew, and a sort of arty-crafty fairy-like, almost psychedelic construction in the centre, like a frame for a TV pop singer.

'Why's there such a hell of a draught?'

'To replace the printed-off air in the focus, of course. Not to mention the printed-off bods. Otherwise there'd be a sort of implosion each time.'

'Oh, the air goes with me! That's great!'

'At Development, the reception end, you know, they suck the air out instead.'

'Do I lie down or what?'

'No, just walk inside that egg-shaped frame. That's the focus. Take your stuff in with you. When you're ready, making sure all your fingers and toes and luggage and hair and so on are tucked inside it, just nod and we'll print you off. Don't bother to stand still or even hold your breath – so long as you keep inside.'

'What'll it feel like?'

'You won't feel a thing – honest!' And he and Deutero-Fitch walked out. The door 'bonged' to.

Four delicately curving, narrow arms or ribs of plastic, meeting overhead below the roof but touching the floor well out, enclosed a space like a slender egg nearly forty feet high and nearly flat at the base (a little depression, perhaps twenty feet in diameter, on the tiled floor). This base was solidly covered with the same plastic. I stepped through between two arms, placed my cases one to left of my feet and one to right, folded my plastic mac and laid it on one case, took out my wallet and the chequebook, made sure everything was all right, and replaced them. I almost looked for a passport. I took a deep breath, looked at my watch – 4.35, the second-hand prancing round towards forty seconds – and nodded vigorously. Nothing happened, except that my heart was pounding sonorously away. The door opened and another of the staff came in. 'Welcome to you,' he said. 'Welcome to your first run, your first edition.'

'It didn't work,' I said.

'Oh yes, it did. You're in the catageon now. Never seen me before, have you?'

'I suppose not. I thought you . . . Weren't you out there a minute or two ago?' (Now I came to look at him, his scarlet plaque was the wrong shape; it was square.)

'I was out there, yes, but not Down Under. You're in the other world now, boy. You've made it. This is the Developer end of your world's convertron. Come and have a drink. I expect you could do with one.'

'I was expecting to feel dizzy, hear a bang or something.'

'I know; they all do first time. I've been back and forth a couple of times now. You get used to it. By the way, be careful what you say about the two worlds. Most of the reception committee are ananthropes, but one or two – with yellow labels, you know – are catanthropes. To them, this is the real world, and the one you came from is reversed. Better stick to neutral terms. *We* usually call the other universe Down Under, or Over There, or *La Zone*, and to say "printing" is safer than "printing off" and "reprinting". Come and meet my three editions – or should I say reppies?' He winked. 'Oh, a minute – these bags. Bring 'em along here. Now open them and lay them on that metal shelf, with your mac. The machine will unpack them, then it will check the contents with your lists and repack. Won't take long. You'll collect at the other side of this wall after the party.'

The outer chamber was devoid of the gadgets it had had when I arrived, and empty of everyone else. I began to believe. As we went out into the corridor a sort of crematorium hatch swallowed the shelf with my bags and mac.

The 'party' was in a large room just beyond. Over a dozen people, three of them women, were standing around, some with drinks already in their hands. 'Fact is, couple here got engaged, so we're throwing a little celebration. So you've got company this round.' And he introduced me. There were four Sams, red 1 to 4; three Johns, yellow zero to 2; two Mays, yellow zero and 1; Harry, red 1, who seemed to be engaged to Fay, red 1; and two Jims, red 2 and 3. All *their* badges (and my new friend's badge) were square, not round. My new friend himself was Frank red 2, and numbers 1, 3 and 4 were also there.

'Do I get a badge?' I said.

'No, only con and recon staff get them. Here's your drink. To your future!' And he winked and went off.

'I suppose,' I said, finding myself facing the two miniskirted Mays, 'one of you's been Down Under for a time.'

The two girls giggled inanely. 'Yes, and the other's going too.'

'I just left my reprint behind so I had a parallel situation,' I said, accepting my second drink, something short like the first.

'Parallel times never greet,' said May zero (at least it sounded like that) and flounced off, leaving May 1 contemplating me quizzically. 'I hope you'll have profited by your stay,' she said cryptically, and with a slightly acidulated smile slid off at a tangent.

The drink was powerful all right. I attended to it for some moments, then found my eye caught by my Frank 2. 'Hello,' he said, 'you look a bit lost. Don't worry about the future. You're kipping with us for the present, and we'll give you the gen tomorrow. Just now we're off the hook a bit for once.'

'I'm rather at sea. Can't seem to speak the language, somehow.'

'No, well, life here takes a little getting used to. Keep your ears open and your mouth shut among the natives at present. Anything you want cleared up from your pre-print briefing, by the way?'

'Someone said something about Ovay Shtoyzer. How do you spell it?'

'Sh, not so loud. The yellow boys might be hurt. *O, w, e, h*; *S, t, e, u, s*, double *o*-umlaut. He wasn't exactly a shining example. Over here we prefer to call it a slinger: you know, you hurl the sling twice round your head and let go the third time round. It's a graphic metaphor.'

'Where's the other convertron? They said there were two got built. Is it in here?'

'Yes, what Down Under would call the reconvertron, to go back to them, is in another part of the building.'

'No, I mean the, er, primary one, both ways.'

'Oh, the primary con–recon pair won't get built yet. Not till 1989. The anageon pair don't even get built till 1990, so the catacosm will really be the first of the two universes to start this thing going – as far as we know, that is. Yes, it makes you think, doesn't it! Anyway they aren't going to be here, they'll be about two hundred miles away.'

'Funny Britain thought of it first.'

'Bri— Oh I *see* what you mean. Well, did it? We don't know. Erm, Japan, and even the, er, States, may have some, they say. But no one knows. It's all kept so hush-hush. No one's telling, if there are any elsewhere.'

I downed a third drink and began to feel better. Frank drifted off again. The party began to spin. Someone, I think it was John yellow zero, a big man like the other two, was teasing the engaged girl Fay. 'Wait till you try the milk-round, girl, wait till you start this multi-printing lark. That'll corrupt you!' he boomed; ' "Gomorrah, and Gomorrah, and Gomorrah, creeps o'er this pretty face from Fay to Fay." ' Laughter from the other two girls.

One of the reds, Sam 4 I think, came over and said he'd show me my quarters presently. He had a crinkled, wise sort of face; a man of fifty or so (at that stage we didn't consider anyone over forty half-dead). We chatted of this and that, mainly my past interests, but I don't recall much about it. I had a fourth drink, or it could have been a fifth. After a bit he fell silent and I heard, back to back close behind me, the same booming voice as before. It appeared to be intoning ' "These ragmen have I roared against, my Bruins." '

'There you go,' said someone else, 'quoting again. Who said that?'

'D. S. Herriot, you palestine!'

I shook my ears a bit. The drink seemed to have got into them, unless this joker had a twisted mind. Decidedly I'd had enough. 'I'm kind of tired – do you think I could collect my bags and go to ground now? If it's not taking you off too soon?'

'Fine. There's your bags on that shelf, shut and ready. Oh, and a mac. Just down this passage, now.' And he conducted me by the arm down a long corridor which seemed to taper into nothing (walled in metal and without cameras, I think), and finally let me in at a door marked 136 (at least that's what it said next day). It had hot and cold, and every mod con was round the corner. 'Ring if you want anything, ring twice in the morning for breakfast – about 8 a.m. Pleasant dreams!' And he was gone. The bags were okay, as far as I could focus them, better packed than I could manage, but in the same basic order. I switched on the wall radio. Something that sounded not unlike the climax of Ravel's *Bolero* came from it. At the end a voice said, 'That was the overture to *La Ragazza se Lagna*, "The Heaving Bagpipes", by Tetrazzini.' I switched off hastily and had a long, long drink of water from the tap. It wasn't long before I was in bed and asleep.

Next morning, with a slightly thick head, I faced the reception committee. The two Mays had gone, I was glad to see; and the booming John yellow zero, though he was there, wasn't booming any more. Fay was there at one end and her fiancé at the other. Sam 4 seemed to be presiding.

'Well, Fitch,' he said, 'the computer must have taken to you; it thinks you'd do best as a computer programmer in the town. The place it had in mind uses the same language as your firm's Over There had. Does that appeal?'

'It'll do all right for the present,' I found myself saying. 'I've certainly thought of sticking to programming work there. My firm's way of treating its computer was a bit amateurish, but they were coming to rely on me. How do I get taken on in this place you speak of?'

'Oh, we'll fix that up for you. We've got contacts in a lot of firms, including that one. We'll recommend you as a trainee programmer. Here's your false past, in these papers, in case someone asks you. Our computer worked that out too. We have to do that sort of thing, as it wouldn't do for the general public to know about time-reversal and convertronics in this era.'

I took the papers, intending to swot through them at the first opportunity. 'When do I apply?'

'Oh, not for a few days, I expect. We'll fix up an interview for you. Meanwhile you'd better stay with us for a bit, until you can find your way around. Maybe we can fix up lodgings for you.'

'Isn't it all plain sailing? I could fix myself up, I should think.'

'Not quite,' said Frank 3, unexpectedly striking in. 'You need to get acclimatized. It isn't exactly identical with Down Under, you know. But you'll pick it up. We would have gone into it last night, only we had this party. This morning I'm afraid we have to sandwich you in between two committees, so there isn't enough time for details.'

'You'll pick it up,' echoed Franks 1, 2 and 4. Johns zero to 2 were busy taking notes. So were one or two others. I suddenly thought of the jury in *Alice in Wonderland* and wanted to laugh. However, the rest of the interview, such as it was, went off easily enough. One or two people asked questions. Then Frank 2 spoke up. 'I think you'll do. But remember, this isn't the universe you're used to. We speak English here, and the basic world history and structure are the same, down to quite little details. Only some of our mental outlook here is subtly different. That's why you need to be cautious at first.'

'Yes,' said John 2 suddenly, sounding just like John zero, boom and all. '*La Zone* has some quiddities of onlook which you'll have to shed before you can fit in here.'

'What sort of difference is there?'

'Hard to explain,' said Frank 1, 'but you'll find out soon enough. Anyway, we wish you good luck. You're a reasonably flexible fellow; perhaps you'll settle here eventually.'

I looked at him but kept my mouth shut. Evidently my dossier hadn't mentioned that I had been introduced to the convertron by my own first reissue; or the information had failed to make an impression on Frank 1; or he didn't want to bring it up in front of the catanthropes.

'Well, thank you, everybody.' I got out at last, and shook hands all round.

Next day I was introduced to the outside world by Frank 2. This cata-convertron–reconvertron Centre proved to be inside a huge factory building. Frank had got me a map of the town, which (I suppose) was the same in gross as its counterpart (whose identity I am determined to keep to myself) on *this* earth, but the fact that the ana-warehouse was a cata-factory was an indication that everything was not the same, and anyway I wasn't familiar with the ana-town either. Everything looked like industrial urban England of the 1960s, however: grimy brick, streets littered with paper, grey skies, damp, hurry, every third person with a smoker's cough. We lunched together at a cafeteria, and afterwards Frank had to rush back, but left me, equipped with my map, to find my way home later. I wandered around . . .

The news vendor's placard announcing LIMA HAS THE MEGABON-TOMB and his cry which sounded suspiciously like 'Nightal tale!' shook me somewhat. I bought the paper, got to a park, and started to read it. The first thing that caught my eye was a column averring that Councillor Fishalls stated that negotiations had been opened with the Industry of Foul and Pure. Then there was something about the Chancellor's Taxal Pusilly. There was also a bit about fuel rationing. TWO MERITAN DIVISIONS FOR NIET-FARM? asked a headline. Further down its column, I learnt that a Niet-Bom explosion had wrecked a motel. The thing about Lima's megabon-tomb was tucked away in a back page. Riots in King-Kong.

Trembling, I got up and walked rapidly through the park. I was ordered off the paths, which were certainly highly swept and garnished, by an official. 'Can't you read?' he said. There were indeed notices, KEEP TO THE GRASS, and almost everyone was doing so. It was much more pleasant, and the grass seemed to stand up to it well. I saw now that the seats were all on the lawns and off the few paths, which seemed to be purely ornamental. In fact, now I came to look at it, entrances were all grass-covered. What I had taken for gravel paths, but which did not lead to the edges at all, ran round in elegant curves and circles.

After crossing the park, I found myself by a magazine stall. Copies of *Hunch, Ova, Good Horsecoping, The State Newsman, Boater, Parry-Snatch, L'Illumination, Arabella, Sie & Wir, Confianza, Chime and Chide, Live, Dime, Height of Pry, Charade, The Amateur Pornographer, Men Lonely, House and Bound, The Scientific Armenian, The Sly Nuditist, The Agronomist* and *The Psychedelegraph* met my eye. On impulse I bought *The Psychedelegraph*, a colourful parade of rather mysterious revelations; its language foxed me. My map included bus routes, and once I had grasped that the rule of the road was right except for buses, whose routes ran down the middle of the larger streets like an old-fashioned American railroad, I was able to locate the proper place to get a bus, and even to get off at the right stop but one. (The drivers' seats were all on the right, by the way, which must have made passing difficult.) I crept back into the Developing Side canteen in the cata-con–recon Centre, and had some tea. I still had my reading matter.

The canteen had the radio news on. There was more about Niet-Farm. Lima, which turned out to rhyme with rhymer, might well, it said, have the 'megabon tomb', which was pronounced like bun and Tom.

I sought an interview with Frank 2, but he was on duty. I didn't run into him till after supper, when he was hurrying down a corridor. 'Look here,' I said, trotting along beside him, 'I don't think I can take it here. This world is crazy.'

'Not crazy, just different. No crazier than Over There, at any rate – only in a different way. You stick it out. You'll get the hang of it. We ought to have given you a fuller interview the night before; it was that party. But you'll adjust. Can't stop now. Sorry, old man.'

I had another early night, but my dreams were a turmoil and I kept on waking up.

Next day I wandered out. I couldn't stand any more shocks of that sort, so I looked the other way whenever I passed a newspaper man. I only had one bad turn that morning: when a van passed me with ——, SHOPLIFTERS, LTD on it. After another cafeteria lunch I suddenly got an idea. I went into a bookshop (there in the entrance were *Ova, House and Bound, Hunch* and the rest: I shuddered) and went in. After a bit I thought I had found the section I wanted; but no, it said *Fictionaries*. Finally I found a corner labelled *Book-of-the-Words*. There they were: *Inglish Lexicon*, most of them were called. I selected a large one, then ranging further, got hold of a phrase book 'for alienists'. I managed to discover their prices and to pay for them. Then I went straight home and studied, and studied, and studied.

I got them to postpone my interview for my job for three weeks, on the official pretext of difficulties at my present employment (a fictitious journalism job). I went to the same bookshop and got another of these books on 'Inglish' for 'alienists' (which evidently meant foreigners). At the end of a fortnight I thought I had some idea of how to get along without putting my foot in it, if not actually how to win friends and influence people. I started to talk to passengers in the bus, table-sharers in restaurants, seat-sharers in the park – timidly at first, later with more confidence. No one actually assaulted me, though I got some queer looks. Occasionally, however, my confidence got a bit of a bump – as when I saw the news that Le Gôde had vetoed Tribain's joining the Modern Carcass.

Well, I got my interview, and a pad at a place up the road. I got the job, to my surprise; perhaps there was a shortage of programmers. Most of the time I was on my own, so I hadn't much difficulty with the catanthropic English (or Inglish). After a bit I struck up a mild friendship with a guy named Zoe (the *e* was silent) (and there was nothing kinky about him), who worked in the same firm. We used to have meals together at the same cafeteria, round the corner.

'You know, Fitch, I've been reading some of that stuff in *The Scientific Armenian*,' he said one lunch. 'They state time runs backwards as good as forwards, and some of those particles – hypatomic ones, I mean – are truly running backwards.'

'Do they now? What else do they say – state, I mean?'

'They state there might be another universum, justly like ours, only running backward. The patacosm, they baptized it.'

'Oh . . . what do they call – name – this one, then?'

'The paracosm. The contra-particles in this world are particles strayed over out of the patacosm, they state.'

'Paracosm and patacosm. I see.'

'Fascinating stuff. Only I don't see how they may ever tell if it's truth. You know, they state one day we might be able to enter the patacosm and disappear out of this one, whenever we liked.'

'Really?'

'Yes, that's why they name it the Faustaean universum – *F*, *a*, *u*, *s*, *t*, *a*, *e*, *a*, *n*; you know the nurtury rhyme:

> Doctor Fausta
> Went to Glausta
> In a power of pain;
> He fell through a bubble,
> Turned into his double
> And never was seen again.'

'Well, well! Come in useful, if you were in some trouble.'

'You mean, if you could get into the other universum?'

'That's what I was thinking.'

'That's what the rhyme would mean, if it applied. But in effect I think that's a piece of science-fancy, really. Getting into the other universum, I mean. You know, there's a deal of science-fancy in what scienticists state nowadays.'

'I'd like to see that article.'

'Aykay, I'll let you have it tomorrow.'

I changed the subject. When I got hold of the magazine, I got quite a shock. The nurtury rhyme was quoted in small print in a footnote. There were a few sly suggestions about passage from one universum to the other. The reference, via the rhyme, to a bubble, and to a double, may have been pure chance, but it looked as though someone was trailing bait, hinting at the reconvertron business, perhaps in order to get potential recruits, or else clients who would pay. The nursery rhyme was a bursary rhyme. (Hell, the catageon was corrupting my thinking!) Anyway, it isn't Gloucester in Britain, I can assure you, the town where the ana-convertron–reconvertron is. Honest. I noted the author was actually a Meritan, jotted down his name and university. Perhaps, on second thoughts, he was signalling the location of a Meritan con–recon?

Meanwhile the Meritans continued unsuccessfully to pour men, flightcraft, 'tombs', 'battilery', small arms, pukatives, deflorants and ingenderflam into Niet-Farm. The Niet-Bom continued to butcher villages. The warring states of Hegirea, unanimously blaming Tribain for their dissension, cut off her fuel supplies. General Dayassa alleged that black mercenaries had 'tombed' the Yegmev. Yellow-versus-Pink riots broke out in Meritan cities. It was believed that outrages against Tribish diplomés in Lima were inspired by an agent from Tuba, last seen in Albion. Millions of Green Knights (teenagers) all over Lima, plastering slogans over every available building surface (and several human surfaces), destroyed most of the ancient historical monuments and more of the records, shouting the historical Thought of Meritan Chairman Lord: 'History is Bunk'. Reports from Cape Hennessy were that plants sent round the moon in a capsule returned growing in a spiral; the cost of this latter project was ten times that of the annual aid sent from Merita to the under-enveloped countries. M. Dabrey at his trial criticized Tribish economic policy. The Union of Rational Teachers in Tribain called for a work-to-rule in selected areas. Railway staff in Tribain refused to supervise passengers' meals. 'Pilot-Radio' stations, hovering over Tribain, were declared illegal. There was another round of outrages in the Creator District of Eden.

Once, on a visit to the Reception Centre, I asked Frank 4 why the great big world outside seemed, if possible, even crazier than affairs at home in Tribain, which, even if they appeared a bit dotty now and then, more or less made a sense of their own. In general, you see, despite those oddities, the ordinary run of home news was really much as it always is in my own familiar Britain, in broad outlines: the usual go-slows, strikes, official and unofficial, the usual threats of violence, the usual aggressive protests against aggression, the usual number of children murdered by sex maniacs, young women strangled and/or assaulted, old women battered and robbed, babies and dogs starved or beaten up, telephone booths wrecked, cemeteries desecrated, schools ransacked, trains derailed, cars smashed up, hold-ups. And this was reflected in what I could perceive around me too; with my ear to the ground, I sensed everywhere the normal indifference to the inconvenience of other human beings or the sufferings of the unfortunate. I noticed everywhere the usual louts (rich or poor) excreting litter, the usual graffiti, pornographic or political, the usual din, the usual dinginess and muck, the usual disregard for anything but money and sensation. Just the normal human pattern, same as back home. But when it came to the news of foreign goings-on, that seemed to me to exhibit a lunacy of an altogether higher order. (Litter was 'cast-offs'; graffiti were 'escrementi'.)

'It's a relativistic distortion, a sort of redshift. The further away from your immediate neighbourhood and experience, the swifter things seem to recede from normalcy. The deflexion towards insanity is a function of distance – of alienation, if you'll pardon the transcosmic pun. If you'd printed off in Lima, for instance, no doubt the goings-on in Tribain would appear to be pure madness compared to what was happening around you. Mind you, editions printed outfrom the catageon find just the same distortions Down Under. They can get along with their immediate ana-surroundings; but the outer world seems more lunatic the further they look. You ask the Johns!'

I did not. I got back to my place.

The next time I called in at the con–recon to report progress was a month later, after which I stayed for a snack and gossip in the canteen. Opposite me was a man more than twice my age. His get-up, though obviously an attempt at current fashion, was somehow subtly wrong. I introduced myself. He bobbed his head sideways once or twice but made no other move. 'Redging,' he murmured.

'Where are you from?' I said.

'Print-in. Just returned up back out of the Zonio.'

'Then you belong here?'

'Belong? Oh, exact. But not this time-belt. Had quite a run

Below. You're a placey way prior to me; unless you're a para too?'

'Para? No, no, I'm an imprint – edition is it? – from Down Under. Only been here a few weeks.'

'Down Under? Oh, you intention Below?'

'I suppose so. The other, er, universum. You've had a lot of experience, then?'

'Guess out you could expression it this way. Happy to be on this present decade, believe me!'

'How did you get to this point of time, then? I don't get it.'

'Making the decades Below, of course. Printed out of way to head of you. Things here were off, very off; decisioned trying out Below. Not much change. More and more off. See you don't credit me? I was a babe when printed. Besides along of this, I took in a rejuvenation course. Suspensioned eight months on it. Worth it for a ten years' minusing.'

'Why did you come back?'

'History. Knew the Golden Age was on this present time-belt, high prior to was born. Sold down on most of my clobber, buyed in on a reprint for myself, and zing, here to love it!'

'What was the world like? When you left it Below, I mean.'

'You're requesting in for me to information you on the future, do I receive your message?'

'I'd like to know what's coming to us, certainly.'

He shot me a wary eyeful. 'I don't motivation like informationing you in upon this. Not cert they permission it here. If you want in for finding it out, you'll have to make the decades here first. Negation, you won't, you're a patanthrope, a Belower, didn't you announce?'

'I'm a print-off, yes, or whatever you, er, call it.'

'No joy then, you won't see it back Below, you'd be out onto the past. Still, if you live it on just here, you'll see our version. Much the same. Adhesion down onto it some thirty years and you'll see what I got out from out of.'

'You mightn't find *this* time so wonderful after all. Are you going straight out into it?'

'Negation. They want in for me to stop off in mid of them a pair of months in minimum. They say my speechways necessitate revisioning.'

'I do find it difficult to understand you, rather; and you must find *me* a bit difficult?'

'I home approx onto most of your program, but it has me extrapolating up on areas. Very old metal, it rings to me. But too, they opinion I'll have to get accustomated to the spaciousness, the hand-waggings, the do-it-yourself, the mechanism-poverty, the go-out-and-get, the quiet.'

'They do, do they?'

A tiny buzzer sounded from somewhere near his open collar. 'Excuse, have to home in on an appointmentation.' And he was gone. I stared thoughtfully into my cup of citron tea. My appetite had vanished, I found. I did a little diagram with my spoon handle on the tablecloth. If I reprinted without staying long, his very much *non*-Golden Age would be in full swing in my own anageon before I reached middle age, and get 'more and more off' as I got really old; unless of course the two worlds developed differently, and evidently they didn't, as far as general outlines went. If I 'adhesioned down' in this world, on the other hand, I would reach middle age about the time he was goaded into leaving it. Of course it was true I hadn't met, or heard of, a vast horde of reprints refugeeing from the future, from either world; I had only met him. Perhaps he was biased, a misfit. Still, he'd deliberately stuck it out for thirty years more just in order to get back to my time (and taken advantage of some kind of youthifying procedure). And maybe not many people were free to face the problems of printing off and making a new life for decades on purpose to skip back thirty or forty years in history? I mean, Golden Age or no Golden Age, they had families, safe jobs and so on.

By this time the tablecloth was getting illegibly wrinkled, and my citron tea and Guelph rarebit were both cold. I left. Outside, the news vendors' placards proclaimed DOCTORS STRIKE OVER DRINK-TEST DECASUALIZATION. A headline in the paper said, MERITA: LORD'S STRIKERS DEMAND TRIPLE HOLIDAY PAY. As a result of the hoof and snout epidemic, Tribish meat prices were rising to those current in the Modern Carcass. I dropped into the nearest bar and ordered a volga-and-skoda. Who should I see there but one of the Johns. He had his badge off, so I couldn't tell which.

'You know,' he said in an undertone over our third round, 'the Crippen Paxton has just turned up. Guess where it was.'

'Not the faintest.'

'In the patacosm, of course. Only they found the same thing happened there, so they got scared and brought it back. Then they mailed it to the Minster from an alienist address.'

'How did it get past the computer and all that?'

'Hand luggage, and a load of influence. All the same, crime doesn't pay up in the con–recon business.'

I looked at him covertly out of the corner of my eye.

'. . . by the Western Symphonic Orchestra, conductor Desto Weniger,' said the radio's cultured tones. Someone hastily switched to pop.

'How are you making on? I've seen you in the Centre rather a deal.'

'I don't find it easy to fall in step with this world. I like to have a base of operations where I won't put my foot in it so much.'

'You mean, you like to have a foot on the ground where you won't put a leg wrong, don't you?'

'I suppose so. I can't get quite in tune with your world.'

'For a pata you're doing all right. You need to be bolder, man, step on a bit. It's no use waiting for Doggo. You must grasp the bush by the thorns.'

After this evening I tried to take his advice. I started to take the girls out at the office. They thought I was a bit old-fashioned, and not only about sex. But it seemed to increase my fascination for them (or as it has recently become the misleading fashion to say, *their* fascination for *me*!). I guess they thought I was something of a poppet, something that wanted showing around.

I was sitting at a café table waiting for Thoria to turn up and idly scanning the evening paper. A Triton Nationalist in Nimportou had written an open letter of challenge to Le Gôde. Jack Dammet in the Treasury said there would be no tax relief for stricken doctors' families, but three words would end the bank lock-out. A neo-nazi resurgence was reported at Irrstadt. The expulsion from Eden was in full swing; sniping had begun again from the organization Es Seif (The Sword), and a Tribish soldier in Eden was heard to say 'That flaming Sword'll have us out without any breakfast.' A carriageful of football supporters, who had done five thousand pounds' worth of damage on the train, was given a police escort to a match. At the Union (Enosis) debate, General Stivas declared his faith in a communion of faiths, but the Imam Paysel asserted that the Orthodox had no place in the island; interviewed later, however, on *48 Hours*, General Stivas said that the Imam's brinkmanship in bringing up a host had outraged Orthodox Catholics throughout the world. Interviewed on TV again, Kurdish students said the only way to peace was war. Meanwhile back in Tribain, the Forward-Drivers' party in power, imposing a go-slow economy after invalidation of the pound, refused coalition with the Brakes-On party in a National Cybernation, even if the go-slow policy should bring the country to a standstill.

'Having bad dreamsies, sonny boy?' said Thoria's voice in my ear. 'Don't you know your old mum, then? Snap out of it, for Hell's sake!'

She was wearing an aquamarine wig, some beads, a lot of *décollation* (as they called it here) – in her case it amounted to what they called deep 'declivity' – and a mega-skirt apparently made of Scotchlite, slit at the side nearly to navel height. I found the effect rather terrifying. After a few drinks and the beginning of a meal, however, I felt I was afloat all right even if it was out of my depth.

'Tell you what – how around the Dizzique tonight?' she said a little later.

'I thought somewhere quieter.'

'Not in your life, sonny boy. It's the lights and the music for me.'

The Dizzique was crowded. We were out on the floor at once. Thoria's mega didn't seem to hobble her much. In between bouts, an eternity and a half later, she suddenly waved across the room and yanked me over. There, quite at ease in spite of his age, was one of the Johns. 'Hi, Johnnyo!' cried Thoria. 'Meet Ian.'

John blinked his eyes at me, a sign I took to mean 'Don't recognize me' (although it might have had something to do with the 'Ian') and held out his hand. 'Just came in,' he said to Thoria, and to me, 'What'll you have?'

To Thoria he gave her usual, to me and himself a volga-and-skoda. Was it the same John I'd met in that pub? He started a long inconsequential chatter to Thoria, fed me the odd sentence, asked me what I thought of the place, told a few funny stories, and faded out suddenly, said he had to dog a man.

Next time Thoria and I made an evening of it, she again suggested the Dizzique. John was there before us, presumably the same John; anyway, he greeted us like long-lost friends, and half an hour later swept us into his autobil and along to his place, a high flat in the middle of town. Plenty of jazz and booze, rather flashy decor. When we left he invited us to a party there six weeks later.

The news went on as usual. Human Wrongs Year opened. The Emperor of Hélas was found AWOL by a tribunal of his generals. A plebiscite of the Divided Nations vetoed the vote of Algebra Tariff to stay with Tribain. The Aldborough airport project was shelved, to the relief of naturalists of the Ouse Conservancy Society; the Stampead Airport was abandoned, and a pressure group started campaigning for one at Thamesmead. Clannie and Boyd fashions became the 'rave', as they called it; even Thoria, who was a bit independent, tried them.

Some trawlers were lost off Cecily and some submarines off Islandia, where there was a very nasty earthquake. The Tip Tribain movement got a lot of publicity and so did the landscaping Operation Cleanup, but somehow I never seemed to see either of them in actual practice, except that a lot of replacement parts for Tribish gadgets became unobtainable, because they turned out to be made abroad. The hero of the Winter Olympiads was Milly, until threatened with deprival as an alleged professional. The Chemico Olympiads, however, were to be boycotted by South Capricorn and Tuba because yellow Capricorn states were taking part. H. Wilson the 'Great Brain' robber, now wearing a beard, was arrested in Candia.

Thoria, despite luminous eyelashes, was a bit quiet and moody going along to the party. There was a lot of music and some dancing going on. John, who was talking on one side with a bulky man with a bullet head, and a thin man with a bluish jaw, came over with both hands outstretched, kissed Thoria, pulled me into a group of drinkers and disappeared with Thoria. I was a bit mad, but two of the drinkers were real dazzlers of girls, and I found it easy to keep my eyes on them. One was introduced as Cat – it turned out later her name was Catriocia, pronounced Katrisha. She was black-haired (short-cut), pale and petite, with a little black shift and delicious bare arms. The other was one of the two Mays from the party at the con–recon, but transformed by an orange hairdo – unless it was a wig – and a lot more good-looking than I remembered her. She gave no sign of recognition, but was quite amiable. After being rather thrown around by Thoria it was a nice change to find I was making a hit with Cat. The rest of the group gradually melted away and we started an earnest talk on the sofa. Out of the tail of my eye I saw John – if it was the same John? – making little signs to the thin man across the room. The thin man slipped out and I went on exchanging views about life with Cat. I was already in a sort of trance. I was an iron filing and she was the magnet. I hardly looked up when Thoria tripped over my feet, on her way across the room with the bulky man. They went on. I started showing Cat around the flat a couple of Nirvanas later, and we passed the thin man and Thoria at the telephone in earnest talk with someone. 'Who's the thin man with Thoria, do you know?' I said in passing.

'He's some crony of John's. John names him Patch.'

'He was with a big sort of man with a, er, football-head earlier on; do you know *him*?'

'I know the one you refer, but I never saw him before tonight. What's in here?'

'Here' was John's bedroom. We retreated in some confusion. John was in it, with bullet-head, packing up some bulky objects about the size of suitcases, or maybe unpacking them – we didn't stop long enough to find out. We settled down gazing over the lights of town from John's balcony. I believe there were two other couples there but I never really took them in. We got a bit entwined. An eternity after that we were wandering back and John stopped us in the corridor. 'Oh, Fitchey,' he said, 'Thoria had a bad headpain. We couldn't find you, so I took her home.'

'Thanks – I'm sorry – she all right?'

'Yes, only a headpain. She asked not to bother you, you might as well stay on. You don't *look* anxious to quit early!'

Cat and I started dancing, and presently, when the crowd was thinning out a bit, I got her to come out with me. I got hold of a locomotor-taxier, and after driving around a bit took her home in it. She insisted on saying goodnight outside her flat, which she shared with May, apparently. I paid off the taxier, which had run up quite a bit of a fare, and walked home to simmer down and to register in my mind the whereabouts of Cat's flat. We'd fixed up tomorrow night for a meal and dance.

Next morning the news said that jobless white Lenians with Hindi passports were being denied entry into Hindya because Hindyan food-supplies and educational facilities were already strained to breaking-point. Three white murderers were hung in Dodecanesia, in defiance of a royal reprieve in Tribain;

Dodecanesia looked like becoming a commonwealth. Programme-news followed: Gerard M. Hopkins's 'Four Quartets' plays, *Taking to a Scrounger*, were to be repeated, this time on TBC3.

Cat had obviously been to the hairpresser. She looked bewitching, but slightly alien, in a micro-shift of silver. The dance woke us up, though. Afterwards she asked me in (May was off that weekend) and left me for a moment while I stared, I remember, at a pretentious full-page advertisement in *We* for Starbuck Martyr Oloroso. We drank randies, however. Perhaps that was what got us into bed.

The next few weeks were a cross between a roller-coaster and being becalmed in a fog. Part of me kept going on the everyday material plane. The rest was fathoms deep. Meanwhile the outer world rolled on. There was an outbreak of congregational violence in Tribain, apparently intended to inhibit free speech. Mauretania celebrated her independence. There were Polovtzian riots. Grobnik won against Winchester United. The President of Sloczo-Chekhovia resigned. Gone for ever, hoped radio commentators, were the days of a mono-glyphic Ominoust flock under the commination of Crussia. There was a gold-selling panic, till the bankers took gold off the money-standard. Anti-war aggressioneers in Peyton Place kept thousands of police busy on several Sundays, while the criminals had a field day, stealing the treasures of St Paul's and the House Guards. Jenkins resigned because of Brown's swingeing budget, but remained Leader of the House. The proprietor of a Yoho 'Donkey-Club' was prosecuted for refusing to employ three coloured girls as 'Neddy-Girls'. Euphonic plague spread in West Niet-Farm. A Germite plane landed mysteriously in a Clashire field and a rash of angina cases spread through Clashire hospitals. Hoof and snout reappeared in Tribain. Euan Parnell made a speech about 'rivers of blood' flowing through the campuses of Tribain, and a mob of London Doctors of Philosophy processed to Parliament to support him. What did I care! I was astride a dream. As for Thoria, she just dropped out of my life. Occasionally I saw May, with whom I now got on quite well. Once, turning up rather early at Cat's flat (to which I now had a spare key), I found May and John apparently shunting the furniture around. They were just pushing a bookcase against the built-in cupboard, and looked rather bothered. I lent a hand. They said Cat and May had got tired of the cupboard and never used it anyway. Cat came in from outside and lifted an eyebrow, but said nothing. May and John vanished and we had the flat to ourselves.

I was going off for a fortnight with Cat – it was now summer – but unfortunately about this time the Forward-Drivers having lost so many by-selections, they decided to work to rule and the country came to a standstill again. We hired an autobil, however, and got away. We had to go far north to find a beach (which is what we fancied) without tar, jellyfish, or three-families-two-transistors-and-an-ice-cream-van to the square yard. We struck lucky for the weather, too, which is more than all the other millions on Tribain's shores did.

When we got back I found an unknown Circadian had assassinated Dr John Wycliffe Queen, and President Thompson had cancelled his visit to Monolulu. Gimson had reshuffled the Tribish Caballist. Racism was suspected when the driver of a train was killed by a stone flung over a bridge, because two of the passengers in the train happened to be coloured. The death penalty was proposed for genocide, defined as killing a person whose genetic skin colouring differs from one's own. The Government staged a sit-in in the House of Lords. A minor canon was fasting in the Great Hall of a northern university in order to demonstrate against the oppression of students by university authorities in general. Twenty-five university staff and their wives and families 'took over' (as *Look Forth* put it, meaning, squatted obstructively in) a Students' Union for a week, in protest against the students' political victimization of a visiting right-wing speaker; some of the papers forgot to report that 300 of their staff colleagues had signed a document deploring this takeover. A university porter who washed a painted slogan off a wall was accused of Fascist brutality on this account: 'It's a clear case of moral violence!' shouted twenty Anarchists, mostly from other institutions, interrupting a concert held in aid of spastics, so that the audience of 500 had to go home and their money was refunded. Following the collapse of the tripartite Gallic Revolution, reactivist leader Manuel Lohn-Bandit from Paname was invited to Tribain by the TBC and government, to confer with militant leaders from other countries. At the height of his triumph in the Caledonian binaries for the Meritan Presidency, popular Roddy Hennessy was shot dead by an Assyrian who wished to celebrate the anniversary of the Philistine Jehad; the Divided Nations immediately cancelled their debate on Philistine. Monaphra said they would shoot down any plane that dared to bring food supplies to the starving Negentran infants. Meritan children of fourteen were forbidden to buy revolvers except by mail order, despite an outcry from the Bring Back John Birch Order of Bison, the Man a Minute Militiamen's Klan, and the Drum-Minorettes of the Meritan Revelation. In Tribain the biochemical warfare establishment at Towton Bourne began holding visitors' days, and members of the public were invited to 'adopt' a guinea pig or a rabbit there. Among Crussian movres and counter-movres, popular President Dutschke, said the headlines, was given a 'blank cheque' in Prague.

I went over to Cat's flat one evening soon after and found a note saying she'd be out for an hour, please wait. (May was away for a month.) I played a few records and after a bit got bored and started rearranging the furniture. Then I thought I'd shunt the bookcase sideways a bit that May and John had pushed against the cupboard the other day. I thought I could manage it on my own, and as I heaved vainly at one end, one of the cupboard doors swung open. There was some grey packing paper inside, but no shelves. The paper was rather roughly shoved up behind the cupboard doors and it half fell over.

The whole cupboard was full from front to back and from floor to ceiling with gold ingots.

I revolved a few things in my mind. Thoria, May, John, the thin man and the big man at John's party, the telephoning and the packing in John's bedroom then; John's remarks about the Crippen Paxton and crime not paying in the con–recon business; the gold crises in the world, the catageon anyway (didn't know what might be going on in the anageon in the same time-section). After a bit of thought I put everything carefully back, bookcase door and all, and left Cat a note to say I couldn't stay. I wanted to think things out for a bit. Looked like she was being fooled by May, who was probably in the plot.

By about 11 p.m., after walking round and round and round, I thought I had better let Cat into the secret, and I went back to the flat. I could see there was a light on in her bedroom so I let myself in quietly, not to cause a scandal and so on. She'll be reading in bed, I thought, I'll give her a nice surprise. I opened the door softly.

There was no doubt what she and John were doing on the bed.

Somehow or other I found myself in my place – I'd slipped out softly and hailed a passing taxier, I suppose – and ringing up Frank 2 at the con–recon, after their switchboard had got it into their head who I was. Yes, he said, I could come over right away; he was on duty all night. I felt I trusted him. I'd kept the taxier waiting while I packed and left a cheque. In half an hour I was closeted with him. I told him everything I knew; he did a lot of telephoning and intercom speaking, then he drew up an affidavit and got me to sign it. He said they would stage an 'accident' or a 'nervous breakdown' for my place of work, and reprint me back to the anageon. I mean, I'd had it as far as this universe was concerned. He said they'd had their suspicions something was going on, but the Johns had charge of that side of things. He said he thought they must have been doing a 'perpetual-motion spin' with the gold, reselling and rebuying the same gold and continually printing it across from one universe to the other and back again. All sorts of jugglery.

Frank 2 got me and my stuff in the egg frame they had at that side, with two copies of my affidavit and his own signed comments appended. 'We'll stop the gold drain racket pretty quickly,' he said, 'and as to your personal life, you'll have to write this off to experience. You'll come up fighting in a month or two. Not all girls are tarts, you know.'

'Can I do anything to help?'

'No, keep your nose out of it; there's murder and worse on the fringe of this sort of business.'

'But what'll I do for a life? There's my ur-doppel, I can't dog him for a year.'

'Fitch zero, you mean? Stay around with the con–recon boys Down Under for six months or so. Show these documents to George 1 – that's the man who briefed you in their prelim-room. (He won't know you, because he's a year younger than he was then, of course, but that won't matter.) Don't show them to anyone else, and don't say why you came back. I think I know who the Johns' opposite numbers are, but I won't tell you. Better be on your guard against everyone but George. Do what he tells you, and after a few months you can travel around and see the world before boinging Fitch zero, so you can indoctrinate him and close the loop.'

And that's what I did. More dead than alive, about five in the morning, I reprinted back here. I said could I see George 1 before going off, and they said he was asleep, so I camped out in his office till seven o'clock, when he showed up and woke me up. I told him the whole tale. He nipped off with my documents, sending in some brandy and hot coffee nearly treacly with sugar, which saved my life. When he came back two hours later he said they couldn't disturb the temporal pattern, so they would have to let things ride at this end for two years, but they had fixed up for the Centre Security boys to keep close tabs on every operation of the gang, and would meanwhile organize suitable counter-measures through world bankers and so on. As to my disappearance from the catageon, I had a good personal reason which John and Cat would guess at, and the best thing was to leave Frank 2 to run the catageon end, as a direct message would be two years too early.

They gave me a job in the Centre. I got to know the organization pretty well. Naturally I'm not giving away any details in this write-up. I'm going to store it there or in my bank – haven't decided which place. Hope it's legible, finished off in this reporter's notebook in the breeze. I had talks with George about the curious parallelism of the two worlds – of course I was living nearly an ana-year earlier than the cata-year I had known, but you could see what was in the wind, after the psychotron effect of my little loop. I had some theories about the whole set-up and George thinks there is something in them. Then I wangled a job as a roving reporter in Europe for six months, which redoubled my cynicism, I can tell you, and which also kept me away from proto-Fitch. Now I'm on that fell-walking tour which is going to start the cycle rolling. I'm sitting on that moor summit writing up my last notes, waiting for him to walk up the slope towards me. There he is, a speck on a track far below. He'll be up in a quarter of an hour. When I talk with him later at his digs – my digs – I won't tell him my project. Too confusing. I'll just say, which will be true, that I'll stay in on his firm for a bit. But I've greater ideas in mind, and I think the con–recon will finance them. Here's my theory in a nutshell, before I stand up to watch him climb the slope. Here's the psychotron effect as it seeded my brain:

Shakespeare says:

> As flies to wanton boys are we to the gods,
> They kill us for their sport.

(or as I once heard it on the radio in the Yonder, where it was part of *The Apophthegmata* by Davy Jones:

A s'prize to war-torn guys, I weep the sods
Dave billed as not their sort);

but it would be truer to say the 'gods' are psychopaths who put us, both ananthropes and catanthropes, through our antics, in order to fall about giggling. Nothing else can explain actions and attitudes so vicious, short-sighted, humourless, senseless and downright insane as we poor sap(ien)s indulge in. I intend to devote the rest of my life to finding out just who are these witless galvanizers of humanity, on both sides of the glass. Then perhaps we can be set free. (The gold gang will be mopped up a year after I rejoin, but that's a mere detail . . . So is the transcosmic 'resonance' we shall set up with the writer of that article in the catageon's *Scientific Armenian*, if we can manage it.) I shall try, probably with George's help, to promote a research project based on the convertron–reconvertron Centre. We shall feed in significant data from both universes into the con–recon computers, if we can buy enough time, and see if they can point a finger at our puppet-masters. As far as I can see at the moment, however, both Dr Fausta and Dr Faustus inhabit a world given over to devils; not the wickedest, not the greatest, not indeed traditional anti-Christian devils at all; merely the silliest: irresponsible flibbertigibbets, the nadirs of inanity, gnats of nothingness. These are our animators.

Take It or Leave It

2000. 223. 08.42. Out of bed wrong side today. Trouble was, drier was cold. Following my shower, a freezing gale. Called up the man but took two hours to get through, and when I did get his ugly face on the screen he said it'll be ten days till they can show up. Maggy says why not use the holiday wraps – towelling should absorb enough moisture if you rub and pat a bit – and pep the washroom up to 30. Suppose that'll do. Have to. Then meanwhile the hairstyler got a bit cranky and aligned my second lock in front of my shoulder instead of the sine curve I've been used to, sod it. Johnny had to open his pharynx about it, too, young bug: 'Your hair's skew, Dad!' Denise kidded me it was the sparrows. Maggy says I must have moved. One of these days *I* can tell, this is going to be. I hope *you're* functioning anyway, sodding tape-set; play you back and see . . . Good. And then when I pressed the news button I thought, I bet this'll be black and so it was; this is, as black as they ever leak. As usual, the British news was cushy, only the exter news leaked much. Thousands dead in American riots, some of them fried by the cops and feds. (Ours only rinse, never heard of frying here.) Same thing in Japan and China and Russia, more or less. Between the lines, inter looked bad too: 'The disorganization in Mersea is under active control. Prospective traffic from other megalopolises is advised to contact the police by prior call, during the next ten days.' I've heard that one before. No motivation to visit in Mersea, luckily. Then the weathercast: why they have to keep the rain off the south and west and let it chuck it down all over Midlandia and the north I don't know. I suppose the agric zones have to have their sun, but why at our expense? Depressing, I call it. All very well for the uppercrust with their ion fountains and their sunlighting.

Another day. Looks like showers. Feels like showers, too, from the ache in my bones. Sun's still up in the north at the day-ends, shouldn't be summer's end for a month or two. How you feeling, Maggy love?

Well, stir the kids and see if they can't find some hips. In spite of that cat last night, my innards are grumbling, dunno 'bout yours . . .

Look sharp, John. That hedge'll have something on it by now. Watch out for the Gibsons, though. Now they've settled in the old helicopter, their Larry goes prowling early, and he's grown up real strong. I've seen him down that far. Couple of stones sent him off last time, but it won't always, and if you and him was to meet up there suddenly on your own, I wouldn't back you, boy. Take the big catapult and four, five stones, do for a cat as well if you see one. The old fence post'll come in handy too. We'll be OK, with the aerial and the branch.

Wish my father had bought me a non-wind waterproof watch. It would have lasted through the river, and I'd know where we were so to speak. I think Mike Gibson must have one. Seen him looking at his wrist.

Have to look out a new battery if it gets much colder. You don't know how to start a fire properly, do you, Jane? Denise'll show you next time. First cool day after a dry stretch, we'll have one; some of the doors and chairs'll burn nicely, on the drive. Keep the bugs away too, if we leave a bit smouldering on the porch; too many in already. So long as we can keep the ants out. Plug the crack in the door with clay, Denise, and open the other door if it gets hot.

09.10. Johnny and Denise blasted off to the schoolab. Never guess they were fraternal twins if I didn't know. The pre-inductee centre's only five hundred metres off, but I worry sometimes. Jane's infant centre doesn't operate since the barons wrecked it the other night, but she looks in on edscreen here instead. Just now she's working on her 'tartriper'. This is what she used to call her talkwriter. She needs motivationing, though. According to Maggy it's correctioning she wants; Maggy's too hard on her.

Maggy's set the clensomat and called up the instruction program she's on about now – what is it? Light-sculptation. I suppose this means she'll be on at me to get her a light-sculptor for Christmas. It's time I called up supplies, not to mention the programming for the old megastore. This batch has to be a bugged sample. Which reminds me: I have to check again for bugs on our own cartons; I don't fancy guinea-pigging for other firms. Maggy doesn't know all their little dodges yet. Then I'll have to mission the megastore this afternoon, I suppose.

I do hope Denise and Johnny are all right . . . No one would take them for fraternals, she images at least a year older, so we get all these disapproving stares when we're togethering, from people that don't have big families. Maggy decisioned to have Jane prior to her implant skinpill (she was getting allergic to the sniff method) – she said a third would keep the twins from fighting, when it grew up a bit, and it's true they don't resonate . . . Someone actually propositioned Denise by paternoster three the other day. It's these eyes, this height, this sexational hair. Took her for an inductee, shouldn't wonder. Better than sexmurder, anyway.

Time for calling the megastore. My sight-aid? Here . . .

That ceiling's leaking. The rafter's rotten above, I think. What say we look around for another pad? House-hunting's hopeless, I know; places standing all occupied. Still, search around might turn up

something. Don't say anything to Jane; I'll just have a wander, soon as John gets back.

Isn't that Mike Gibson up the hill? Coming through the old gap? Hope he hasn't seen John. Denise, climb upstairs and have a look round. Give that whistle if you want me up. Hell, there goes another meal; I'd have hit it if I hadn't been looking after Gibson; cats always shoot past the gate now. Try and get that thrush, Maggy, your aim's better.

10.05. Mail buzzer. First for six days. It was from Jim. A bit cagey, but clear Jessie's not herself and something shorted with Bill. Jim never got this tape of mine, day 205, seems. It was the mail strike, I bet. I'll try a remake. Reach him in five days, say. Or shall I just call him up?

10.31. No good. Been trying half-hour now. Half the channels are this way nowadays. I wonder, now, would it be quicker just to transportation it and visit with him? Let's see: the block; the transit, say half-hour; the integrator, say twenty min; the HVT, one hundred fifty kilometres, say half-hour with acse and dece; at his end it's multimode – say another half. Half-hour visiting – or say hour with lunch. Be back mid-afternoon, look in the megastore, OK, Maggy . . .

10.41. She thought she could negative-pressure me, huh. No, I must mission him. Two-legs better. Calling-up's hopeless, this channel. So long as he's in. Can leave a notation, if he's out. Take my notation-set, in case. Or get a spare one at a store his way: I'm not a nupe-watcher, if I'm shedding all this credit another nine pound won't sink me. Even get a cassette and leave a tape after all. What'll I get into? The yellow has this hole the time the barons – Maggy forgot to put it in the automend. No negentropy, this ma has; place is like a disability home. The old green, then. The red waywear, and carry floorwear, because he likes his floor cold. And sod it, I'll take you; might want to record something while it's hot, in transit.

But Jim's I'll buy, if necessary. Set the responsomat for the megastore, in case. Be off in a micro.

Got him! . . . Give it to Ma, Jane. Well you hit it, you eat it; you can pick it too! Hey, was that . . . What is it, Denise? See something? . . . Yes, working round the back he is. Maybe it's a dog he's seen. Or a fox. Well, I wouldn't whistle; never hear us through the pane, catch is all rusted up, and I don't want to smash the glass just yet; besides, John's blocked by those two buildings; he'd never hear anyway. Still, might turn Gibson. You run downstairs and scream through the doorway – just once. Then if I whistle scream again. Quick now – he's creeping back.

Whhh!!

Too sharp he is, give me that aerial and a cata. Run up and lookout till one of us comes back.

11.17. Ran up against Mike Gibson from the next block; he was queuing for the transir. Why don't you visit with us more often? he said. Says Larry's doing fine. Told him I was off to Jim's, but the transir intervalled us too far to finish the story. This higher-pigment type had slid between us, what Maggy's programs call a real overtan – h'mhm . . . Mike, as I was saying – oh here comes the terminal.

11.38. This must be a hill over there. Wonder where it is. It's all cultured too, and the lumimobile gives it panash. Sodding rain, you need a splash of colour . . . Travel broadens the mind . . . Should've brought the instruxopak . . . I'll turn on the woosic.

12.11. This auto method's fine. Last time it was self-drive waycars all the way. Of course you can personalization this kind too. Nice and low-volume too.

Do you know, I could have sworn this ma in the integrator called me a garnet, under her breath. Just because of this lot re the higher-pigment type . . . How about the car woosic, now?

What the hell are you skulking up there for? . . . Mind
your own business and I'll mind mine! . . . You move a
step and I'll murder you, you thug! . . . You dare move
another step and I'll bash your face in! . . . Keep off our
manor, you thieving bastard or I'll bash your head
in! . . . Don't you dare come down any further! . . .
You come past that house and I'll lay your face
open! . . . And you're another! . . . Scared are you, got
to have your bloody brat to face me out, have you? Ya,
Larry, that's right, come rushing down, two against
one, that's right! . . . All right, don't you two come any
further! You keep to your own manor, let me stay in
mine! . . . Attack women, would you? Threaten a
woman, eh? Maggy's worth two of you. Give it 'em,
Maggy! . . . By hell, this is our house and the man that
lays a finger on the hedge'll be the last thing he ever
does! . . . Go home you bastards! Ya! Home! Ya!!
Home!! Ya!!! Home!!! Virus get you, you bastards!!!

Hell, that was a near thing. I'm hoarse – aren't you,
Maggy? Thank you for turning up. I think John got
away. Here he is, round the back. My, we drew 'em off
OK, didn't we? Lucky they hadn't any catas. Johnny
my son, you made it. What, you got a – two hedgehogs,
by hell! Smashing! Did they see you really, do you
think? Who cares anyway, we're all safe and sound,
and two hedgehogs to the good. John, you're a master!
No, Denise, they won't dare come right down. I think it
was your mother that really put the fear of hell into
them. Now what do you say to a fire and a clay bake?
Johnny can keep a lookout at the front, just in case.
Denise, you can be cook.

13.02. I'm at Jim's. I'm putting *you* on, so's we can have a
record of our visit. Jessie's off to rest, but we can dialogue.

'You saw what she's like. It started over Bill.'

What happened?

'They beat him up. Bill. Barons. Working for the estate mafia *and* having a bit of fun on their own this time, I opinion. Last winter. Left him for dead near the lift shaft. Health squad got him in. Ended up in a cereb forty kilometres out—'

How's this? Where did you say?

'A cereb – a casualty home. He's not classified for rehabilitation, only minimal prosthetics. So he's there for good. I've been businessing all on my own ever since. Jessie visitationed twice: *this* set her back. Then she started thinking the mafia were after Juju – and him no more than an infant. Besides, I've always kept right side of them – monster gifts from the store, forgetting to program debits, exetra. And I'm all right with the block king too. A JCO he is – Junior Cleansing Officer. He's all right if you stand dead still when he passes by, and stand him a drink at the drinkateria. It's the ones with sexational wives and daughters need to worry . . . No, the block king and the mafia are on my side. No fear there. Couldn't get Jessie to see it, though.

'Then she started saying she was a wicked woman, she'd neglected Bill, been the cause of it all, wasn't worthy to live. By spring, I couldn't do anything with her: she wouldn't take any telemedication or even let me connection the diagnosticator. In the end I hooked the doctor (twenty thousand to care up on to, he's hard to get) and he got her certified for temporary care. I was at my wit's end re Juju; even when she was here I was scared she'd do something to him; but in the end I got Cousin Amy to mission up and care on to him. I only managed to visitation Jessie once, prior to the HVT engineers' strike. Then she came back around day 180, but she's still to be sedationed. They say she classificationed against metapsychic drugs, otherwise she'd have been rehabilitationed long ago. Agitated depression, they call it. Juju's picked up a mob of fears from her kinky ways.'

But she'll reclamation in time, with you, I expect?

'A year or two, they said. And then things aren't ideal here.

The block alarm is pooff. Someone smashed it. If the corridor TVs haven't registered the trouble, you have to call up the cops yourself – if the channel's functioning. Takes ten minutes to get through, average. And they won't act if they think it's a mafia job.'

Sod it, I've left it fine. Got to get back and take in the megastore today. Your wall-chron's slow by my wrist-chron. Listen, try and call me up every five, ten days. You might get better luck than I did on the channel. I'll just look in on Jessie and off.

Maggy, I think I've found it. About an hour from here. It's an old garage block, top of a hill. The house is fallen in, but the garages are OK. Face south-east. Good view all round. Marshy below the hill. That'll keep 'em off. Woods, old orchards, on the slope. Nettles, badgers, birds, cats, berries, apples, pears, snails, owls. No good hanging on here. Set off now. In twos, Johnny in the rear, keep each other just in sight. Whistle and we'll freeze . . . I don't care if the Gibsons do think they've scared us out, Virus get 'em. Get moving now.

23.17. It was so late when I got away, I decisioned a detour via the megastore. Found Pete missioning there. He was saying the mail was so slow and the set so blinky, he was considering tabling purchase of a private lasercom just to liaise with Droffield's and Willenhausen's. They're both in eyeline, all three being so high. I said right, go ahead, peg in my name with it. The versionizer hasn't come yet, how we're going to cope with the Jap mergees I don't know; they aren't in resonance with Commart English.

When I homed in on the unit Maggy was connectioning her matebureau business. Jane was culturing the creepers. A sparrow shot past me . . . Time Jane initiated tapping a non-talk write-set. Must call up one her size keys.

Anyway I was glad to shed my wear and relax. Maggy had a horror story, though. 'You know a man got caught today,' she said, 'in a paternoster, a vertipater, not a horipater, crushed, killed? Well, what they're saying at the salebox is, it wasn't an accident. They say the block mafia are running a transplant supply, undercover.'

'How do they calculate it could have been done?' I said.

'Someone pushed in with him,' she said, 'staged the rest, they say. They say they've a health squad in their pocket, zipped him off. Been a crop of "accidents" like that. Always young, healthy ones, ideal for transplant donors.'

'They're fictioning!' I said; but all the same . . . Then to cheer her up, I asked re her horoscope. I'd just missed out on the horocast. It was a bright one for her *and* fair for all of us, as it happens, so we dialogued this-ward a bit. The twins came in, so *this* was all right. Then there was a screen-and-button 'puterpoll for Midlandia parliament on the alternatives for the new airport site. Maggy and I voted for the Northsea platform and new HVT links. Johnny and Denise griped it isn't fair, they should poll too; serious. The rest of the evening we had educasts and spottoquiz. The colour was a bit blinky, though. Have to file a mendation order. Time for bed.

See what I mean. Got possibilities. No ants either. We'll use this big one for us, see, the front rolls up and down, and there's a peephole in the roller. Next one for stores. This one here for wood and such. Escape staircase'll do for lookouts, over by the house. Salvage some things there, chairs, exetra. Might manage to knock a hole from one garage to the next, in case of trouble. Soon get dark now – you settle in, I'll have a quick butcher's round the house, what's left.

2000. 224. 23.35. Must have been religion day or something. First a Jove's Witness, then an Anglican Methodist, then a Yogist called up. Made short work of the AM; but the Witness and the Yogist persistented. The Yogist call must have been a computerized interview – you could tell from the pauses. Clever how the 'puters analyze your vocabulary and switch in the right reply. Only this must have been pitched for high persistence, it wouldn't take no for an answer. Endwise I had to operate the control and fade him out in mid-gesture. Then sod it if a neo-Marxist didn't screen up. He was personalized but even more persistent. Had to control him out too. Following this an Ortho-Catholic who was easy stuff, especially as he called just following an aggressive redecoration rep who brain-rinsed me to exhaustion; to rehabilitation, I'd just ingested a pep with a real kick, when the O-C screened up.

Next thing was a door call. Imagine our surprise when Uncle Ned and Aunt Olga screened up. When they came in they said they were transiting and could they visit a couple of days with us. I had to miss my hour's exercise at the autosquash court, sod it. Aunty said, My, wasn't Denise a 'sexy' bird already; she's going to be quite sexational, I opinion, and she imaged this then, with some jewellery that really resonated. They're all in bed now. Uncle's aged up, really in the higher-succession bracket, you'd opinion: at sixty-odd he images well over seventy; almost ready for a gerry, a retiring home. Aunt Olga actually wears wear indoors now – to act parallel with him, I suppose – although she's only forty-five; brought a shift and floorwear with her. First news we watched, Uncle started on his usual gripe re the news being anaesthetized, not like in his young days. Thank goodness this is only a couple of days they're staying. I was hoping to see the musical of Kafka's *The Castle*, but now they've come we had to switch to another channel and see the underwater ballet of *West Side Story*. Maggy doesn't even *like* underwater ballet. The sparrows didn't either, they kept nuisancing around during it. One positioned momentwise on Aunt's head. The block's infested with them. The twins fed their predecessors when they were infants and now they're triple-hardened.

Uncle keeps on boring us re he used to roar round Brands

Hatch when he was young, or how there used to be woods where our blocks stand, or recalling back to the rationing when he was an infant, in the Welsh mountains because grand-mother was evacuated there in the 1939–45 war. Aunt Olga isn't on the same wavelength: edgy and never announces. She was a great free-sexer for years, prior to settling down with Uncle. I suppose that's why she doesn't interface with infants or pre-inductees – Jane especially just emigrates when she's around – and why she images so dehydrated.

Following the children had blasted off to bed, though, she told us she had it on the salebox grapevine that the Heyns-Suit Babies are demanding all the key positions in forecasting, industry and government, otherwise they'll organize a brain drain. Where would they go, I said, to the US? No, she said, to Scandinavia apparently, Japan, and NZ. Seems the Panpacific Alliance has them drooling. These HSBs think they've got it made, as Uncle would say, but who wants all these brains around? I wouldn't give a nupe for them. We'll outvote them a thousand to one at next week's centregov screen referendum, anyway.

Living off the fat of the land, we are. Oh my stomach. Acorns. Truffles. Garlic. A thrush and a pheasant. Not to mention these dogs . . . Maggy, come here, Maggy, come on now, yes, come on . . .

2000. 225. 19.45. My hairstyler's off the blink now, thank goodness . . . That cartoon of *Moby Dick* was a riot. Went on too long though. The whale had some funny numbers. Some-thing more serious, though. I didn't tell Uncle and Aunt – they're next door just now – but I saw Larry Gibson on my way back from the megastore where I'd missioned to get away from *them* for a bit. Larry was in a crowd of all pigments, all queuing for the vertipater. Quite a sexational low-pigment bird in partywear was standing in front of him – and the wear was more minus than plus, of course. I was orbiting and trying to get through transit. The crowd pushed him and he just about knocked the bird down. He turned round – there was a higher-pigment type just in rear of him – and shouted, 'Get back you!' A neon-dearth-al-looking lower-pigment type close by, who I think was trying to make the bird, shouted out something, and Larry ripped out some object, rammed him in the diaphragm, and pulled twice. It was all over so quickly. The neon-dearth-al collapsed, blood all over the place, screams everywhere, the cops homed in in microseconds (the corridor TVs will have picked it up), and there's Larry standing shaking over the corpse. What he'd done was use an instapeg wall-hook gun. One peg must have cut a big blood vessel, the second must have targeted on the vagus nerve or something. Says he, 'Bastard called me a racist!' Cops quizzed me. I said, yes, it sounded just like this. Course, this would be justifiable homicide. But I knew sodding well he was sodding well errored – it was only 'rapist'. Anyway they took my word for it. By good luck, the bird had stayed grounded, and she relayed me to the nth. The 'puter'll never convict, now.

I had to tell somebody or something, so now I told *you*. Shaking, I was, had to have a pep when I got in. Just told Maggy quietly Larry had killed a man up the corridor, and I hoped it would be OK.

Denise shouldn't have gone off like that, even with the fence post with her. Been all day now and she'll never make it in the dark. I'll sit up a bit and wake you later, Johnny. Let Ma have some sleep till dawn. Might hear something, perhaps.

2000. 226. 13.18. The supply-tube milk's changed. The flavour's queer and it's more green. Have to try with natural cow milk for a bit, if we can call it up. Anyway, this is something: the old couple are gone. I opinion, if it wasn't for the drier being cold they'd have stayed much longer. I put in ninety minutes autosquash to make up for yesterday exetra.

The lunchtime edscreen is on early literature. Maggy likes it, but me-wise it's a drag. I could never understand these great historical novels like *The Sotweed Factor* and *The Spire*, and I don't make much interface with socio-philosophy ones like *Ulysses* or *The Trial*. Anyway I'd sooner call up my lunch and ingest it in peace. I don't mind listening to a magazine in parallel of course.

Maggy keeps impacting with Johnny for saying 'followings' instead of 'afters'. Personally I don't mind what a pre-inductee says. Anything for peace at meals. It's different with Jane, she's still an infant. This lark re speaking right, it's all alf garnet, I don't resonate with it.

The megastore held a telecommittee this morning. We decisioned to production several new lines. They agreed to the lasercom too. In the middle in came Jane and started announcing. I had to alarm Maggy to come and incentive her off. As Maggy was calling over for the matebureau, Jane wasn't very popular.

I was going to visitation my cousin Michael at his disability home. He's an LSD baby – his parents used the stuff. Born too early to get classified for prostheses. But when I called up the spa they said his viability had diminished and he wouldn't survive long; he was sedationed and wouldn't be worth seeing now. That's what they *said*, anyway. *I* opinion they've initiated culling the inmates.

I know why Denise ran off like that: you were trying to mate with her, last night in the garage after that blowout we had. I didn't realize then, but I know now. Don't say no, your face gives you away. Trying your own sister, you – you – I've no words . . . I bet she was a match for you, anyway, for all she's no older than you. I'm right, aren't I? I heard the roller door in the middle of the night. She must have gone then to hide in one of the other garages. Or else that's when she went off for good.

2000. 226. 22.51. Denise has sprung it on us that she's going on this world nature tour. It's in thirty days, and durates a hundred days. She'd connectioned it herself without asking us, and showed us her classification card today, so it was all fixed. Most on these tours are inductees, say thirteen to twenty-two, and handpicked too. Many of them are Heyns-Suit Babies. She's only twelve and no HSB. All the same she was classified OK. It struck me it might be a kidnap syndicate forgery, so I connectioned a recall from the original 'puter, but the data were OK. Recall systems are spoofproof, so this is final, I suppose. And as things are, there's no appeal unless we can incentive her to reverse. I don't think this is worth it, nor does Maggy. But I must say it's a trauma.

Come here, boy. This bloody leg's broken, I'm sure. Virus take that bloody bird's nest. Wish I'd never gone after those eggs. If Denise had been here I'd have sent her up, she was nimbler. If I could have brought myself to ask you, John, but we weren't on speaking terms. It'll never heal. You three ought to have left me there, instead of heaving me back. You'll never thrive with me lying here. Don't say anything to Ma and Jane. Let them sleep.

2000. 227. 12.10. We have to evacuate this unit. It came on the screen, early. The whole block's being traded in for a new gerry, a retirement home. And the next block's being switched for a reciddy, a psychopathology home. We've all been given fifteen days to move. Maggy fed our requirements by call-up into the 'puter system, to integrate on to our classification. Including the desired move radius, which we settled at two hundred kilometres. It turned up only nine units within a range of 60 to 70 per cent on the desirability scale, and this is the best it could do. Six were filled units with families leaving inside four days, three were new units. Two of the three were pods in

163

pod-batteries, the third was an unbooked unit in a new block. I spent the rest of the morning trying to call them up for teleview. I got five: the two pods and three filled block-units. We visitaped the views and tonight we'll run them through for the twins, but I think we'll take one of the pods. (One of them's in the state of Yorkshire, but their laws aren't too tough.) It'll be a change; the only thing is, a lot of the facilities and supplies are only piped to the battery centre. And they say these centres have pigeons the way we have sparrows. But we're sick of the block life, maybe the pod-batteries won't be so mafia'd and kinged, and we might resonate well with community life.

We'll have to try and call up the other four by the end of tomorrow. *Then* we'll have to get the schoolab facilities confirmed. *Then* we'll have to decision on which unit. *Then* we'll have to trade off our immobiles exetra locally against replacements in target. *Then* we'll have to fix goods transportation. *Then* we'll have to lodge all the addresses for readdressment-service, friends, firms, unaymit. I can hardly face these fifteen days. And Denise off fourteen days following then. Have to recall confirmation that her route's been recast. The cold drier'll stay cold now, sod it.

Now they're all gone: Maggy to milk that cow with the calf they found, with the old bucket; Johnny to hunt; Jane to look for berries. Parked me out on the cobbles. My innards must be busted, keep passing blood, can't keep anything down. I thought we'd make it, after Maggy and me lasting through the Virus, but it was too good to last. I hope you're all right somewhere, Denise; I hope nothing happened to you . . . Just a drag I am, lying here . . . Those bloody rats in the ruin, I can hear them, they won't get me either. Here goes. Bit of window glass here. Left wrist. Ahhh! Ahhh! Ahhh! Done it! Done it! Goodbye, Maggy. Aaah.

Mouth of Hell

When the expedition reached the plateau, driving by short stages from the northern foothills, they found it devoid of human life, a silent plain variegated by little flowers and garish patches of moss and lichen. Kettass, the leader, called a halt, and surveyed the landscape while the tractors were overhauled. The sun shone brightly out of a clear sky not far to the south, for the quasi-arctic ecology was one of height, not latitude. Mosquitoes hovered low down over tussocks below wind-level, beetles and flies crawled over the flowers. Beyond a quarter-metre above the ground, however, a bitter wind from the north flowed steadily. The distance was clear but it was difficult to interpret what one saw, and the treeless waste held no clues to size. Ground undulations were few. There were no signs of permafrost beneath. After a time a fox could be made out trekking southward some way off. Some larger tracks, not hooved, showed by the edge of a bog pool. If one wandered far from the vehicles and men, the silence was broken only by the thin sound of the wind where it combed a grass mound, the zizz and skrittle of insects, the distant yipe of fox or other hunting animal, and the secretive giggle of seeping water. Here and there on the north side of a mound or clump traces of rime showed, and a few of the pool edges were lightly frozen.

Returning to the main body, Kettass ordered the midday meal to be prepared. He thought about the situation. The wind was a trouble: it was steady and merciless and evidently below freezing point. One could bake at one's south side and freeze, literally, on one's north side. As the hour wore on, the wind increased and became, if anything, colder as the sun grew hotter. But a fringe of dark grey cloud began to climb along the southern horizon, like a ragged curtain seen from upside down, climbed and spread, until its outer streamers menaced the sun. Kettass got the party going again, and the little group of tractors trundled carefully, picking their way towards the clouds.

After two hours, 'Afpeng spotted a herd of greydeer and the party stopped. A long stalk by 'Afpeng, Laafif and Niizmek secured three carcasses which were strapped to the vehicles, and the party moved on. The clouds continued to grow and by evening covered half the sky, to the south, the icy wind from the north meanwhile growing in strength. A camp was made, using the tractors as weather walls to supplement the canvas. The deer were cured and their flesh preserved, against a time of shortage of food.

During a wakeful night the wind blew steadily on, slackening only towards dawn. The night was clear and freezing hard. In the morning the sky was cloudless and the whole plateau covered with white frost.

'What direction now, chief?' asked Mehhtumm over breakfast.

'Press on south, simply.'

In two hours the frost was gone. The beetles came out from their hiding places, the sun beat down, the ground was warm, but the wind blew fiercer than ever and as cold. Far ahead, cumulus heads rose fully formed from the horizon, and soon towering thunderclouds covered the southern sky. A screen of false cirrus spread and became a grey pall, shutting off the sun. The wind grew and turned gusty at times.

'Have you noticed the ground?' said Mehhtumm in Kettass' ear some hours later.

'The slope? Yes.' And the chief halted the convoy. It was just as though someone had tilted the world slightly. They were pointing down a gentle slope, nearly uniform, which spread east and west as far as eye could see. Behind to the north, the same slope. The change had been too gradual to notice before. Kettass had the troop deploy into a broad arrow with his vehicle in the lead and centre.

In the next two hours the tilt became more and more pronounced. Pools had become moist watercourse-beds. Kettass' altimeter showed that they were down halfway to sea-level. Yet the vegetation was hardly changed. The mosses were richer, the ground almost hot, but the icy gale hurtled at their backs as if to push them down the hillside, a hillside that stretched mile after mile to either horizon. They were shut in north and south by the tilt of the ground, now visibly a curve round which they could not see. 'Ossnaal's face was a grey–green, and Kettass wondered why one who could be so cool on a rock face should be so easily affected by this landscape. Not that 'Afpeng looked too good, and no one was happy.

'Where's it going to end, eh?' muttered Laafif.

The thundercloud had become a vast wall of dark vapour, lit by frequent flashes. An almost continuous rumbling came from the south, and their sets crackled. Kettass ordered the vehicles to run level with his own. The slope was now a clear threat to progress.

An hour later Kettass stopped the vehicles again. The slope was dangerously steep. Although it was barely noon the light was poor, under the pall of cloud which now arched over most of the sky. Plants were more lush but more isolated, so that much rock and gravel could be seen. The biting wind rushed on.

'Looks as though we'll need our climbing suckers after all,' suggested Mehhtumm. Pripand and Ghuddup were muttering together beside Vehicle 5 and looking darkly about them. 'Ossnaal's face was white and everyone looked anxious.

'If only a handy hollow or ledge would appear, then we could park the tractors,' went on Mehhtumm. Kettass said nothing. He was considering the altimeter.

'Must be *below* sea-level,' he said at last, 'yet no trees, nothing but this arctic wind, keeping vegetation down, I suppose, and no sign of a bottom.' Then: 'Immobilize here, everybody. Keep two vehicle-lengths apart. Cast out grapnels as best you can. Pull out the packs and climbing equipment, just in case. Pitch tents, but well east of the vehicle line, and choose vegetation areas: the gravel may be in the track of floods. Same thing with the stores. After all that's done, a meal.'

Before the meal was ready the gale was suddenly full of soft hail, which turned to cold rain. The afternoon was punctuated by showers of this sort. The grapnels saved two vehicles from rolling off in a shallow spate.

Kettass held a council of war. 'Seems to me,' growled Niizmek, 'there's no bottom in front of us. We could send one or two ahead to report, and camp here till we know more.'

'What do you say, 'Afpeng?'

'Strike twenty kilometres east or west, in case there's a spur or a chimney?'

''Ossnaal?'

'I think . . . I don't . . . It's a waste of time trying east or west. You can see there's nothing however far you go. It's go on or turn back.'

'You can't take the lot of us,' Laafif snapped; 'you can't get enough stores down with us, without tractors. If the ground isn't reached soon and this slope steepens, we've had it. Only two or three men can get down, and then only for a few kilometres' travel.'

Ghuddup and Pripand, mechanics, said nothing.

'I think,' now put in Mehhtumm, 'we might send a patrol party first tomorrow, to go up to half a day down, return by twilight, and report. Then you can decide, eh, chief?'

'Probably best, but I'll sleep on it,' said Kettass.

Few slept that night. The wind was moist, the ground cooled off, the thunder ceased after midnight but the storm of wind roared on. Next morning again a clear sky, apart from some tumbling clouds low down on the southern horizon (which, owing to the slope, was not very far off). It was chilly but not freezing. Kettass chose a party of three after a breakfast at first light among the long dark purple shadows cast across the tilted ground by vehicles and tents. Mehhtumm was to lead; for the other two Kettass asked for volunteers. To his surprise 'Ossnaal and Ghuddup spoke up. 'If we're not able to use the tractors I'll be at a loose end. Pripand can keep an eye on them. I like climbing, if we get any,' said Ghuddup. 'Ossnaal assured Kettass he was fit; 'I want to find out what we are really coming to.'

The trio set off almost at once; besides iron rations and water, ropes, karabiners and the newly devised suckers, they carried oxygen. 'You don't know how deep this basin is going to go, and what air you'll encounter,' Kettass pointed out.

At first they were in communication with the main party, but at about five kilometres reception grew too faint, partly from the crackling that came with the morning's cumulonimbus. Before this Mehhtumm reported that the air pressure suggested they were 2,000 metres below mean sea-level, that the slope was over $50°$ from the horizontal, that the surface was rock and sand, interspersed with unusual and highly coloured lichen, that there were numerous small torrents east and west of them, and that mist and cloud had appeared, hovering off the edge not far below. After that, silence . . . until a hysterical signal, eventually identified as Mehhtumm's, in the deep evening twilight.

Soon after they lost radio contact with the camp, Mehhtumm, 'Ossnaal and Ghuddup paused to stare at the cloud formations. Swags of dirty grey, like dust under beds, floated in the air level with their eyes and a kilometre or so south. Lightning from the formless curtain behind turned them into smoky silhouettes. The cumuloid heads above had largely vanished in the general mass of thundercloud. The tilted horizon terminated in a great roll of clear-edged cloud like a monstrous eel, which extended indefinitely east and west. The ground air, at any rate, was here free of the gale, but the rush of wind could be heard between the thunder. The atmosphere was damp and extremely warm. The rock surface was hot. What looked like dark, richly coloured polyps and sea-anemones thrust and hung obscenely here and there from crannies. The scene was picked out now and again by shafts of roasting sunlight funnelling down brassily above an occasional cauliflower top or through a chasm in the cloud-curtain. Progress even with suckers was slow. Mehhtumm got them roped together.

An hour later the slope was 70°, with a few ledges bearing thorn bushes, dwarf pines, and peculiar succulents. The torrents had become thin waterfalls, many floating outwards into spray. A scorching breeze was wafting up from below. Two parallel lines of the roller cloud now stretched above them, and the storm seemed far above that. The smooth, brittle rock would take no pitons.

A curious patternless pattern of dull pink, cloudy lemon yellow and Wedgwood blue could just be discerned through the foggy air between their feet. It conveyed nothing, and the steepening curvature of their perch had no visible relation to it. Altimeters were now impossible to interpret, but they must clearly be several kilometres below sea-level. Crawling sensations possessed their bodies, as though they had been turned to soda-water, as Ghuddup remarked, and their ears thrummed.

Mehhtumm and Ghuddup ate part of their iron rations and swallowed some water, but 'Ossnaal, whose face was a bluish pink, could only manage the water. They took occasional pulls of oxygen, without noticeably improving their sensations.

Two hours later found them clinging to a nearly vertical rock face which continued indefinitely east, west and below. The patternless pattern below their feet was the same, no nearer visibly and no clearer. The waterfalls had turned to fine tepid rain. The air behind them, so far as it could be seen (Mehhtumm used a hand mirror) was a mass of dark grey vapour, with much turbulence, through which coppery gleams of hot sunlight came rarely. The traces of sky above were very pale. The naked rock was blisteringly hot, even through sucker-gloves, but carried a curious purple and orange pattern of staining, perhaps organic. The crawling sensation had become a riot of turbulence in their flesh. Their ears were roaring. Something stabbed in their chests at intervals. Their sense of touch was disturbed and difficult. It was lucky they had suckers. Yet with all this, an enormous elation possessed Mehhtumm, an almost childish sense of adventure. 'Ossnaal was murmuring continuously to himself. Ghuddup was chuckling and apostrophizing the 'Paisley patterns' of the abyss.

Half an hour later 'Ossnaal gave a shrill cry which could be heard in the others' earphones, and went into some sort of fit. Fortunately his suckers held.

'We must get him up somehow. Can we move him foot by foot?' shouted Mehhtumm. He felt curiously carefree and regarded the crisis as an interesting abstract problem.

'I'm not going up!' snarled Ghuddup.

'You can't go down and you can't stay here. Our only chance is to try and get him up bit by bit. Maybe he'll come to or faint, and we can manage him that way.'

'I'm not losing our only chance of seeing what's below,' snarled Ghuddup again. 'The hell with 'Ossnaal, and the hell with you too. You're yellow, that's what you are, a yellow skunk, a yellow Paisley skunk!'

Mehhtumm, in a dream, saw Ghuddup, who occupied a central position, saw quickly with a knife through the ropes on his either side. The long ends flailed down. 'Ossnaal's twitching body hung from three suckers of his four. Ghuddup spidered nimbly down and was soon virtually out of sight, but his muttered obscenities could be heard in Mehhtumm's radio. Mehhtumm tried to collect his thoughts, still dreamlike. Finally he arrived at the conclusion that he must go for help, as he could certainly not manoeuvre the sick man by himself, and together they would probably perish uselessly. He pushed 'Ossnaal's left hand hard against the rock to fasten the sucker, tested the other three and shifted one. There was nothing to belay to. Extracting a luminous-dye marker from a pocket, he splashed the dye vividly over 'Ossnaal's suit and around him. He waited close to 'Ossnaal for two minutes, trying to rouse him by shouting his name. Finally the man quietened, and muttered something in response to Mehhtumm's shouts of 'Hang on; don't move!'

Mehhtumm began clambering upward, marking the rocks with the dye-splasher. Half a minute afterwards a sound and a movement beneath caught his attention, and he looked down in time to see the body of 'Ossnaal plummeting into the abyss. An invisible Ghuddup was still muttering in Mehhtumm's radio, and it was half an hour before his voice faded.

The rest of the upward journey was a nightmare, and took Mehhtumm far longer than he expected. After about three hours his head began to clear as his body reverted to normal, and the full realization of what had happened came to him. The first terrible doubts of his own action flooded in. There was nothing to be done now but to make as good speed as he could to the camp.

He had been calling for an hour before he was heard on their radios. Kettass sent Laafif and 'Afpeng to collect him. They managed to rendezvous by radio, and brought him back, weeping like a child, in darkness.

'Sounds like some sort of gas narcosis to me,' Kettass said later to a recovered Mehhtumm.

'Yes, could even be nitrogen narcosis; except for 'Ossnaal. There could have been something else wrong with him – would you think?'

'I should never have let him go. He looked peculiar for some time . . . We shall have to write off Ghuddup as well, poor fellow, if we can't trace him in the morning.'

Next day in the early sunlight Mehhtumm, Laafif and Kettass went down unroped and marked with dye. The oxygen apparatus of each was adjusted to give them a continuous supply as a high percentage of their inspiration total. They followed Mehhtumm's markings. It was agreed that the first man to notice any specially alarming symptoms, or to have any detected by the others, was to climb up at once, but that till then they would keep close together, and that the remaining two must come up together as soon as either began to succumb. What happened was that Laafif, becoming confused despite the oxygen about 100 metres above the fatal spot, started to ascend. Mehhtumm passed the spot and, despite a persistent impression that he had become a waterfall, silently climbed on down, passing Kettass rapidly. He was 400 metres below, muttering to himself and glaring about him, when he and Kettass heard something between a sob and a laugh in their radios, and Laafif's body passed them, a few feet out, turning over and over. It became a speck above the carpet of coiling vapour which had replaced yesterday's colour pattern. The cries were still sounding in their radios minutes later when reception faded.

Kettass, dimly retaining a hold on sanity, eventually persuaded Mehhtumm to return, convincing himself and the other through a swirl of sensations that it would be no use searching for yesterday's madman over several thousand vertical metres of rock. Mehhtumm said later that at that depth he had kept on seeing little images of Ghuddup, brandishing a yellow knife, hovering around him.

They got back in the late afternoon, and next day a silent expedition set off for home, one man per vehicle.

It took five years for authority to build two suitable VTOL craft capable of flying and taking off efficiently in both normal and high-pressure air, and fully pressurized within. Mehhtumm was dead, killed in a climbing accident on Mogharitse, but Kettass secured a passage as film-taker and world radio-commentator on one craft, and Niizmek on the other. The broadcasts were relayed from a ground station set up on the plateau, which picked them up, or rather down, from the ionized reflecting layer of the atmosphere, since the basin depth would cut off direct craft-to-layer-to-receiver broadcasting; even so, only about a quarter of the material came through.

The two craft landed in summer on the plateau near the 15° slant zone. Flight between about 11 a.m. and midnight was considered meteorologically impossible owing to the severe up-currents and the electrical disturbances. They took off at 7 a.m. just before dawn, using powerful searchlights. Kettass' craft, piloted by an impassive veteran of thirty named Levaan, was to sink down past the rock wall near the original descent. The other craft sped west looking for a change in the geography. The two were in continuous communication through the pilots' radios (on a different wavelength).

Levaan tried his radar on the invisible floor of the basin. 'You won't believe this – we have forty-three kilometres beneath us.'

Kettass was speechless.

'There's a secondary echo at thirty-seven km or so – could be the cloud layer below. Let me try the lidar.' He aimed the unwieldy laser gun downwards. 'Yes, that'll be the cloud layer all right. And that blip over there, that's the roller cloud, or rather an incipient roll – I don't think there's anything visible to the eye.'

'The – the ground echo: what does that make it in depth?'

'Given our altitude above MSL that makes the basin floor over forty-one km below sea, and nearly forty-two beneath the bevel of the plateau.'

They began to descend. All trace of the event of five years ago was lost. The craft sank nine or ten kilometres, as indicated through the vertical radar. Kettass informed the world that the tinted rock was continuing and took a few film sequences. The sun poured across over the impossible vertical face. At fifteen kilometres down the colours had broken up into isolated dots and patches. The empty parts of the sky had turned a milky white and now began to change to brazen yellow. There was still no visible sign of a bottom, none of the patternless pattern described by Mehhtumm, but the fog below was brilliant in sunlight, yellow sunlight. Even in the air-conditioned cabin it was exceptionally hot wherever the sun struck.

'Perspective makes the wall appear to curve in above us and below us,' Kettass was saying to his microphone. The view was indeed rather like that seen by a midge dancing a few inches in front of a wall made of barrel staves curving towards him, except that the midge would have been no thicker than a fine hair. The sky met the cliff line dizzyingly far overhead. No less than three parallel lines of black roller-cloud (very slender) were now silhouetted against the yellow sky, while a fourth roll was indicated by an Indian file of fishlike silhouettes along-side them. Not very far beyond hung the shaggy charcoal bases of the first cumuloids, behind which the brassy sun beat down. Black ghosts of the clouds grew and gestured, many kilometres high, on the cliff wall. At times Kettass had the illusion that the craft was flying banked sideways, and that the cliff wall was the horizontal floor of the world.

Descent began to be very bumpy. The other craft reported no change at fifty kilometres west. At thirty-six km down the open sky was now a blood-orange hue. The fog, which had become exceedingly turbulent, was close below, and after cautious exploration Levaan found a hole through which pink, green and indigo masses could be dimly seen, crawling in the quivering air currents. At thirty-eight km down, battling against strong updraughts, they sighted far below a vast vista of dully red-hot lava, cold greenish lava, and what looked like violet mud, in apparently kilometres-wide slabs and pools, lapping right up against the thirty-to-forty-km-high vertical wall on one side, and ending in pitch darkness many kilometres southward. Occasional flashes of forked lightning played near the cliff base. Besides the distortions of the air currents, the whole floor was in slow motion, spreading, rocking, welling, bubbling.

Levaan broke in on Kettass' commentary to say he dared not stay longer, as the updraughts were becoming too violent and the fabric was groaning. The other craft had just sighted the end of the basin and wished to make its own commentary. Risking a breakup in the turbulence near the roller cloud level, Levaan's craft rose to pass it, and swung back to rendezvous. Niizmek and his pilot Fehos had sighted a step-like formation closing in the western end.

Next morning the two craft switched roles. Fehos and Niizmek descended into the pit, some way out from the wall, while Levaan's craft flew east to find how the basin ended on that side. But Fehos' transpex imploded at thirty-nine km down with a crack heard on the radios of the world, and the craft, a squashed insect, plunged into the magma. After that Levaan would not fly his craft below twenty-five kilometres.

They established that the cliff line stretched 163 km east to west, or rather slightly north of east to slightly south of west, and that the western end, later known as the Terraces, consisted of a series of nearly vertical cliffs of from 2,000 metres to 3,000 metres high each, separated by sloping shelves and screes several km across. The eastern end, the Staircase or Jacob's Ladder, proved to be a rather similar formation like a file or grid whose ridges or bars were 500-metre-high 30°-lean overhangs (over the basin) of hard rock, alternating with boulder-and-gravel-filled hollows of soft rock, the whole system being tilted down southwards at an angle of 35°. The southern edge was a vertical wall like the northern, nearly parallel to it, but peak-bordered, higher by several thousand metres, 146 km long, and some 200 km away. After a few months press and radio exhausted their superlatives and wisecracks ('Nature's Mohole' was the type) and took up Slingo, a new parachute waltzing craze sweeping the world.

Thirty years later Kettass, a hale septuagenarian, was taken down the Terraces' pressurized cable railway by his son-in-law, daughter and three grandchildren, and, looking through the triple transpex wall, gazed in silence upon the oozing magma from 700 metres' range. He did not live to travel the tourist rocket route built five deaths and eighty-three strikes later down Jacob's Ladder, but two of his granddaughters took their families down the North Wall lift. That was the year Lebhass and Tollhirn made their fatal glider attempt. By this time, three other deaths and 456 strikes later, heat mills, for the most part automatically controlled and inspected, were converting a considerable fraction of the thermal energy in the basin to supply two continents with light, heat and power. A quarter of the northern plateau was given over to their plant, another quarter contained a sanatorium and reserve for hardy tourists, and the other half was a game reserve and ecological study area, but the jagged mountains of the south, scoured by their own murderous southerly winds, resisted general exploitation.

Lost Ground

'Eat up your bacon now, May,' said Miriel. 'Daddy's ready to run you up – don't keep him waiting.' May, humming irrepressibly to herself, picked up her fork and began toying with the crisp fragments. 'May!' said Miriel sharply again. The ten-year-old's brown curls tossed, but she fell to. Philip, his dark eyes scanning the faces of his mother and sister with the air of an anxious dog, spooned in his porridge. He was only in his third year. Roydon, shifting about a little in his chair, was hidden behind the paper, uneasily aware of its sour biscuity odour in the sun. STRIKE DUE TO LAST BITTER SPELL? read one of the headlines. LATE RAGE-STORMS STALL OHIO said another. Roydon frowned, inserted a tiny earphone into one ear and switched on the minitape recorder which he had set to the last forecast.

'A system of depressions and associated troughs will follow one another in quick succession over Scotland and the north,' it said. 'Insecure, rather sad feeling today and tomorrow, followed by short-lived griefs, some heavy, some stormy, with cheerful intervals. By midweek the griefs will be dying out, rather sooner in the south. Drives weak to moderate, veering creative to instinctive. Temperament chillier than normal for the rest of the week, but serene; however, some early-morning fear in the latter half of the week is expected to form in low-lying areas, dispersing slowly each day.'

Roydon snapped off the recorder and removed his earphone. 'Better give May a slow pep-pill before she goes. The forecast's a bit gloomy; I shouldn't be surprised if there were griefs on and off this afternoon too.'

'OK. Here you are, May; swallow that with your tea,' said Miriel. 'And you might as well have one yourself, darling. I can give Phil a quick quarter-dose if he goes out to play.'

'Oh *need* I, Mummy?' from May. 'The school's OK, and they always pass the stuff round at break.'

'Yes, May – I think Miss Weatherbridge is a bit careless about these things; she has a lot of other things to think about, after all.'

'Oh, all right!'

Roydon dumped a singing May from his little city-car, the green one. The pep-pill was already lifting his spirits, protected as they were by the car-aerosol. He had to check himself from chanting rowdily and dodging about in the workwards traffic. 'I should have waited till lunchtime and had a quick one,' he thought. 'Miriel coddles me – and I take it from her.' The vision of her brown oval face old-fashionedly curtained in the straight fall of soft dark hair hovered between him and the traffic for an instant. After eleven years it was still a mystery and an enchantment to him. He opened the draught and let the sadness seep in for a little. A few of the schoolchildren waiting to cross at the next school were in tears. 'Feckless parents,' he thought. They would be all right after a minute in the air-conditioned school.

In the studio office all was bustle and confusion. Panset, the chief, was in and out constantly. Mood-weather bothered him comparatively little, except that in periods of unusually warm temperament he usually had to take a tranquillizer outside. The pep aerosols were functioning nicely all over the building. The night's programme of current affairs was beginning to take shape, but must rest in a half-cooked state till late that afternoon, when Roydon would leave it in the hands and mouths of the studio people. He rang up Miriel at lunchtime to say he might be later than usual, the way things were running.

'Are you coming out for lunch, Vic?' he called to his mate

across the table, fixing him unconsciously with a characterist-ically searching gaze under his thick brows. 'I'm getting sick of the canteen stuff.'

'Better pep yourself up again, then, Royo, there's a nasty grief outside,' said Ken Mattock, coming in breathing deeply and erratically through pinched nostrils.

'Oh, the corner place will do us. That's not far, we'll survive it, eh, Vic?'

'I'll take a quick booster first if you don't mind. I'm a bit low this morning,' said Vic, helping himself from his pharmapouch. 'Right – that'll fix me. I'm ready now.'

That night, a rather disturbed May eventually persuaded to bed, Miriel broached the subject of school precautions again. 'You know,' she said, 'I don't care for the way they hand out their peps and tranqs – much too rough and ready. I delivered May after lunch in the red city-car: she was quite upset coming in. I had a word with the head. I'm going to keep her carefully drugged up and the school will have her for lunch in future. That means she won't be so easily exposed.'

'You coddle her too much,' said Roydon.

'No, Roy, I can't have her education going to pieces because of all these ups and downs. It may be all right for some parents, but not for us. We have her future to think of.'

Roydon gave way. He sighed for the Golden Ages of his parents' memory, when the world's atmosphere had nothing worse than true weather and a little fallout for men to contend with. A feature item on the chaos in Africa and India, scarcely mitigated by pharmacological aid, underlined his thoughts. The Indians and Africans were trying to ride out griefs by hectic dance-sessions on the lines of the old Mediterranean tarantella remedy, and angers and fears by great choral chants, but these folk remedies were naturally very chancy. Only the most advanced nations had been able to meet the new emo-tional influences in the air with air-conditioning and with drugs subtle enough to act quick enough or slow enough and without seriously affecting judgement or the body's reactions. His own

World-Day programme came through and he watched it dutifully and critically. It was followed by a *Men of Science* interview with a microdiathesiologist.

'You see,' explained the pundit, 'the mood-climate differs not only from country to country, but from place to place, from street to roof, from valley to slope, and often in quite spectacular ways. Take the corner of a high building or the top of a cliff. This sort of site is subject to great turbulence. While the general mood-weather round it may be gloomy one day or one hour and optimistic the next, the mood at the acron, as we call it, is often switching minute by minute from despair to ecstasy and back again. Hence the semi-mystical nature-loving joy one moment and the suicide leap the next.'

'But such violent changes are not met with in other places, are they?'

'Not commonly. Indeed the micro-sentiment at many spots is more stable than that of the general mood-weather at man-height. The surface of marshes is nearly always depressed and fearful. Those of a park or a well-kept garden are warm, friendly, serene. And of course there is a third class of micro-diathesis which varies on a twenty-four-hour cycle. A wood or a lake at noon is usually gay and serene, at midnight amorous in moonlight but hostile and intensely fearful in darkness. The nature of the cycle in this case depends on the illumination.'

Roydon, yawning ostentatiously, switched the set off at this point. Details of this sort were rather beyond him, his yawn implied. But his heartbeat was accelerating. Programmes like this one he found disquieting. The world was dangerous enough without these local effects. He preferred not to know. The shelter of Miriel's arms and hair blotted out the world and its perils.

Three years later it happened. Roydon, now in the studio team of *World-Day*, and normally working from 3 to 11 p.m., was rung at the studio one March afternoon at five.

'I thought I told you not to ring me at night – it's far too hectic here!'

'Roy, Roy, it's Phil! He – he –'

'He had an accident!' shouted Roydon. He recalled that Phil was usually brought home by some rather older children from infant school. Sobbing, Miriel told him that Phil and his friends had run into an unexpected pocket of terror in a dip in the road coming home. They had scattered, Phil darting insanely across the road, it seemed, and straight under a car. It was all over in a moment.

After the funeral, which ironically took place on a gay, serene morning, Miriel, who had kept herself on a tight rein, seemed to go to pieces. She refused all drugs, scarcely roused on the most cheerful of days, and gave herself up to a sort of resentfulness of sorrow. Roydon's parents, who had stayed on for some days, took May under their roof not far off; and for the rest of term were to fetch her to school and back. Roydon managed to secure leave and took Miriel west to a wild part of the country neither of them had seen before, which she could not associate with Philip. They left the two city-cars behind and hired a runabout. Gradually she began to pick up, but there was a ghostly something about her look, an air of looking through or past Roydon, which worried him. It was a fine spring and the mood-weather was optimistic, with only the occasional grief. Roydon let the griefs wash over Miriel when they were out walking, and sometimes over himself, as he felt they would help to purge the emotional load.

The first Sunday they went to church. The rather meagre congregation huddled in the cool Early English interior. The sermon was uninspiring. But there was a soothing quality about the grey–green gloom and the thin arches. The motor of the tranquillizer-cordial hummed gently in the silences. Afterwards Roydon was rather sorry they had gone, for they were strolling through the churchyard when Miriel stopped with a shudder. The funeral was too recent. Drunken gravestones, their inscriptions worn to rivers in the soft local stone, leant around them. But she had stopped at a very tall and broad headstone.

'Look,' she said uncertainly. 'Roy, you could have had an ancestor here.'

'Well, could be, certainly ends with "Back", and it certainly has an R as second letter, and the length looks right. Can't make out the forename, can you?'

'No, I don't think I can. And what a long inscription.'

'From the few words I can make out, it was one of those paragons of all the virtues. Local bigwig, I expect. They used to make them out to be saints on their tombstones in those days; whereas they probably fathered half the brats in the parish really, and twisted their tenants. I must have a look at the parish register some time, just in case he really had the same name. Still, it's not absolutely unique as a name.'

'What is all this about the Snevley Fields?' said the big man at the bar.

Roydon turned half round from his half-pint. Miriel was upstairs. The big man, who looked like a landowner or businessman, was talking to a squat little fellow who might be a farmer or a lawyer.

'What do you want to know about the Snevley Fields?'

'Something queer is going on there – what is it?'

'Something decidedly queer is certainly going on there,' said the squat man, who, like the big man, had a whisky in front of him. Roydon cocked his *World-Day*-educated ear. 'It seems that all Morris's cattle have disappeared there. So has Midgley's dog. Midgley was walking the Carruthers side and his dog went after rabbits. That was a week ago and no one has seen the dog since.'

'But it's perfectly open country, no badger holes or fox holes either.'

'Exactly. And no cow holes! . . . Midgley's a bit scared to go in himself. As for Morris, he thinks the place is bewitched.

Talks about fairies and I don't know what. Won't stir near there. A bit superstitious, old Morris is.'

'Was it in daylight?'

'We don't know about Morris's cattle. But Midgley's dog went early one afternoon.'

'Any clues?'

'No! Only thing is, the Snevley Fields seem to have been re-hedged by someone. The old hawthorn's given way to hazel, Morris says. He looked through binoculars. Says it goes beyond the brook too.'

'Snevley's is let, isn't it?'

'Yes – to someone from Scrutton. But they haven't been there for weeks.'

'You talking about them Snevley Fields?' put in a long man in an overcoat, drinking stout on the far side.

'Yes, and Harry says it goes on beyond the brook.'

'Too true; and another thing,' said the long man: 'you know that brook runs straight down a fair way between them two hedges? Someone digged it that way long since.' The other two nodded assent. So did three other listeners. 'Well now it don't. It runs all squiggly-squaggly. And them hedges – they've gone!'

There was a heavy silence. 'I know another man as lost a dog thereabouts,' called a dark man in a corner. Silence. Heads turned. ''Twere Ted. His bitch were round Parker's Knoll, a week come Friday 'twere. She were chasing rabbits too. Ted says he had his eye on her, and she just vanished.'

'How d'you mean, vanished?' put in the big man.

'Vanished in full view, right in the middle of the next field. Here, Fred, turn up the aero-whatsit. That crossness is seeping in again – I can feel me hackles rising.'

''Tis the whisky in you, Bill,' called the squat man amid general laughter, but the landlord picked up an aerosol hand-sprayer and pumped the cordial-tranquillizer over the room.

'Well, as I were saying. She vanished in full view. One moment she were there, going hell for leather in the middle of

184

a field. Next moment – she weren't there. Never came back no more.'

'That's a hell of a lot of land that is. From Snevley's to Parker's Knoll.'

'And from Goff's Brook to t'other side of Snevley, I shouldn't wonder,' came from a small man who had not yet spoken.

Roydon, who was used to interviewing, or failing to interview, rural types, held his peace, but after a moment or two found occasion to ask the barman the name of the long man and the squat man, and still later buttonholed the landlord and got from him their addresses (they turned out to be the village grocer and the local garage man) and the approximate location of Goff's Brook, Snevley's and Parker's Knoll. He represented himself as an amateur landscape painter with some ideas about later fishing.

Next morning, with a strong instinctive drive prevalent and a cordial temperament abroad, Roydon took Miriel out on foot looking for the mystery area. The forecast was fairly optimistic and he thought it would be good for her to tramp around with him while he tried to work up what promised to be something of a news story. In two hours they were in sight of the farmhouse known as Snevley's. Beyond it down a slight slope were the Snevley Fields, a set of meadows already powdered with buttercups. The pair paused. 'Let's work round this field and up to that copse. We might get a better view of that break in the hedges they were talking about.'

When they reached a field corner next to the copse, where a distinct drop in the emotional temperature could be felt, Roydon took some photographs. The chilliness was becoming palpable hostility, and his wife was unprotected by drugs. 'You stick it out here, Miriel. I'll walk uphill and see what can be seen from that tree.' Roydon strode off. A brusquely suspicious mood dominated the summit. Reaching the tree at the top he turned. Miriel was not to be seen.

Roydon, shouting her name at the top of his voice, glared

round an arc of countryside. Away down a narrow meadow between two hedges he thought he saw a flickering speck running, running very hard. An instant later it was swallowed up, in the line of the nearer hedge. Perhaps it was a rook in the air between. Moving cloud-shadows confused the view. After a minute of calling, Roydon ran back down the long slope and at length arrived, gasping and dizzy, his knees aching, at the spot where he had left her. There were some snapped twigs, and after staring around he thought he could see the imprint of her shoes in the earth not far off, pointing homeward. But beyond this on all sides tall wiry grasses swallowed up everything. The feeling of hostility grew, mingled with acute fear. The wind hissed among the twigs and grasses. 'Bitch, bitch!' Roydon found himself muttering. He forced himself to swallow a pill, but found minutes later that it must have been a slow-acting one he had chosen. Hoarse with shouting and cursing, he began to stumble back the way they had come, convinced that she had started home. As he approached Snevley's a squall of rage and grief burst upon him. Sobbing and swearing, tears coursing down his cheeks, he ran round the yard and burst in through the open doorway. No one was at home. He rushed through the rooms without finding anyone or any trace, tried all the cupboards, and finally ran out again and on to the village. At last, in a state of maudlin warmth now that the pill had taken effect in more cordial surroundings, he stumbled into the inn. Miriel was not in their room. No one had seen her. Someone brought him to the police station, in whose tranquillized air he told his story.

'That settles it,' said the sergeant. 'I'm ringing HQ. These disappearances are beyond us.'

Roydon found himself at the receiving end of the interviewing on that evening's *World-Day*. Ken had shot up from London by jet to see him personally. By next day the CID and half the newshawks of the west of the country were in the district. No one dare enter the 'Forbidden Zone' and a cordon was to be thrown up by the army. During the week a helicopter and a set of tracker-dogs on the end of microphoned long lines were brought up.

The tracker-dogs found nothing, but two disappeared, their lines neatly cut. The helicopter only discovered fields empty of all but birds; but two locals (Midgley and the squat man) who were persuaded to go up in it, averred that (so far as they could tell since they had never flown before) the country had changed quite a lot. The area was closed off now with rolls of barbed wire, military posts established round it, and a desultory watch was kept up, with an occasional searchlight at night. 'I'd sooner run straight acrost a bleedin' minefield 'n gow in theer,' Roydon heard one soldier say to another.

'Reckon it is a minefield – only the other sort. I reckon it's holes in it, bloody great pits, all camouflaged up,' said the other.

Roydon flew up to London. He meant to resign. The city seemed to him meaningless, like an undubbed film in a foreign language. Its noise and bustle seemed to be all on the other side of an invisible barrier.

'Look here, Royo,' said Vic, taking him aside near the studio. 'A team of investigators is going up there; why not join them as a reporter? Panset'll recommend you, he says.'

'Who are they?'

'Scientists of some sort. You know they got some anomalies with their lidar probe when Ken was there – or perhaps you don't? Some of them think there's something odd about the spacetime geometry of the region. That's the line they're working on now.'

May was adopted by her aunt and uncle. Roydon was attached to the group of scientists, shut up the house, and returned to that accursèd green countryside to which he was now bound, as with the thongs of a rack, by ties of fear, hatred, memory and love. He came gradually to follow, in a hazy way, the investigators' reasoning and the drift of their experiments with masers and charged particles. So it was that six months later Roydon himself, carrying out a prepared 'interview' of the group's spokesman on TV, gave the public its first picture of what was happening.

'A set of anachronistic cells or domains has come into being on the landscape, covering a wide area. Each cell has reverted to an earlier point in time – we are not at present sure exactly what point – and its neighbour cells have similarly reverted, but apparently with no discernible pattern. We have a patchwork quilt of time-levels.'

'How far back are these time-levels from ours?'

'We don't know. Some may be only a few seconds or even microseconds. Others may be a few weeks, years, even centuries. Some are certainly many years back. The change in visible landmarks fits that, according to early tithe maps.'

'But if we can see the country, how is it we can't see the persons and animals that have disappeared?'

'We think they have moved out of the area, but in the time of the cell in which they found themselves.'

'Does the first cell you meet fix your time-level, then?'

'We don't know. It may – or it may not.'

One day Roydon, allowed past the army posts as one of the team, slipped quietly away towards the spot where he had last seen his wife. He was certain now that she had run off further into the area and believed he might have caught a glimpse of her running and not of some bird flying. But the landscape was confusing, was difficult to identify. Where he thought to have found the field corner below the hill there seemed to be a long stone dyke with stone steps jutting out of it, and a fence to one side. He climbed over the dyke, keeping bent low in case he was spotted from outside. He was determined to follow Miriel and search, if need be for years, in this past world. The atmosphere was serene, with a slight intellectual drive in it. He combed the copse, returned, walked along the fence, slithered down some rocks which he never remembered seeing before, ran into a richly cordial atmosphere, skirted a round dewpond, and past a gnarled old thorn came face to face with a stinking old man in tatters, who touched his forehead and sank on one knee.

'Where do you come from?'

Roydon had to repeat this three times before the man answered: 'Scrootton, ant plaze thee, serr.'

'Have you even see a young woman in strange dress in these parts?'

'?'

'Have – you – seen – a young – woman – near here – ever – wearing – strange – dress?'

Roydon had to repeat this once more, then: 'Noo, serr, hant nivver seen noo witch, serr!' and the creature took to his heels. As Roydon stared after him he vanished in mid-stride. Much shaken, Roydon walked slowly onward, stumbled over some gravel, was pushing through some lush undergrowth, and found himself on a sheep track among tussocks of grass. A grotesque sight met his eyes a few yards further on down the track. A thin man in a sort of sacking hood, ragged hose like ill-fitting tights and bare feet, was perched on a short ladder leaning crazily in towards the track. The ladder was leaning on nothing, and indeed its poles ended at their tops in a curious vertical chopped cut, which kept changing its pattern, yet this ladder stood still and only rocked slightly with the man's movements. It was some time before Roydon realized that the changing texture at the tops of the poles coincided with their growing slightly shorter or longer as they rocked. The man kept descending and coming up again with bundles of what looked to Roydon (who had seen a museum of antiquities) like thatch-ing straw, and thrusting them above the ladder, where, to-gether with his hands, they disappeared. His handless arms, each obscenely terminated by a fluctuating blue–white and crimson cross-section, would ply about for a time, then the hands would reappear, but not the bundles. A great heap of these bundles lay on the ground. The place was thick with flies and gnats. The ladder-man was humming an endless, eerie, plaintive chant. Behind him was the rim of a forest clearing.

Two lean dogs like lurchers, but with longish pointed ears, were slinking about near it. The trees of the forest seemed to be chopped short at about ten feet up. The ladder-man and his dogs were all totally oblivious of Roydon's shouting and gesticulating. Something, however, held Roydon back from passing under or beyond the ladder. Perhaps it was that only ten feet on the far side of the man the forest clearing swung in abruptly to march right up to the sheep track. This part of the beheaded forest, moreover, was frost-laden, from the boughs to the ground, and devoid of undergrowth, and a light snow shower was scudding down from nowhere. Through this wintry woodscape, lit by a ruddy glow from the east, a pack of huge savage hounds presently broke, baying fiercely, and plunged obliquely towards the still oblivious ladder-man and his dogs. Instead of overwhelming them the pack vanished one by one in the still air of the clearing, and the silence returned piecemeal hound by hound.

A last hound, a straggler, was still bounding up, when the man called out, as if to someone well beyond Roydon's shoulder: 'Pest taak they, Will, maak hast, 'tis aal boott nohn!' He paused, apparently listening, then broke into a snort of laughter and resumed his whistling and humming.

An obscure trumpeting, mingled with cries, broke out deep in the frosty wood; crackling branches and rhythmical thuds intervened.

Seized with a kind of panic, Roydon turned down the track, thrust through a dark thicket, and found himself without warning in the middle of a curious wide tunnel or cave apparently made of blackish glass, and dimly lit from nowhere in particular. There was a marked cheerfulness and a strong organizing drive in the air. Coming out into the daylight he saw a wide flat level strip, like the track of a gigantic snail a hundred yards across, made of the same material, stretching out from his feet. On its edges a number of glassy boxes and tubes, on spring legs or spikes, were standing, some winking and clicking busily. The strip looked rather as if it had been sprayed on.

'What kind of a past era is this?' he thought. Beyond the strip were banks of rich shrubs powdered with exotic butterflies. The growl of a helicopter came from the west, and Roydon took cover beneath a shrub, disturbing the butterflies somewhat. When the helicopter appeared it had an unfamiliar look, and most of it was formed of greenish and blackish glassy material. After it had gone Roydon walked on above the shrubs. Then he took cover beneath the shrub, disturbing the butterflies, hearing the machine. When it had gone he began to walk on. Then he took cover under the butterfly-laden shrub, keeping the helicopter under observation. When it had departed he walked on, shaking his head uncertainly. There was something he could not quite remember. A déjà vu sensation. Odd. He recalled the tunnel and the strip. What an odd strip! What kind of past age could this be? And what peculiar gadgets these are down its edges. Why do they click and blink like that? . . . He found himself walking about the shrubs, feeling unaccountably odd and dazed. Then he saw Parker's Knoll or what should have been Parker's Knoll, miles ahead. It was topped by a device like a glass water-tower. The entire landscape between seemed to be dotted with tallish block buildings of greenish opaque glass, with banks of shrubs between. Men, women and children, in closely clinging clothing with a dull whitish lustre, were moving about. The sound of their voices came to him. The sky was pullulating with aircraft like a swarm of insects, and droned and screamed with them, but the voices could be heard quite clearly nevertheless. Only the strip and its neighbourhood seemed deserted. Then he saw a sort of Parker's Knoll, but decorated with a glassy tower, and the people in their clinging clothes, and the aircraft overhead. He shook his head to clear it, and saw Parker's Knoll, topped with a tower, and the population, and the crowded skies, and heard the noises. Roydon sat down, and in between the first bending of his knees and being seated had a visionary flash of millions upon millions of – what? Of the same event, which he instantly forgot. He sat down and tried to collect his thoughts. Could it be that he was somewhere in the future, not the past? Could the helicopter have come out of the world of that future? The machine came back and for the second time (was it the second time?) Roydon took cover, but he was astonished to hear a loudhailer of sorts address him:

'We can detect you under that growth. Who are you? Can we help you? . . . Who are you? Are you Roydon Greenback? Please come out from under. Please come out from under. We would like to help you.' There was something peculiarly vulgar and sprawling about the accents of the speaker, and his vowels were difficult to recognize.

Roydon clambered out and waved. After a moment he called out, 'Yes, I am Roydon Greenback. Who are you? Where am I?'

The helicopter descended some way and a rope ladder was lowered. 'Please climb in.'

'I am looking for my wife.'

'We don't know where she is, but perhaps we can help you. Will you come with us first?'

Silently, Roydon climbed up the ladder, which was at once extraordinarily smooth and very easy to hold on to. As he went up there was a sort of blink, and looking down by the helicopter hatch he was astonished to see that the landscape was once more deserted and green, indeed rather lush, except that the glassy strip and a few of the shrub-banks up to a little past where he had sat down were still there below him. A big gloved hand hauled him in.

'Roydon Greenback. Well. You are something of a legend to us, the man who entered the poikilochronistic jungle to search for the woman he loved. Well, well. As luck would have it, you got into a domain that started at plus-sixty-one years and has been running a cog-slipper static ever since. So you levelled up with our time. You are sixty-one years behind us in source. We shall take you to our world of sixty-one years ahead.'

The voice was no longer sprawling, but the same slipshod quality seemed to slur its vowels, and what with this and the unfamiliar vocabulary Roydon could hardly comprehend two words in three. He looked at its owner, a tall red-headed man of middle age with shaggy locks and a long beard. His clothes, like those of his companions, seemed to consist of a translucent skin-diving suit with pockets, but without mask or oxygen, and, encasing the hands and upper arms, long translucent gloves. There were half a dozen persons in the cabin, two of them women.

'I am Paul Sattern, chronismologist in chief. This is Fenn Vaughan, chronismologist-maturator; Mary Scarrick, ento-mologist; Richard Metcalfe, chronistic metrologist; Elizabeth Raine, air chemist; Morris Ekwall, transitional diathesiologist; Zen Haddock, botanist, who also takes soil samples for the podologists; and at the controls, Peter Datch.'

The correct response to an introduction seemed to be a nod. It appeared that Morris Ekwall was concerned, in some esoteric way, with the violent local changes in mood-weather that accompanied the area's time-shifts, while Richard Met-calfe spent most of his time dumping gadgets on the terrain and reading their messages on instruments in the helicopter. What Vaughan and Sattern actually did Roydon never discovered, but the others were concerned with the insects, plants, soil and atmosphere itself. At intervals one or more of them would go down the ladder and come up again rather swiftly.

'Teams of chronismologists,' Sattern told Roydon, 'are engaged in mapping the poikilochronism and its changes; the domains are constantly altering.'

'How do you mean? Do they change their time-level?'

'Usually a domain divides into several quite independent domains, especially if it's a big one; or a whole set of bounds and domains is replaced by new unrelated ones, in one part of the poik. There's not always much visible sign – you have to instrumentate to discern.'

'And Richard here,' said Vaughan, 'is trying just now to

catch them at it. He thinks they don't just go click, they go whoosh – eh Richard?' and he sang, softly:

> 'Micro, nano, pico, femto,
>> it's all the same to metro Met;
> No matter what he pegs down there,
>> he hasn't snapped them switching yet.'

Richard looked pained.

'Are we free of it now?' asked Roydon.

'Free?' said Sattern. 'You mean, beyond the poik? No. It's much bigger than in your day. It's growing about three hectares a year now. Swallowed many square kilometres of our normal-density regions in the last ten years – but slowly. We had to reallocate the population. Devil of a lot of economic and social problems. Lost some strays, too – like you.'

Sattern broke off and gave a terse account of their discovery of Roydon into a microphone.

Roydon, looking over the side some minutes later, saw the hated green, already peppered with odd glassy lumps and bumps, cease abruptly. Beyond was a tangle of curved highways crawling with moving specks. Helicopters seemed now to jostle them on all sides, and above them a dense crowd of swift jetcraft littered the sky. Soon an endless forest of multi-storeyed buildings, glassy in texture, gawky oblongs, jetting into the air, thrust all round them and in every direction. Here and there great banks of flowers or butterfly-powdered shrubs glowed at the buildings' feet, but much of the ground was a close-cropped grey–green herbage. The helicopter dropped onto a squat cube of a building, and Roydon was escorted down into the Chronismatic Centre.

Here he found a small quiet crowd gathered, all clothed like the helicopter party. One wall of the huge room converted itself silently into a coloured vision screen, and for the next hour he was subjected to a merciless interview from the reporters in that screen, with their unfamiliar flat accents and phraseology. After that a series of interchanges took place between the helicopter party, some of the crowd and the screen reporters, who seemed to be in London, with occasional shunts to New York, Moscow and Beijing. The exchanges were largely lost on Roydon, whose nerves seemed to be dancing a jig all over his body. A girl with darkish red hair and green eyes, whom he took for Sattern's secretary, led him off for a meal and a sleeping potion.

He woke on a couch and the purgatory began again. Housed in the building, occasionally treated to visitape recordings of his interview, interviewed anew by scientists and reporters, invited to appear in feature programmes, put through tests of blood-pressure, skin-potential, electro-encephalogram, blood-fluid makeup, olfactronic signature and many others, he collapsed at the end of a week and was kept under deep narcosis for ten days.

He came to to find the red-haired girl, whose name was Sal, contemplating him. 'Someone is asking to see you,' she said. 'Prepare yourself for a shock.' She looked serious.

'Who is it? Are they here?'

'No, of course not. On the screen. It's someone from your family. Think now – who could be alive after sixty-one years?'

'It's not – it's not May?'

'It's your daughter. She was called May. Now remember, she has lived all her life in ordinary time. How old was she when you last saw her?'

Even so, Roydon could not believe for a long time that the rather bowed though well-preserved old lady in grey slacks and tunic could be his own daughter. He was unspeakably embarrassed when after a minute of awkward speech a slow tear or two rolled down the face on the screen. 'You are just like your photo,' she whispered brokenly, then broke down completely and sobbed. 'You never came back – you never came back!'

Gradually he pieced out her history. Brought up for the rest of her growing years with her uncle's children, she had adjusted to the situation but had always mourned her parents, especially

Roydon. An unhappy marriage at twenty had lasted four years. Another at thirty with an older man had terminated with his death seven years before. Her two children – she held up their stereophotograph – were grown up. She brought out stereo-photographs of five grandchildren. Four minutes' link-up with her son and three with her daughter followed. She herself was living in the section of normal-density Britain still known as Aberdeen, where her husband's folk were. Roydon offered to go and see her but it seemed that no ordinary person travelled much today. 'Surface and even air travel are too crowded, and stratocruising is only for long distance,' said Sal, who had come back in after half an hour. May assured him she was content with the screen, and they agreed he should contact her once a week.

Sal, it began to appear, was a liaison officer for the Centre with other institutions. But she took Roydon under her particular care and few minutes of a day went by without her turning up with provender, conversation or means of entertainment. She got him to fix himself up with one of the translucent suits by means of some sort of long-distance measurement recorder. She explained many ways and words that he could not understand. Her green eyes fixing his, she would speak slowly in her husky voice. She kept a sharp eye on his reaction to the mood-weather if he were outside, and produced the antidote.

'The mood-climate's not what it was,' Sattern complained to Sal and Roydon one day, looking in from a conference with the chiefs of other helicopter-parties. 'Spring used to be hopeful, summer serene, autumn regretful, winter gloomy. Now it's all mixed up. You never know what to expect.'

'You're getting more vulnerable in your old age, Paul,' said Sal, grinning.

'Something in what you say, actually. The inocs are wearing off. I must get some boosters.'

'How do you make out here with mood-weather?' asked Roydon.

'It doesn't worry us much,' said Sal. 'We inoculate during childhood; only the most violent mood-storms touch us. Your age hadn't got inocs for that; we'll have to cross-dope you pretty carefully for outside. But the endocrine typometer gave us enough data on you to give you a reasonable safeguard.'

A week or two later Sal told Roydon that Paul Sattern's team would like him to accompany them on trips, hoping he could set them right on some points about the past. He was given unlimited credit for purchase, and the official position of Historical Adviser. Chronismologists were in great demand, as the poikilochronism was regarded as a public danger, and were highly paid, partly because of the risks they ran. QUALIFIED CHRONISMOLOGIST, Roydon read on an old-fashioned plastic news-sheet's advertisement page: 'Vacancies for chronismologists. Higher Sc. degrees essential. Starting credit equivalent £50,000 to £60,000 pa rising by £5,000 pa Minimum service one year.'

'Two other poiks have been detected,' Sal told him, 'one in Bonnium and one in Ceylon.'

'Yes,' said Paul, 'and we think there are some in central Africa and one in Antarctica, only Antarctica is rather sparsely populated, and news from much of central Africa is nil – mood-climate closed chunks of it down. The whole world, including the oceans, might become one vast poik in a few millennia or even centuries, unless we can find out enough about these chronismatic processes to know how to stabilize or reverse them. It's a race against time, in two senses.'

'I had no idea how things were,' said Roydon weakly.

'Well, we have enough to do in our own little corner of ordinary time and space. Do you feel like coming with us tomorrow?'

'I must see,' Roydon thought, 'if I can't get a better clue to where she went. That rook – was it a rook? Can I trace the place? Will they take me there?' Miriel's dark hair and oval face swam up at him suddenly and he groped his way out of the room, muttering something. Paul Sattern looked after him and, turning to Sal with a bitter smile, shook his head ever so slightly. The girl flushed and, biting her lip, picked up a nest of tapes and walked out of the other door. She encountered Richard, the gadget-man, past the doorway. Richard, who had his eyes on her face, turned pale and said nothing, but came on into the room.

'Well?' said Paul.

'Those linking atto-second counters – will they be ready?' uttered Richard harshly, as though the technical sentence was code for something else.

'Of course. You can peg them in a new line from LV_3 to PN_8 tomorrow. But I think the femto-counters may show something yet.'

'Too slow,' said Richard and began a brisk discussion, but his manner was distrait and he jumped when Sal came back in. Roydon, recovering next door, heard much of the discussion, but it might as well have been the conversation of rooks or starlings. Fenn Vaughan strolled in and past the trio, singing:

> 'Where the femto-seconds pass
> Richard sits upon—'

Paul kicked his shin. Fenn walked on whistling. The group broke up in silence.

'What are all those things?' said Roydon. The craft was slowly cruising over the greenery.

'Those are future buildings,' explained Sal, who had pressed Paul to take her along to keep an eye on Roydon. 'We don't know whether they're some kind of plascrete or something new. The three-metre top bound stopped them existing above that at first, but they're growing up now a centimetre a week by infection, and pushing up the top bound. One day they'll be complete. That's why they look like ruins. Dick says the time is plus-ninety-four years in that patch below. But of course it's mostly the same with present and past buildings – if they're new domains, the buildings can't grow above the top bound at first. Look at all that lot to the west; they're all sorts of dates, mostly present to past, but they grew up when there wasn't any building there so they are still incomplete.'

'But surely the whole world from one of these domains must look very queer – masses of foundations and nothing else?'

'No, no, if you went down there you'd see complete buildings, probably a normal-density district, all around you; only the domain part itself would have these shells. Someone coming onto the domain from the world of that date would probably think it was a patch where demolition work had been going on. One reason why we don't often see people near those shells.'

'What's that odd brown patch down there?'

'Oh, that's just the other way. It's minus three hundred-odd years, Dick says. Most of the domains are minus a century or more round here – aren't they, Paul? – which is why they're still unbuilt-up.'

'How big are the domains?'

'Anything from a metre to a couple of kilometres across, and any shape. Dick says they may even start by growing quickly from a mere point, and changing time-level as they grow. That's where his atto-second lines may pick up something.'

Roydon's eyes devoured the hated green. The craft sank and Richard went down the ladder with his first gadget. They proceeded methodically across country like a mathematically minded crane-fly ovipositing on a lawn.

'Why, that – that looks very like the village! Is it part of the – the poik?'

'Yes, been inside it for dozens of years. A lot of it is minus twenty-five years now.'

'Is that why it's got all those odd buildings among it?'

'Yes.'

'Look, there are some people! How is it they don't know they're isolated?'

'Don't you realize?' cried Paul. 'The open domains can be

entered. They're mostly on the poik margins. But most of the inner domains, once entered, can only be left geographically. You can see men and animals crossing them and vanishing. Watch that nineteenth-century labourer on that ploughland. There – he's gone! But he doesn't know that. He's in a complete nineteenth-century world. Once you're down in a patch of, say, minus twenty-five years like the village, you've dropped through a hole twenty-five years deep, and have to walk about on that level for ever. That's the risk we all run if we happen to cross a domain-bound without knowing it. We can't get back. That's what your wife must have done. You were lucky, what with the cog-slipper.'

Roydon shuddered – but not from fear – and choked.

'And of course there's not much sign of a bound in an agricultural area like that when it's mostly minus a century or so; it had been broadly the same for generations.'

'How is it you can see all those domains from the air?'

'The top bound at roughly three metres, that Sal was talking about. It rises to three metres above the tops of old buildings too. All domains are open at the top bound, more or less, and you can see them from above. Sound travels both ways there too. Down below you can only see or hear neighbouring domains from an open one. Some open ones harden up into closed ones, by the way.'

'Don't the villagers and so on see the helicopter?'

'Yes, but they must have helicopters at minus twenty-five years, so they probably just think we're another. If another came by they'd see us go through each other in a ghost-collision that neither lot of us would know anything about – above the three-metre bound.'

'What about the people in the place you picked me up from?'

'That was approx zero. It showed how the area would have been today if there hadn't been a poik at all. The population was real there to themselves, but unreal in our poik-ridden world. Ghosts, if you like.'

'Can I go down by the village?'

'Village? No. It's tricky with people about. Let Richard peg his ninth counter down behind that big barn, on his own.'

At the eleventh descent: 'Why that's the hill I ran down!' shouted Roydon.

'Is that the Spot on the east?' asked Paul.

'I think so.'

'Well, that's where Richard pegs his next counter.'

'Can I go down then?'

'Yes, but don't do anything rash. Tell us what you think and we'll take action.'

Roydon followed Richard down the ladder when they came over the place. 'Wait, Royo, I'm coming too,' called Sal and clambered down third. Richard said nothing, but his face was set as he peered at the ground before fixing into it on its long prong his gadget for recording millionths of millionths of millionths of a second.

'Can't make it out – the dyke's rubble, the fence is all rotted away; brambles and nettles everywhere too, and all those docks,' muttered Roydon. He turned, his eyes searching along what he hoped was the line taken by that hurrying speck so long ago. Richard straightened his back and stared at him, but said nothing. 'The fool thinks,' Richard said to himself, 'because we snatched him from a cog-slipper, that all domain-time is frozen for ever, doesn't realize most of it's moved sixty-one years on, is going onward all the time, let alone what's shunted or rebounded.'

Sal, who, a little way off, was anxiously watching Roydon, happened to glance at Richard and read his expression in a flash of intuition. 'Roy!' she shrieked. At that moment an unexpected and violent gust of instinctive drive invaded the hollow. At the cry, which sounded to him like his wife's voice, Roydon's pale face turned white. He rushed off along the old hedge-line. The hedge seemed to him to swing round and to flicker beside him – was She running along its far side?

Sal, racing at an angle to cut him off, had reached twenty

strides when she vanished. Two seconds later and some way off, Roydon vanished too. 'Richard, you fool, come up!' roared Paul from the helicopter. 'That patch is a maze of little domains. Come up! We can winch you down where she vanished.' But when Richard, white and babbling, was lowered down on the spot, he saw five paces onward the brink of a deep quarry. Below, men in tiny white shorts working ultrasonic excavators, far in the future, were gaping at the broken body.

Roydon's flickering hedge was the edge of a furze thicket. Roydon was running on dry heath. It was very hot. The flickering was the bobbing of twenty-seven crouching heads. A dozen bone-tipped wooden spears flashed towards him, aimed at his hamstrings. Three struck him high in the calves, one went in above a knee. He fell. The skin-clad figures, quacking and barking, loped towards him.

'Leave Richard. We must get that madman!' shouted Fenn Vaughan in Paul's ear. 'I've pinpointed his vanishing. I think I saw something strike him just before.'

'All right. Swing her round, Peter. Let Fenn con.'

In ten seconds the craft was over the point of Roydon's disappearance, a patch of heath. Half a naked, shaggy thigh could be seen, and a queer coughing uproar rose from the ground. Paul and Fenn, stun-guns at the ready, slipped down the ladder.

The tribe was tying Roydon up with leather thongs. He looked dazed. With blood-curdling howls Fenn and Paul rushed on them. A flash of lightning and a simultaneous crack of thunder completed the tribe's panic, and in a torrential rain-squall they scattered over the heather. Paul and Fenn carried Roydon a few paces back inside the domain bounds where the helicopter could again be seen ghostlily through the diminishing downpour, and slashed his bonds loose, looking anxiously about them. From the helicopter's wall the echo of a blackbird's call could be heard ten feet away, somewhere in the nineteenth century. Paul clamped emergency dressings on the wounds. Roydon staggered to his feet. 'Must find her,' he said thickly.

'We've had one death on your account – we don't want three. Up the ladder, you fool, before the tribe comes back.' The sun was glinting on the wet heath.

At that moment an even fainter echo from the helicopter's base reached the group on the ground. 'Miriel, Miriel,' it seemed to say. The men and women in the craft, speechless, were gesturing wildly to one side. 'Up the ladder to the red mark – they'll trawl you over,' shouted Paul. All three clambered post-haste above the red three-metre mark.

'We'll drop you quietly and try to pick up Richard,' said Peter's voice at last. The helicopter drifted some metres north, its loaded ladder swaying dangerously. An old gentleman clad in a sombre jacket, a deal of lace at the neck, and breeches, was kneeling on the ground by a little plot of smooth grass. He did not look up even when the three dropped beside him, and seemed not to hear the noise of the machine, which now vanished southward. A green May morning burgeoned all around him. 'Miriel, Miriel!' he was crying.

At last he looked up at the group around him. He seemed not quite right in the head: at any rate he gave little sign of surprise. 'Here is a lock of her hair cut off when she came to us, here is a lock of white hair when she was taken, here is her ring, her wedding ring. She besought I would bury them near to the place where she came to us, for her body is in Mafford churchyard and her soul with her Maker, but her heart, I fear, is here, though she cherished our people for sixty years. Who are you, sirs? Are you of the company of the blessèd angels? Are you come to take me to Heaven to be with her?'

'She was my wife,' said Roydon quietly.

'Ah, sir, but she was an old old woman when she departed this life on Friday last. How can that be?'

'Never mind; it is true. I should like to see her grave, though I know now where it lies: I have seen it long since. Did she live here all her life after she came to you?'

'Yes, sir, she was, as you might say, the mother of our little flock. Mourned and lamented by one and all, sir, by young and old, by man and woman, and a noble stone they will put up, sir, at the head of the grave. Matthew is carving it but 'twill not be ready for a day or two, I fear. She was the mother of our village, though her heart, I fear, was elsewhere, and that gave her a sadness, a kind of resignation all her days. Resigned to God's will she was, and indeed she loved our people dearly. Miriel has cherished and succoured our village, but she will not come among us again.' And the old man, smiling sadly, nodded off among the meadow flowers.

Roydon picked up the ring and slipped it on the little finger of his left hand. His spear wounds were yelling at him, but in his heart a vast dark grey calm was spreading.

Original Appearances

The first edition of *The Caltraps of Time* contained seven short stories, all originally published in *New Worlds SF*:

'Lost Ground', *New Worlds* 169, December 1966
'Mouth of Hell', *New Worlds* 158, January 1966
'Not So Certain', *New Worlds* 173, July 1967
'Psychosmosis', *New Worlds* 160, March 1966
'The Transfinite Choice', *New Worlds* 165, August 1966
'Traveller's Rest', *New Worlds* 154, September 1965
'A Two-Timer', *New Worlds* 159, February 1966

This new edition contains three extra stories:

'Doctor Fausta', *Stopwatch*, ed. George Hay, London: New English Library, 1974
'The Show Must Go On', *The Disappearing Future*, ed. George Hay, London: Panther, 1970
'Take It or Leave It', *The Year 2000*, ed. Harry Harrison, Garden City, NY: Doubleday, 1970

David Irvine Masson was born in 1915 in Edinburgh, and came from a distinguished family of academics and thinkers. After graduating from Merton College, Oxford, he spent most of his working life as a librarian. Although his output was small and consisted entirely of short stories, he gained a reputation as a writer of vigorous experimental SF. All of his short science fiction is published in the collection *The Caltraps of Time* (1968). He died in Leeds in 2007.

A full list of SF Masterworks can be found at

www.gollancz.co.uk